MW00753048

A Hard Ticket Home

A Hard Ticket Home

DAVID HOUSEWRIGHT

ST. MARTIN'S MINOTAUR ✠ NEW YORK

ISBN 0-312-32149-X
EAN 978-0312-32149-9

First Edition: May 2004

10   9   8   7   6   5   4   3   2   1

For Renée,
as always

Acknowledgments

The author would like to thank Lynne Lillie, M.D., Mark Hamel, Tim Myslajek, Alison Picard, Ben Sevier, and Renée Valois for their invaluable help. I also would like to thank Yvonne Mullin and Renée Valois for the use of their song "Bananas."

A Hard Ticket Home

Just So You Know . . .

It took a few moments before I could force myself to leave the car. It was small, ugly, and old and I hated it—a tan 1987 Dodge Colt with strips of rust running along the rocker panels and back wheel wells. But it was gloriously warm.

I had parked on the shoulder of the deserted county road, edging as close to the ditch as I dared. On the opposite side of the ditch loomed oak, pine, spruce, ash, and birch trees, bending and swaying in the hard wind. About 150 feet behind me was the turnoff that led to the lake property. I had studied the road carefully before driving past. In the summer, it would be dirt. Now it was ice and hard-packed snow, just wide enough for a single vehicle driven slowly. I found the impression of one set of tire tracks going in. None came out.

I was reluctant to use the road. What if Thomas Teachwell was watching it, what if he saw me coming? I wasn't overly concerned that he might shoot me. According to my information it was unlikely that

Teachwell even had a gun, much less knew how to use it—although a man on the run is capable of anything. Nor was I anxious that he might escape. What did I care? But if Teachwell escaped with the money . . . That, after all, was why I had chased him 278 miles north from the Twin Cities on the coldest day in the past two decades. For the money.

I searched my memory for a few motivational phrases. "The job gets easier once you start," was something my mother often told me. "When the going gets tough, the tough get going," was a favorite of my high school hockey coach. "If it was easy, everyone would do it." That was something my skills instructor at the police academy liked to say. None of the clichés inspired me enough to lift the door handle. Finally, I recited out loud the words my father used whenever I complained about picking up other people's trash along the highway when I was slaving away my summers for the county: "Hey, kid. You got a problem with workin' for a living?"

I opened the door and stepped out. The frigid air hit me so hard I nearly fell back against the car. A violent gust gathered grains of ice from the road and swirled them around my face. The knit ski mask I wore afforded some protection, yet instinctively I closed my eyes and angled my head away from the wind.

"Do you believe this!" I exclaimed to the empty highway. Often in the past I've heard people speak of icy winds cutting like a knife. They're wrong. It isn't a knife, it's a club. It doesn't cut, it bludgeons.

I slammed shut the car door and immediately patted the pockets of my bright red snowmobile suit, feeling the weight in both of them. My gun and badge were in the right. My cell phone was in the left. Satisfied, I spun into the wind and trudged, head down, toward the turnoff. I thought about locking the door, but any notion of car thieves lurking nearby was blown away with the next polar blast. Given the current temperature, I doubted the car would start again, anyway.

After a few steps I became keenly aware of my isolation. In front of me the county road stretched like a ribbon of gray and white until it bent behind a stand of trees and was gone. Behind me the gray-white road didn't turn, but merely receded into a distant horizon of blowing snow. My ancient Colt was the only evidence that I was living in the twenty-first century. I longed to see another vehicle—snowplow, truck, car, SUV, even one of those damn minivans. None appeared. I began to question the wisdom of the entire enterprise.

"I'm going to die out here," I told myself. "They're going to find me frozen to a tree like that guy in that Redford movie, *Jeremiah Johnson*."

Still, I moved on. Snow and ice crunched loudly beneath my heavy Sorrels. Mostly it sounded like I was trodding on potato chips, but every few steps I heard a loud, alarming crack that shrieked like the rending of lake ice and made me flinch. About halfway to the turnoff, I left the county highway and moved toward the woods. With my second step into the ditch I descended unexpectedly into waist-deep snow. There was a moment of panic—somehow I had the idea I was sinking into a kind of Nordic quicksand—but it promptly subsided. With hard effort, I plowed my way across the ditch to the steep embankment on the far side. Grabbing hold of the low-hanging branch of a spruce tree, I pulled myself up.

The snow wasn't as deep in the woods, only about a foot. It was hard going, but not as hard as it had been. Still, after fifty yards I was breathing rapidly and I began to feel warm inside my snowsuit. After a few more yards I was perspiring freely. I paused for a moment to rest.

"Can sweating in subzero temperatures bring on hypothermia?" I asked myself. Not having a clear answer troubled me. "Damn, Mac. You should have been better prepared."

I continued walking. My plan was simple if not contradictory: Follow the road to the lake cabin, but stay off it. Keep your distance, but don't let it out of your sight. Make sure Teachwell doesn't see you coming, but don't get lost, either.

The "woods were dark and deep," as the Robert Frost poem suggested. There was no sun, or even the hint of sun, and a subtle gloom fell around me. Yet it wasn't the lack of light that made the woods seem so terribly strange and weird. It was the lack of sound. The wind that had blown so ferociously across the county road was less noticeable here. The trees still swayed and twisted above me, but on the forest floor all was still. And silent. Even my feet trudging through the snow made little noise. The only sound I could hear through the blue ski mask was the muffled timbre of my own breath. I found it very disconcerting. For the first time I understood why some people believe that going deaf is worse than going blind.

After a while, I began to lose sense of both time and distance. I was sure I had hiked a long way, but was unable to determine with any accuracy how far—the trail behind me seemed to disappear into the trees after only a few dozen yards. And while I was positive that the lake cabin was just up ahead, I had nothing on which to base that assertion except my own natural confidence.

I stopped, pulled off one of the large, fur-lined brown leather mittens they used to call "choppers" when I was a kid, and read my watch. How long had I been walking? One hour? Two? Twenty minutes? I should have checked the time before I left the county highway.

There was little else to do—I had limited my options, which, of course, is never a wise thing to do—so I continued hiking forward, although I had to admit my enthusiasm was waning. Ice formed around the mouth hole in the ski mask, and my eyebrows, left exposed by the eye holes, were frosted. I knew cold. I had grown up in Minnesota, after all. Only I couldn't remember ever being colder. Certainly it was too cold to travel by foot.

That's when I realized I had lost sight of the road.

Okay, this is a mistake, I admitted to myself. *They really are going to find me frozen to a tree.*

I held on through a level stretch of woods. The pump jockey at the service station in Ponemah said the cabin was less than a mile from the county road, yet that estimate had proved to be woefully inaccurate. I didn't know how far I had walked, but it was a helluva lot farther than a mile.

Then I was out of the woods. The clearing had appeared so abruptly that I was several yards deep into it before I turned and quickly retreated back along my trail until I was safely concealed by the trees.

I squatted behind a stand of spruce and examined the clearing. An SUV was parked about thirty yards from the mouth of the road. The license plate was obscured by snow but I knew a 2001 Toyota 4Runner when I saw one. Teachwell's. Beyond it was a small, redwood-stained cabin, one of those prefabricated jobs built atop gray cinder blocks. A curl of white smoke drifted up from a metal pipe on the roof and was caught by the wind.

"I don't believe it," I said in a low whisper. Half the cops in Minnesota were searching for Thomas Teachwell—Minneapolis Police Department, Hennepin County Sheriff's Department, State Highway Patrol, Bureau of Criminal Apprehension, even the FBI. Yet I was the one who found him. 'Course, it was plain dumb luck that I knew where to look. I had been in a bar on West 7th Street in St. Paul drinking beers with Bobby Dunston—make that *Detective Sergeant* Bobby Dunston, thank you very much—when this guy on the other side of the bar—a DWI just waiting to happen—pointed at the TV suspended in the corner and said, "I know where he is." One of the local stations was reporting that the search continued for Thomas Teachwell, CFO for a national restaurant chain based in Minneapolis. I had seen the teletype the feds had issued on him. He was being sought for embezzling an undisclosed amount of the company's assets. They used the term "undisclosed" for the same reason they use it when miscreants take down a bank. They didn't want to encourage copycats. Yet you know they had the amount down to the penny. I figured it was at least half a million—why else would the FBI be involved?

"I'm tellin' yah," the DWI repeated. "I know where he is."

"Yeah?" asked the bartender.

"Sure. I know this guy who knows this guy who was paired up with Teachwell on a golf course couple years ago when Teachwell was getting a divorce and the guy said that Teachwell told him that the only thing he regretted about his divorce was that he couldn't visit his brother-in-law's cabin in northern Minnesota anymore. The guy said that Teachwell said that he enjoyed it up there because it was so isolated, because you could go for weeks at a time without seeing another human being."

"Hey, Bobby," I said. "Hear that? Isn't that what you plainclothes guys call a clue?"

"Leave me alone, McKenzie."

"Seriously, Bobby. You should go to northern Minnesota and catch this guy. Think how happy you'll make the feds. They might even give you a new tie to wear."

"One, there's no way this guy's holed up in his ex-brother-in-law's cabin. He's probably skipped the country by now. Two, it's not my case and not my jurisdiction. Three, screw the FBI. And four, I believe this constant reference to my attire is merely a manifestation of your resentment over the inescapable fact that I have been elevated to the dizzying heights of detective while you continue to languish in the lowly ranks of patrolman."

I chose to ignore the last remark, mostly because it was true.

"It's your own fault, you know," Bobby added. "You should never have used a shotgun on that guy."

I chose to ignore that remark, too.

"I'm just saying, you're missing a golden opportunity," I said.

"Think so? Then you go. Catch Teachwell, maybe they'll promote you to sergeant. They might even give you a nice suit and tie to wear."

I put two fingers in my mouth, pretending I was going to force myself to vomit. Still, the idea of showing up Bobby was just too delicious to ignore. The next day I did a little research. I discovered that Teachwell had married and divorced a woman named Yvonne Martinson. Yvonne had a brother named Anthony Martinson, a middle manager for 3M. I conducted a property search on the PC and discovered that Anthony had a cabin on Lower Red Lake in the Red Lake Indian Reservation, a dozen miles west of Ponemah and about an hour's drive from the Canadian border. I had some ATO coming, so I took a day. The sarge asked me what I was going to do and I told him lay on the beach. Since the wind chill was minus 67 degrees at the time, he thought that was pretty funny.

I watched the cabin for what seemed like a long time. Nothing moved except for the white smoke drawing out of the chimney and disappearing in the stiff wind. I began to think that it must be toasty warm inside the cabin and I wanted so much to be warm again. I worked my way to the left, staying low behind the tree line, wishing that I wasn't dressed in red, until I found what I thought was a blind spot, an angle on the cabin where I wouldn't be seen from either a side or front window.

I stopped and studied the cabin some more. To my left was Lower Red Lake, a body of water so large that I was unable to see the opposite shore. There were a half dozen such lakes in Minnesota. Plus about fifteen thousand more where you could see the other side and almost nine thousand miles of rivers and streams. In summer it's glorious. In winter, well . . .

I counted slowly—"One, two, three"—and dashed forward. I used to have good speed. In high school I ran the hundred meters in 12.4 seconds. Only the snow was too deep for speed. I didn't run so much as I plowed. I tried to keep my feet up, tried to rise above the snow and mostly failed. Floundering, once falling, I pushed myself forward—I must have made a terrific target, a slow-moving red blob against pure white. The vague fear of freezing was suddenly replaced by something far more tangible—the fear of being shot. It was a fear I had known before.

Finally, I was there. The cabin had been raised on a hill. The rows of cinder blocks supporting the back of it were only one deep, but in front the gray blocks were stacked six high. I slipped under the cabin and fell to my knees on frozen dirt. I took one deep breath. The noise of it distressed me. I quickly covered my mouth with a chopper, hoping my breathing wouldn't be heard through the floor above.

I began to see things beneath the cabin while I waited to regain my breath—canvas lawn chairs, old planks, a stack of red-tinged shingles, an ax, a metal minnow bucket, a boat anchor, a busted oar, the cracked windshield of a speed boat—only it was the brown earth that seemed most out of place. With all the snow around, it seemed incongruous that this small patch of dirt would remain unmolested.

I pulled off my right chopper with my teeth. Underneath it I was wearing a knit glove, yet even with that protection I could feel the heat leaving my hand and the bitter cold settling in. I unsnapped a pocket of my snowmobile suit and pulled out my 9 mm Heckler & Koch, as fine an example of precision German engineering as there ever was. I had been issued a Glock like all the other street cops in St. Paul, but I had never liked the grip. That's why I was carrying the 12-gauge pump when I killed the suspect outside the convenience store six months earlier, because I didn't like the grip. It was something I still thought about late at night. . . .

Moving in a low crouch, I swung out from under the cabin and edged along the elevated wall to the front. The owners had built a redwood deck leading to the door, and it made me pause. God knew I didn't want Teachwell to hear me coming, and creaking planks would be a dead giveaway, emphasis on dead. I slipped to the edge of the deck where I could get a good look at the entrance. There was a screen door and behind it another door made of solid wood. Around the lock I could see the unmistakable gouges left by a pry bar. Teachwell didn't have a key—he had forced the lock to gain entry.

I crept back to the steps. There were six of them. The door was another six strides from the top. I squeezed the gun tightly. It featured a cocking lever built into the grip. Fifteen pounds of pressure compressed the lever and cocked the gun. When it was fired, the mechanism would recock automatically as long as I held down the lever. Release the lever, and the gun was deactivated. The lever allowed me to carry the Heckler & Koch safely with a round in the chamber. Only it occurred to me as I readied myself to hit the door that I had never fired the 9mm with a glove on.

I cursed silently, removed the knit glove and gripped the frozen metal with my bare hand. My fingers were exposed only for a few moments and I was astonished at how swiftly numbness set in. I transferred the piece to my gloved hand, slapped my bare hand against my chest, flexed the fingers, then gripped the Heckler & Koch again. It certainly was cold. That, as much as anything, propelled me up the steps—I needed to get out of the cold. I flung open the screen door and rammed the inside door with my shoulder even as I twisted the handle. I had guessed right, the lock was broken. The door opened so quickly that I nearly lost my balance. I was four steps inside the cabin before I recovered.

The cabin consisted of one room. There were several wooden columns to support the roof, but no interior walls save for those that enclosed the bathroom. In one corner was a kitchen table, refrigerator, stove and sink; in a second were two regular-size beds and two sets of bunk beds; in the third I saw several metal cabinets, and in the fourth there was a fireplace. The fireplace was working. Sitting in a wooden chair in front of the fire was Teachwell. He held a book in his hand, an index finger marking his place. His expression was one of complete surprise.

I brought the gun up and sighted on his chest, my legs spread, weight evenly distributed, my left hand supporting the right.

"Freeze!"

I couldn't believe I said that.

"What . . . ?"

"Don't move!" I cried.

"Who are you?" Teachwell wanted to know. Teachwell was five-eight and carried sixty pounds more than was healthy. He was wearing a white dress shirt, slacks that looked like the bottom half of a business suit, and wing tips. His hair, what there was of it, was white and his face had the pasty cast of a man who never went outside. He looked about as threatening as a Twinkie, only I was never one to take chances.

"Stand up!" I barked.

Teachwell seemed confused. I repeated the order. He set the book carefully on the chair as he rose.

"Turn around." Teachwell hesitated. "Now."

The man turned.

"Hands against the fireplace."

Teachwell did as he was told, extending his hands until the palms rested on the fireplace mantel. Without prompting, he moved his legs back and spread them apart. Just like in the movies. I closed the cabin door and removed my other mitten and glove with my teeth. I frisked Teachwell from top to bottom, all the while making sure he could feel the muzzle of the gun against his spine. Satisfied, I stepped back and ordered the businessman to the chair.

"Hands behind your head," I added.

Teachwell locked the fingers of both hands behind his neck and repeated the question he had asked earlier. "Who are you?"

"McKenzie. St. Paul Police Department."

"You're a long way from home, Officer McKenzie."

"You, too."

I brushed the hood back and removed my ski mask. The ice that had frozen to my eyebrows and lashes was melting now and I wiped the moisture away with my sleeve.

"Mr. Teachwell, you're under arrest." Bobby's going to love this, I told myself. I recited his rights. When I finished I said, "Now, where's the money?"

"What money?"

"Mr. Teachwell, I have never been so cold in my life," I told him, although I was feeling much better now that I could see the fire and feel the warmth of the cabin. "I'm tired. I'm hungry. I'm a little scared." I waved the nine through the air and shouted. "Where in hell is the money!"

Teachwell's voice didn't reply, but his eyes did. They glanced at a spot behind my right shoulder. It was a fleeting gesture, yet it was enough. I turned cautiously. Two large, blue, hard-sided suitcases on a bed. I backed away from Teachwell, watching him even as I crossed the cabin, found the handle of one suitcase with my free hand and pulled it off the bed—it must have weighed fifty pounds. I was surprised by its weight. I dragged the suitcase to the kitchen area. It required both hands to hoist the suitcase on top of the table, which meant I had to set down the gun. Teachwell was far enough away that I decided to risk it. He didn't move.

After regaining my weapon, I unlatched the suitcase and slowly lifted the cover. My ears filled with a loud rushing sound that was like air escaping from a leaking tire. I swallowed hard and the sound stopped. I purposely blinked my eyes once, twice, three times, closed them for a few seconds, opened them again. There were countless stacks of bills held together with rubber bands in the suitcase. Under each rubber band was a torn piece of note paper on which Teachwell had written an amount;

$10,000, $20,000, $50,000. I reached out and gingerly touched the green bills before pulling my hand back.

"Mr. Teachwell?" I'm sure he heard the admiration in my voice. "How much money did you steal?"

"Six million, two hundred and fifty-seven thousand, one hundred and sixty-nine dollars." His voice was confident and clear, a man proud of his accomplishment.

"Wow," I said.

And then, "Wow," again.

I slowly closed the suitcase. It hurt my eyes to look at that much cash in one place.

"Mr. Teachwell, I'm impressed."

"Officer . . ." Teachwell hesitated, his eyes moving from me to the gun I held loosely in my hand. I waited for it.

"I'll give you half," he announced. Teachwell started to rise from the chair, but I gestured him back down again with the Heckler & Koch.

"I'll give you half," he repeated. "That's three million, one hundred twenty-eight thousand, five hundred eighty-four dollars and fifty cents."

"No way." I didn't dispute his math, only his reason.

"Think of it. Think of all that money."

I shook my head.

"It's all arranged," Teachwell continued. "Tomorrow we're all set to cross the border at Rainy River. From there we go to Winnipeg. In Winnipeg we catch a flight to Quebec. In Quebec we hop a freighter that winds through the Saint Lawrence Seaway and down the east coast. It stops once in New York. We don't even get off the boat. The next stop is Fortaleza, Brazil. From there, Rio de Janeiro. A man with three million, one hundred twenty-eight thousand, five hundred eighty-four dollars and fifty cents in Rio, you'd live like a god."

I unsnapped the other pocket of the snowmobile suit and produced my cell phone.

"Think of what you could buy. Think of what you're giving up!"

I didn't want to think. Thinking would only lead to trouble. If I started thinking . . . It certainly was warm in Rio and I wouldn't mind being treated like a god—it sure beat driving a squad up and down the streets of St. Paul for a living. And after what I had gone through—the ugly accusations, the missed promotions, the publicity—I sure deserved it.

"Take a suitcase. Any suitcase. Just take a suitcase and walk away."

Just take a suitcase. . . . The bills were unmarked. Untraceable. If I helped Teachwell escape, who would know?

Stop it, McKenzie! I shouted at myself and shook the thought from my head. Then I had another thought.

"The money is insured, right?"

"I know what you're thinking. You're thinking that you could turn me in and collect a reward and a finder's fee. Only cops can't collect rewards or finder's fees."

Not St. Paul cops.

Damn, I told myself. I also told myself, *It's been a long time coming.*

I activated the cell phone and pressed eleven numbers in quick succession with my thumb. I did it before I could talk myself out if it.

"St. Paul Police Department, Sergeant Hodapp," a voice answered.

"Sarge, it's McKenzie."

"Mac, I thought you were taking the day off."

"About that. Sarge?"

"Hmm?"

"I quit."

I

Stacy Carlson was nine years old and she was dying. Her parents told me so while I watched her playing happily on the front lawn of their home, and the news hit me so hard I nearly lost my breath.

"Does she know?"

"We haven't told her," Molly Carlson said. "But, yes, I think she knows. We took her to enough doctors, even took her to the Mayo Clinic."

"What did the doctors tell you?"

"Leukemia," Richard Carlson answered from across the living room, answered as if he wished to spare his wife the pain of speaking the word. "They say her body is producing too many white blood corpuscles. They say her spleen and lymph glands are enlarged. They say she needs a bone marrow transplant or she'll die. Only, neither of us is compatible and finding a donor outside the family, that's a twenty thousand to one shot. Leastwise, that's what they say."

Carlson was a big man, big in every direction, 275 at least and not all of it was fat. His eyes were a pale green and what little hair he had was gray. All the other times I had seen him he had worn the faded jeans and T-shirts of a working contractor—a guy who not only designed and sold lake homes, but who also dug foundations and hammered nails. Today he was wearing his Sunday best: black boots, designer jeans, a checkered shirt with imitation pearl snaps, and a belt with a garish buckle declaring his fidelity to Winston Cup racing. He lived in a three-story house that he had built himself in a neighborhood where all the other houses were close to the ground. Somehow he had managed to build it without uprooting the dozen magnificent oak, maple, and birch trees that surrounded it. It was because of the house and trees that I had hired Carlson to build my own lake home.

"You want me to find a donor for Stacy?" I asked.

"We want you to find our other daughter, Jamie," Carlson said.

"Jamie," repeated Mrs. Carlson. Her voice was soft, almost a whisper. She was wearing a powder-blue dress printed with yellow flowers. She was eighteen inches shorter and 150 pounds lighter than her husband, but her hair was just as gray. She sat in a chair, her hands folded neatly in her lap, and watched Stacy through a large bay window. She never took her eyes off the girl.

"We had—we have another daughter. Jamie. She left us seven years ago. Stacy was only two back then. We had her late. She was—a present. Anyway, Jamie left us and never came back. We tried to find her, even thought about hiring a private investigator. Then we figured, well, that's the way Jamie wanted it. Only now . . ."

"Jamie might be a compatible donor," I volunteered. "Jamie might be able to save Stacy's life."

Molly nodded. "Family members are best. And Jamie has a rare blood type, B-negative, same as Stacy. The doctors say, the first thing you need to be a compatible donor is the same blood type."

A missing person. Missing persons made me nervous. Most missing persons are missing because they want to be and rarely does anything good come of finding them. Still, Stacy Carlson was nine years old and she was dying. Her hair was long and blond and tied in a ponytail. Her eyes were vibrant green, her smile was bright enough to melt snow. I couldn't possibly imagine the pain and anguish Molly and Richard Carlson must have suffered as they watched their daughter, knowing she was literally dying before their eyes. When I was in the sixth grade I lost my mother to a brain tumor literally overnight. My father died just five months ago, yet his passing too was fairly quick, although we had both seen it coming. This was something else. Losing a child, slowly . . .

"Tell me about Jamie," I said.

"You'll try to find her?" Molly asked, her face bright with hope.

"I can't promise anything, but yes, ma'am, I'll try."

Molly squeezed my hands like it was a done deal. "Thank you," she said.

"You understand, right? Richard told you I'm not a private investigator? I don't have a license. I don't have legal standing."

"He said you used to be a policeman."

"Yes. For eleven years in St. Paul."

"He said you help people."

"Sometimes. When I can."

"I appreciate this, Mac," Carlson said. In all my previous dealings with Carlson, he had spoken loudly. I figured he always spoke that way, big men sometimes do. Yet in his own home his voice was small. It was what my mother had called "an indoor voice."

"I can't tell you how much I appreciate it," he added. "Only, I'm not asking for charity. I know you usually do these things for free, but I'm a man who likes to pay his own way. Just ask anybody in Grand Rapids. Money's not a problem."

"Don't worry about it," I said. "Money's not a problem with me, either. I have plenty."

"I pay my own way," Carlson insisted.

"We'll talk about it later."

"I know you've been thinking about extending the deck at your place, maybe screening off part of it."

"We'll talk about it later."

Carlson nodded.

"You spell your name S-O-N, right?" I said.

"What?"

"Your name. S-O-N or S-E-N?"

"S-E-N is Danish. I'm Swedish," Carlson answered with a certain pride.

I made a note of it on a yellow legal pad I stole from my girlfriend's office. "How do you spell your daughter's name?"

"J-A-M-I-E."

"Middle name?"

"Anne," he said, then added, "with an E."

I wrote it down. "Jamie Anne Carlson. Pretty name."

"Thank you." Molly smiled slightly and looked down at her hands, still folded in her lap.

Carlson sat in an old, stuffed chair that had carried too much weight for too long and stared at a spot on the wall that no one else could see, leaving his wife to answer my questions.

"It was the year Jamie graduated from high school," Molly said. "Right after the Fourth—the weekend after the Fourth—she just took the clothes that would fit into one suitcase and left. We thought she would come back when her money ran out. She didn't. When she didn't come back by September, we went to the police. They said they couldn't help us. They said since she wasn't a minor and since there wasn't any indication of foul play—that's the phrase they used, foul play—well, they said they couldn't do anything."

"We thought of looking for her ourselves," Carlson said. "Hiring a private detective. But I guess we didn't see any point in it. Besides, we always thought she'd call. We always thought she'd come home."

"Why did she leave?" I asked. "Was she unhappy?"

"She didn't seem unhappy," Molly said.

"Did you have a fight, a serious disagreement of some kind?"

"No. I don't remember a fight. Truth is—truth is, Mr. McKenzie, we don't know why she left. One day she was living here perfectly fine, talking about going to the community college in the fall. Next day she was gone."

"Boyfriend?"

"No!" Molly was adamant. It was the first time she had raised her voice. "My Jamie wasn't like that."

"Something made her leave," I reminded her.

"I guess she just wanted to see some of the world."

"The world." Carlson spat the word like it was an obscenity.

Molly stared at him for a moment before continuing.

"She didn't like it here. She said there was nothing for someone her age to do."

Carlson shook his head in disbelief.

"Plenty to do," he insisted. "It's not like Grand Rapids is some hick town."

"Yes, it is," said Molly. "We like it, but . . . Mr. McKenzie, Jamie was young and she was pretty, she was smart and she was bored. She wanted to leave here and she knew we disapproved, knew we would try to talk her out of it. . . ."

"Maybe so, but she didn't have to just up and go like that. Without saying good-bye. Without even leaving a note. That ain't right."

And she hasn't tried to contact you again, not once in seven years, I thought but didn't say.

"No, it isn't right," I agreed.

"Where do you think Jamie went?" I asked.

"The Cities," Molly said. "Where else?"

In Minnesota? There was no place else, I agreed silently.

"Do you know Jamie's social security number? It'll help me find her."

"I don't know," Molly said. "I know she had one—the government gave her one when she was born. It's probably around here somewhere."

I took a white card from my wallet. I had five hundred printed about a year ago with just my name and phone number. I think I had given out twenty so far.

"If you can find her social security number, call me."

"R. McKenzie," Molly read slowly. "What does the R stand for?"

Usually when people ask that question, I simply answer, "My first name." For some reason I told Molly the truth.

"Rushmore."

"Rushmore? I never heard that before."

"My parents took a vacation to the Badlands of South Dakota. They told me I was conceived in a motor lodge near Mount Rushmore, so that's what they named me. I'm sure they thought it was a good idea at the time. Anyway, it could have been worse. I could have been Deadwood."

Both Carlson and Molly thought that was pretty funny. 'Course, they had never had to raise their hands when teachers called "Rushmore" on the first day of school.

"Driver's license?" I asked.

"Jamie had one. I don't know the number or anything."

I made note of that on the legal pad, too. The Department of Motor Vehicles would be one of my first stops.

"You said she was talking about going to a two-year college. What major?"

"She wanted to be a paralegal and work in a law office."

I made a note of that, then said, "I could use a photograph of her."

"I'll get it." Molly rose from the chair and went into an adjacent dining room.

Carlson watched her leave, then said, "You might wanna try talking to Merci Cole," his voice dropping several decibels.

"Who?"

If I had trouble hearing Carlson, his wife did not. A moment later, she was standing under the arch that separated the living room from the dining room.

"Merci Cole? Why do you say that?"

"Who's Merci Cole?" I asked, writing her name on the yellow pad.

"She was a friend of Jamie's," Molly answered, still watching her husband.

"Friend," Carlson muttered under his breath. It was another word he didn't seem to like. "I didn't say they were friends."

"Maybe not a friend." Molly turned away from her husband. "But they knew each other. Merci ran with a wild crowd—not Jamie's type of people at all. I don't think Merci received much supervision at home. She didn't have a father, she was born illegitimate. Her momma worked all the time at the paper mill. She died—when did she die?"

"Two years, three months ago," Carlson said. Molly seemed surprised that he knew the answer.

"They became friendly when they were both up for queen at that festival they had at the end of the school year," Molly added. "Spring Fling. They both lost. People said it was because they were both tall with blond hair and green eyes. They split the vote and the girl with dark hair won. The girls spent a great deal of time together during the contest. They seemed to have this, I don't know, rapport." She turned toward her husband. "But I don't know why you think Merci had anything to do with Jamie leaving."

"I didn't say she did."

"Well, then . . ."

"Well, then—they both left at nearly the same time."

"So?"

"So, I don't know, maybe they ran into each other."

"Merci was a thief," Molly said.

This time Carlson didn't argue. Instead, he found his spot on the wall and stared some more. Molly sighed in resignation and went back to watching her daughter through the window.

"Tell me about it," I said. "Anybody."

"Merci was a waitress at the diner near the mill," Carlson said. "Leastwise she was until she and the Steele boy, Richie, ran off with money they stole from the till. Didn't take the deputies long to catch 'em, neither. They didn't even get as far as Duluth. Oh, they swore they were innocent, said they didn't steal anything, said they were running away to get married. But the money was sure enough missing and they were sure enough leaving in a hurry. After she was arrested, Merci used her one phone call to contact Jamie. Jamie used her savings to bail Merci out."

"Why would she do that?" I asked. "You said they weren't close."

"I don't know," Molly answered.

"What happened after Merci was arrested?"

"The Steele boy, his father is big over at the paper mill," Carlson continued. "So you know the cops went easy on him once the old man replaced the money that was stolen. Merci they told to get out of town. They said if she wasn't gone within forty-eight hours they were going to arrest her. So off she goes."

I nodded. It was a typical tactic of a small town police force. Whenever the rurals have a problem that isn't worth their time and aggravation—or when the fix is in—they just tell the suspect to grab the next stage out of Dodge and don't come back.

"That was toward the end of June," Carlson said. "Week or so before Jamie left."

"One thing has nothin' to do with the other," Molly insisted.

"I didn't say it did," Carlson said.

I jotted the facts down on the yellow pad along with a question: *Was 18-year-old Jamie's sense of justice so offended by the treatment of her friend that she would abandon her family and home?*

Molly shook her head at her husband, then gave me the photograph, a two-by-three high school graduation shot. It showed a young woman posed against a dark, marbled background. She was beautiful. Bright green eyes, hair like a palomino pony, skin—you knew not so much as a pimple ever dared blemish that skin. I looked from the photo to the Carlsons to the little girl playing quietly outside and then back to the photo. How did Richard and Molly Carlson ever produce a child who looked like this? Twice?

"I'll be in touch."

Molly squeezed my hand. Again she said, "Thank you."

I shook hands with Carlson and went to my Jeep Grand Cherokee parked in their driveway. Stacy waved as I drove away. I waved back.

Ten minutes later I parked in front of the Judy Garland Museum, Judy singing "Somewhere over the Rainbow" on a weather-battered speaker, the ticket taker singing along. Kirsten Sager Whitson was leaning against the building, waiting for me.

"Sorry I took so long." I gestured toward the museum. "How was it?"

"Okay," she answered without enthusiasm. I reached for her hand. She pulled it away and filled it with her purse, making it seem like a casual gesture instead of the deliberate snub I knew it to be. She moved quickly to the passenger door of my SUV, opening it before I had the chance to do it for her.

A visit to the museum—Judy Garland had been born Francis Gumm in Grand Rapids; her family later moved to Duluth—had been Kirsten's idea, an alternative to meeting one of my "cases." Kirsten didn't approve of my occasional forays into detective work and said so.

She thought they were common, even used that word once. "Common." I reminded her that I was eleven years a police officer. "How common is that?" Only that was before Teachwell and, in Kirsten's world view, didn't count.

Teachwell's company and insurance carrier had agreed to pay a finder's fee of fifty cents on the dollar with the stipulation that I keep my mouth shut about the size of the theft—thus avoiding a possible Enron-like meltdown of the company's stock. After the government took its 36.45 percent, I was left with approximately two million in income-producing mutual funds. Kirsten expected me to act like it. Only I had been unable to cast off the shackles of my blue-collar upbringing. She had used those words, too. "The shackles of your blue-collar upbringing."

"What do they want you to do?" she asked when we hit Highway 169 going south toward the Cities. I told her. "You're going to do it, aren't you? You're going to find the girl."

"Sure, if I can. Why not?"

"You don't need to do this."

"No. I could turn the car around and go back to the cabin. You and I can spend another week fishing and swimming and lolling in the sun. But I thought it was starting to get a little old toward the end, didn't you?"

"No. What I mean is, you don't need to do *this*. You could get a real job if you're bored."

"Doing what? Making more money?"

"There's nothing wrong with making money."

"Of course not. Except I already make $170,000 a year just for getting up in the morning. I realize that's not much if you're a shortstop for the Texas Rangers. On the other hand, I don't have coaches yelling at me or fans booing because I hit a single instead of a home run. Anyway, my needs are few and relatively inexpensive. I have more than I'll ever need."

"I'm not talking about money."

"I thought you were."

"I'm talking about getting a job that you can care about, that has value, that gives you pleasure. Like, like . . ."

"Like helping people with their problems?"

She didn't have anything to say to that.

"Kirsten, I was a cop for eleven years. It was the only real job I ever had. I liked it. I liked catching bad guys, I liked being a peacemaker, protecting the peace. But mostly I liked helping people. It got to be a habit with me."

She didn't have anything to say to that, either.

During the 200-mile drive up from the Twin Cities Kirsten had been all chit-chat, conversing in depth on a number of topics that meant nothing to her. Same thing at the cabin. Now she sat in stony silence, staring out the passenger window. I didn't push, yet by the time we hit McGregor, midway between Grand Rapids and the Cities, I was feeling anxious. I figured she wanted to tell me something and was having a difficult time getting to it. I also decided I definitely didn't want to hear it.

Kirsten agreed to stop for a sandwich, and I pulled off the main drag and parked in the gravel lot of a restaurant called Jack's. Across the highway from Jack's was a small office building. A few decades ago Jack's was called Mark's and the office building had been a mom-and-pop tavern called The Wheel-Inn. It was there that I had witnessed Neil Armstrong's first steps on the moon. My parents and I were returning from a camping trip not far from where my lake home is now and listening to the event on the radio. As the historic moment approached, my father stopped at the first public place he saw with a TV antenna. We sat in the tavern for over three hours eating hamburgers and drinking root beer while waiting for Armstrong and Buzz Aldrin to leave their landing module. I don't remember much about the historic moment—I was so young. But I remember the root beer and I remember my parents. Dad cried and Mom laughed.

"Are you coming?" Kirsten asked.

I closed my door and locked it with a button on my key chain.

"Are you pregnant?"

Kirsten's mouth hung open for a moment and I thought I had guessed right. I was actually disappointed when she finally shook her head and said, "No."

"What is it then?"

"Nothing."

"Hey." I rested my hands on top of her shoulders, leaning in, and giving her my most reassuring smile. "It's me."

She stepped back until her shoulders were no longer within reach. My hands fell away.

"Oh right. Like suddenly you're the Great Communicator."

I was surprised by the sharpness of her words. "Where did that come from?"

She crossed her arms.

"Kirsten?"

"It's not you, it's me."

"What's you and not me?"

"Do we have to talk about this now?"

I gestured toward 169 with my head. "We're running out of highway."

Kirsten stepped away from the restaurant door and walked to the center of the parking lot. Gravel crunched under her feet.

"Something's changed," she said.

"What's changed?"

"Something."

I shook my head dumbly, my mouth open. I felt numb, except for my stomach—my stomach was suddenly very active, performing all kinds of gymnastics.

"You spend too much time on the fringe, McKenzie," she told me at last. "The people you associate with—they live in rooms they pay for by the week."

"I don't know what that means."

"The coke-heads, the pushers, the prostitutes, the criminals and low-lifes and, and—two weeks ago we were supposed to go to the Guthrie Theater but we didn't because instead you were parked outside a motel with a camera because a friend wanted to know if her husband was cheating on her."

"The woman was from the neighborhood; I knew her growing up."

"That's what I mean. The people you deal with. In your world, in the world where you do these favors for people, everyone is so, so—wrong."

"A middle-aged couple from Grand Rapids is wrong?"

"You know what I mean."

I took the half dozen steps to my car door without realizing I had done it. The vehicle was now between us. I looked over its roof at Kirsten.

"I don't want to deal with it anymore," she announced with a voice as hard as the look in her eyes.

"Would you be happier if I was a stock broker?"

"Yes."

"A lawyer?"

"Yes."

"The artistic director for the Minnesota Opera Company?"

"Yes."

"I can't be those things."

"I think maybe we should start seeing other people."

"Are you already seeing other people?"

"Oh yeah, right. Typical male reaction."

"Is that a yes or no?"

Kirsten moved to the Cherokee, leaned against it. Her arms stretched across the roof toward me. I took both of her hands in mine.

"I would never do that, Mac," she said, softening her voice for effect. "I care for you too deeply. Besides, you carry a gun."

Kirsten smiled. I guess she thought she had made a joke.

"If you tell me you just want to be friends, I might use it."

See, I can be funny, too.

"You'll always be more than that," she said.

"Then why are you dumping me?"

Kirsten didn't answer and I found myself gazing at the office building across the highway again. Suddenly, walking on the moon didn't seem like such a big thing.

I dropped Kirsten at her handsome Cape Cod located on the parkway that ringed the Lake of the Isles in Minneapolis, the house with the Victorian-style gazebo in the backyard. She kissed me good-bye. Not one of those quick pecks people in a hurry usually give each other. This one lingered long enough to cause a stirring in the nether regions.

Sure, I thought as she bounded away, her designer duffel bag over her shoulder. *Break up with a guy and then kiss him to the depths of his soul so he knows what he's losing.* 'Course, Kirsten insisted that she wasn't dumping me, that we weren't breaking up. We were merely seeing other people. So there was still hope. Yeah, right.

Twenty minutes later I reached my own home in Falcon Heights, a large English Colonial with a sprawling front porch. When I bought it, I thought it was located in St. Anthony Park, an exclusive, quiet, exceedingly old neighborhood of St. Paul tucked unobtrusively between the St. Paul campus of the University of Minnesota and the city of Minneapolis. It wasn't until I made an offer that I discovered to my horror that the house was on the wrong side of Hoyt Avenue, that I had inadvertently moved to the suburbs. Still, I'm a St. Paul boy at heart and whenever anyone asks, that's where I tell them I live.

I parked in my garage and entered the house through the back door.

The first thing I did—before flicking on a light, before opening a window, before checking my mail and newspapers stacked in a box on the porch—was to turn on my CD player. Immediately, the grandiose sounds of opera spilled out of nineteen speakers strategically placed in various nooks and crannies throughout the house—Maria Callas singing an excerpt from *Madame Butterfly*. There was a purity to the music that I rarely heard in any other form. Still, I wasn't an opera fan. I listened to it because Kirsten listened to it. It was Callas, in fact, who had brought us together.

I had attended a Christmas party in the offices of my accountant, where I had discovered a remarkably handsome woman arguing with a man I didn't know. From what they said, I gathered that Callas had once been quite fat—as opera divas often are—when she first established her reputation. Afterward, she carefully and deliberately shed a third of her weight, turning herself into the sleek, fashionable woman who attracted the attention of Greek tycoon Aristotle Onassis, among others. The topic of debate was whether Callas sounded better when she was fat or when she was thin.

"What do you think?" the woman asked abruptly.

"It might be sexist," I told her, "but things tend to sound better when they come from an attractive package. You, for example, remind me of a Mozart aria."

She laughed and told me that was the most original line she had ever heard. One thing led to another and there I was, listening to Maria Callas on a late Sunday afternoon.

"Why do you need to see other people?" I asked the empty house. Its answer was no more satisfying than Kirsten's had been in McGregor.

I poured myself a Pig's Eye beer and drank it way too fast. I poured myself another. I figured I had two choices. I could sit around and feel sorry for myself or I could work. I chose feeling sorry for myself. That lasted until the telephone rang.

"Are you all right?" Kirsten asked.

I was so surprised to hear her voice my heart skipped a beat and a voice shouting from the back of my head told me that it had all been a terrible mistake—*of course she loves you.*

"Sure, why wouldn't I be?"

"I thought you might . . ." After a long pause she added, "I knew you would be okay, I was just checking."

"Thank you for your concern," I replied stoically. Sure, like I was going to tell *her* I was hurting.

"Mac?"

"Hmm?"

"Mac, you're not like anyone else I know. All the men I know, they have a-gen-das"—she sounded the word out—"they have plans, they have mission statements. You don't. No, come to think about it, you do. You do have a mission statement. But yours is so simple and concise. Live well. Be helpful."

Why are you telling me that? I asked myself but didn't say.

"You're a good guy," she added. "There aren't many like you out there."

"Thank you."

"Umm, I have to—I have to go, now."

"Me, too."

She said, "I'll talk to you later," but it sounded like "good-bye."

And that was the end of that.

I hung up and listened to Maria for a little while longer.

"Screw this," I announced. I went to the CD player and replaced Maria's disc with another. A moment later Bonnie Raitt filled my house, asking, "What is this thing called love?"

What indeed?

———

I poured a third Pig's Eye—promising myself this would be the last—
and settled in with my telephone directories. It's rarely that easy, but you
have to begin somewhere and after seven years maybe Jamie wasn't hiding very hard. It was seven when I started dialing, eight-fifteen when I
finished. Everyone was home—it was Sunday night in Minnesota, after
all. There was one honest-to-God Jamie Anne Carlson listed in the Twin
Cities, only she was sixteen years old. Her father, a doctor, had given her
a phone with the stipulation that she stay the hell off his. There were
thirteen 'J' Carlsons in the Minneapolis white pages and eight 'JA's—
including a Jean Autry—but no Jamies. The St. Paul white pages listed
six 'J's and two 'JA's. None of them was the woman I was looking for.

I returned the phone books to their proper place under the junk
drawer in my kitchen and moved to what my father used to call "the
family room," just off the dining room. Boz Scaggs followed me, having
replaced Bonnie Raitt in the ten-disc CD player.

I fired up my PC and accessed the Web site of the Minnesota
Department of Public Safety. I found the screen for motor vehicle information and completed the request form, asking for Jamie's driver's
license information. The request cost four dollars, would take at least
twenty-four hours to complete, and left me wondering what to do next.

The concept of the right to privacy is a treasured hallmark of the
American way of life, institutionalized early on by the founding fathers
in the fourth and fifth amendments to the U.S. Constitution. It's also a
myth. In this era of advanced computer technology, guys like me can
examine private information contained in vast databases that most
Americans don't even know exist. Give me a name—just a name—and
in seventy-two hours I can learn if the guy's married, his wife's maiden
name, the names of his children, where they go to school, and if he's
shacking up with some bimbo at the No-Tell Motel. I can obtain finan-
cial records including bank account numbers, deposits and balances,
insurance policies, medical history going back ten years, employment

histories, credit histories, court judgments, worker's compensation claims, property records, even high school and college grades. I can learn which credit cards he carries, what magazines he reads, which restaurants he frequents, the charities he supports, the organizations he belongs to, as well as his long-distance and intrastate toll calls. If he's online I'll know which Web sites he visits and what chat rooms he hangs out in. I can even find out if he wears a toupee or bought the Mario Lanza CD that was advertised on television. Yet it all seemed like so much work for a guy who broke his promise and was now working on his fourth beer.

Besides, there were two databases that might tell me everything I needed to know in a hurry if I could tap them—the National Crime Information Center and the Minnesota Bureau of Criminal Apprehension's Criminal Justice Information System. I used to have a pretty reliable source in the Ramsey County Sheriff's Department who would access this information for me—I paid him fifty, sometimes a hundred bucks a pop. But that was when he was a sergeant making thirty-nine seven a year. Now he's a newly promoted lieutenant pulling down forty-four five and he's above it all. Not only that, he threatens if he catches me using someone else in the department he'll bust my balls—how soon they forget.

I considered several other likely candidates who could help me and settled on Detective Sergeant Robert J. Dunston of the St. Paul Police Department. I called. The phone rang five times before a woman answered, "Hello."

"Hi, Shel. It's me."

"Rushmore." She's the only person who gets to call me that. "When are you going to take me away from all this?"

"From all of what? What's going on?"

"Bobby's in one of his moods again. Right now he's upstairs lecturing the girls because they didn't turn on the porch light."

"Put him on the phone."

A few moments later Bobby was telling me what he told his two daughters.

"How many times do I need to say it? Keep the front door locked, keep the back door locked, turn on the lights. How many women need to be raped, how many need to be killed before they catch on? Do they need to see pictures, 'cause I have pictures."

"Crime scene photos? You're going to show crime scene photos to an eight- and ten-year-old girl?"

"If that's what it takes."

"Bob, you're losing it."

"Am I?" He took a deep breath. "Maybe I am." Slow exhale. "It was awful. The worst I ever caught. What he did to her." His voice dropped several octaves like he was afraid someone would overhear him. "Mac, he removed one of her breasts with a steak knife, the other he peeled the way you would fillet a fish. Cigarette burns all over her body, a knife protruding from her vagina. He tied her to the bedposts with twine and sealed her mouth with duct tape. . . ."

I closed my eyes at the horror of it. Sometimes I didn't miss police work at all.

"I never saw one that bad before, not even in training," Bobby added.

"Who was she?"

"Katherine Katzmark. Know her?"

"Name sounds familiar."

"She was an entrepreneur. Rich. Owned a catering service and a chain of kitchenware stores that sold imported place settings, cutlery and that sort of thing—you know, Worldware—and something else, I don't remember. By this time tomorrow I'll know everything about her."

I didn't doubt him for a moment. Bobby was an extremely thorough investigator.

He added, "I only came home for a few hours of sleep," in case I thought he was sloughing off—the first twenty-four hours in a murder investigation are crucial.

"High profile case," I volunteered.

"Tell me about it, the media is already . . ." He paused, sighed some more. "You try not to take it home with you, you know? But I pull into the driveway and the light's not on."

"I know."

He paused for a moment and then asked, "What did you want, anyway?"

"I was going to beg a favor but I'm embarrassed now, what with your other troubles."

"But not *too* embarrassed."

Of course not. I told him the reason I called and he recited the department line concerning the unauthorized use of criminal records along with a lecture centering around the fact that he was far too busy to do my *favors* for me. I agreed with him and apologized.

"Ahh, screw it, I'll call you tomorrow morning."

"Bobby?" I asked before he hung up.

"Yeah?"

"Could you pull Merci Cole, too?"

"Sure. Why not? It's not like I have anything better to do."

I then asked him to put his wife back on the phone.

"Rushmore?"

"What the hell, Shelby. You and the girls can't be bothered to lock doors and turn on lights . . . ?"

2

Bobby Dunston's call caught me just as I was stepping out of the shower. I was dripping water all over my bedroom carpet when he told me, "I pulled the information you wanted."

"Thank you."

"Why don't you come downtown about twelve-thirty and I'll give it to you. You can buy me lunch."

"Sounds like a plan."

"You can do a favor for me, too."

"Sure."

He hung up before I could ask him what favor.

Jerry Jeff Walker was on the CD player, singing about getting off that L.A. freeway without getting killed. I hummed along while I drank my coffee and read the newspapers.

Both the St. Paul *Pioneer Press* and the Minneapolis *Star-Tribune* were filled with stories about the brutal slaying of Katherine Katzmark. They emphasized that she had been an attractive woman. They remarked on the three businesses she had owned. They also made mention of the fact that she was the only female among the eight founding members of the Northern Lights Entrepreneur's Club, a growing organization of young businesspeople that was challenging The Brotherhood—as the Twin Cities' more senior movers and shakers were known—for political and economic dominance. It was just-the-facts-ma'am reporting, but there was an interesting if not insidious edge to it that disturbed me. The papers seemed to suggest that Katherine had been raped, tortured, and murdered *because* of her looks, her three businesses, and her involvement in the club—that her brutal death was punishment for having the audacity to shine in a male-dominated world.

Or maybe it was just me.

Without thinking, I reached for the phone. I was going to call Kirsten to ask if she had the same take on the articles as I did but then I remembered—we don't have a relationship anymore. I cursed softly and returned the receiver to its cradle.

I was surrounded by eight large windows arranged in a semicircle in the breakfast nook that I had added to the house, each window over-looking my backyard. The yard was nearly a hundred feet deep and at the back of it was a small pond with a fountain in the center that my father had installed—I had told him we could pay someone to build it for us, but he was a guy who liked to do things himself. In the pond I could see five baby ducks frolicking under the watchful protection of their parents.

The mallards had arrived in the early spring at just about the time my father died and had somehow discovered the pond despite the fir trees that shaded it. Soon after, the five ducklings appeared. I told my father about the ducks while he lay in a hospital bed and he made me promise to take care of them. He was a guy who took care of things, of people. If you needed a ditch dug, a roof shingled, furniture moved; if you needed a few bucks or a shoulder to cry on; if you needed a volunteer, you called my dad. I learned from him.

I began by feeding the ducks from a distance, but eventually they took dried corn out of my hand. I called the adults Hepburn and Tracy. The kids I named Bobby, Shelby, Victoria, and Katie after the Dunston family and Maureen after my mother. They seemed quite content in my backyard and I dreaded the day they would all fly south for the winter. I asked a friend at the Department of Natural Resources about it and he told me if they survived the trip the ducks would probably return in the spring to establish new nests.

"In a few years you could be up to your butt in mallards," he said.

That was fine with me. I liked the ducks. One of the things I liked most about them: They mated for life.

The St. Paul Police Department is located across from the Tastee Bread Company in downtown St. Paul, I-94 cutting a valley between them. I parked neatly in the visitors section of the asphalt lot after dodging a half dozen vans and panel trucks that were parked any which way the drivers pleased. The trucks were emblazoned with the logos and call letters of local TV and radio stations. Reporters for the stations as well as the two Twin Cities daily newspapers and assorted weeklies milled together in the foyer, standing apart from the officers who came and went, while they waited for someone in authority to make a statement. Most of the officers viewed the reporters with derision if not outright contempt. I recognized some of the cops from my eleven years on the force. Some of them recognized me.

They were friendly enough. They slapped my back and shook my hand and joked about the times we shared and how bad things were getting in the department and how lucky I was to have left when I did and said we should all get together and raise some hell. Only I knew nothing would come of it. I was no longer a member of the fraternity. I had quit. Pulled the pin and walked away. I might have gone back if someone invited me, only no one did. So, I stood by myself in the foyer, waiting for Bobby. It was the curse of the self-employed—or unemployed, as the case might be. Working alone you often become lonely. There's no one with whom to discuss last night's Twins game or politics or even the weather.

"I feel like a kibitzer," I told Bobby later as we left the building, walking south on Minnesota Street.

"You are a kibitzer," he said abruptly.

"Thank you for understanding."

"What do you want me to tell you? That you're an integral member of the St. Paul Police Department? You're not."

There was anger in his voice and since I was reasonably sure I hadn't put it there, I asked, "What's going on?"

Bobby threw a glance over his shoulder at the TV vans.

"In about ten minutes, Deputy Chief Tommy Thompson is going to blow my investigation to hell and gone."

"How?"

"He's going to tell the media that Katherine Katzmark's boyfriend is our only suspect."

"Is he your only suspect?"

"So far."

"Are you going to arrest him?"

"Hell, no! Right now there's plenty of evidence to prove that he was in Kansas City when the murder took place and absolutely none to prove that he wasn't. He's the one who discovered the body. He's the one who called 911. He's cooperating. He's answering questions. But once he hears what Thompson has to say, you just know he's gonna lawyer-up and then I won't get jack from him.

"Bastard Thompson—he wants his fifteen minutes of fame so bad. I begged him, Mac. I actually begged him not to mention the boyfriend. 'But we have to give the media something,' he says. Yeah, right. Something that'll get him on the evening news before the chief comes back and takes over."

"Where is the chief?"

"Fishing. In Florida."

"Lucky him," I said.

"You know what this means, don't you? From now on I'll be expected to prove that the boyfriend killed Katherine. Forget developing other leads or investigating other suspects, just get the boyfriend."

"Maybe he did it."

"What do we know? We know that Katherine was a white, upper-class female who was killed in one of the safest neighborhoods in the Twin Cities, so right away we figure she was killed by someone she knew."

I had the distinct impression that he was talking more to himself than he was to me.

"We know that in spite of everything the bastard did to her, the ME says she was strangled—manual strangulation—which means the killer probably had a strong personal attachment to her.

"We know that the killer was unafraid of discovery. He did nothing quickly. He spent hours in that house, which indicates that he knew something of her habits. What's more, everything he used came from Katherine's kitchen—the twine, duct tape, steak knife—he knew it was available to him before he arrived."

Bobby was on a roll now.

"And we know the way he hacked her body, the way he displayed it, concealing nothing—he wanted people to see what he had done to her. That indicates rage. A crime of passion. And yeah, all that would seem to indicate the boyfriend."

"He wouldn't be the first killer to"—I quoted the air—" 'discover' the body."

"Except he was in Kansas City for a convention. He flew down there Thursday morning and we know he flew back early Sunday afternoon. In between . . ." Bobby shrugged. "Kansas City is four hundred fifty miles away. That's a lot of hard driving there and back in the amount of time he had."

"Unless he flew."

"Doesn't matter. Fly or rent a car, he'd still need a credit card—after nine-eleven no one's accepting cash. We're checking. So far nothing. But we're still looking. In the meantime, I sent Jeannie down to KC to interview hotel employees and any conventioneers she can find, check his alibi."

"Who's Jeannie?"

"My new partner. You haven't met her yet. You'll like her. Young. Beautiful. Smart as hell."

Bobby stopped walking. I was two steps past before I realized it and turned toward him. He was pointing a finger at me.

"I'll tell you one thing—I don't care what Thompson tells the media. I will not play favorites. I'm not going to arrest just any dumb moke to clear the case. I'm going to get the right person for it and I'm gonna put him away forever."

I draped my arm over his shoulders and led him across 10th Street. I tried to recall my first impression of Bobby Dunston and failed. I couldn't remember how or when we met—probably school. It seemed we were always in the same class together, always played on the same baseball teams and hockey teams. We even went to the same college—the University of Minnesota—each selecting the school independently, not at all surprised to learn the other had made the same choice.

"We've sure come a helluva long way since we played ball at Dunning Field," I told him.

"Naw," he said. "It just seems long."

We continued walking together in silence. Finally, I asked, "Where are we going?"

Donahue's hadn't changed much since the early 1950s when the purple neon sign above the door blinked HOME COOKING. The sign was still there although the neon had long since burned out. So were the original booths and tables, just as worn with age and use as the sign. The walls were adorned with a series of Chinese landscapes that seemed as out of place now as they had fifteen years ago when I was introduced to the restaurant. I was still on probation and Colin Gernes, my supervising officer, sat me down at the counter and announced, "Got a rook here, Liz."

Liz was a big-busted woman of indeterminate age, dressed in a black and white uniform. "Fresh meat," she said contemptuously. Five minutes later she slid a platter of sliced roast beef served with mashed potatoes and gravy in front of me.

"This one's on the house, Rook, with some advice," she said. "Find another line of work while you still can."

"Too late," Gernes told her. "He busted a suspect for B and E this morning and he liked it. He's a thirty-year man for sure."

I learned later that Liz had a husband who put in twenty-six years with the cops before he was killed in the line of duty by a seventeen-year-old coke-head. You'd think she wouldn't want anything to do with cops after that, but she did. She took her husband's pension and insurance and bought Donahue's, where she dispensed good food, hearty laughter, caustic advice, and simple wisdom to the men and women who worked at the St. Paul Police Department three blocks away. That and a strong shoulder to cry on. When her huge heart finally burst at the age of seventy-two, they fired exactly seventy-two shots over her grave. Four hundred active and retired officers attended her funeral. No governor, no mayor, no councilman, no police chief was allowed to speak a word.

"I haven't been here in years," I said when we found a booth under a faded print showing a dozen Chinese peasants trapping a tiger beneath the Great Wall. I didn't know they had tigers in China. The restaurant was half full. Most of the cops had stopped coming after Liz passed. I read the menu the waitress gave me. I don't know why. I already knew what I was going to order. "Hot roast beef with mashed potatoes."

After the waitress took our orders, Bobby told me that there was no paper on Carlson, Jamie Anne—she hadn't ever been arrested for anything, not even a traffic summons. He had run the name through DMV. The only match was sixteen and brunette and living in Minneapolis—the doctor's daughter, I presumed.

"What about Merci Cole?" I asked.

Bobby gave me a folded sheet of paper.

"My, my, my."

Merci had a long list of prostitution gripes, one DWI, a couple of dis cons and one Class A felony—possession with intent. She did eighteen months at Shakopee and was released six weeks ago. Her last known address was on Avon near University Avenue in St. Paul, a neighborhood with abysmal property values.

I refolded the sheet and stuffed it in my pocket.

"I appreciate this, Bobby."

"No problem. You can do me a favor, though."

"Sure."

"I'd like to use your lake home. . . ."

"Of course."

"When this is done . . ."

"Anytime you want."

"Get away for a few days."

"It's yours. In fact, I'll tell you what. I'll get you a set of keys. Whenever you want to use it, don't even ask. Just go."

"That's decent of you."

"Think of it as a resort. Use the boats, the tackle, eat the food, drink the beer—don't worry about anything. It's on me. And hey, if you and Shelby want to go alone, have a nice weekend of passion, huh? I'll be happy to take the girls."

"Nice weekend of passion," he repeated quietly, nodding his head like he could already see it. And then, "How's Kirsten?"

"It's not my turn to watch her."

"Trouble in paradise?"

"It looks like we're through. She says she wants to see other people."

Bobby nodded.

"What does that mean?" I asked.

"Huh?"

"The head nodding, what does that mean?"

"It means I'm not surprised."

"Oh, really?"

"She's money, man. She's Lake Minnetonka, she's Vassar, she's opera."

"I have money."

"Yeah, but she was born to it, she was raised by it. You just lucked into it. Answer me this. Would she have gone out with you if you were still a cop living in Merriam Park?"

"I like to think so."

Bobby shook his head.

"Don't get me wrong, I liked Kirsten when I met her. But the thing is, this is a girl who never rode on a city bus, not once in her life, while you and me, we're the guys who tried to sneak on and off without paying, who slipped slugs into the doohickey that collected the fares."

He had a point.

"You'll find another girl," he added.

"You think?"

"God, I hope. I've been living vicariously through your sexual exploits for years."

"What sexual exploits?"

"C'mon, Mac. You've got it made."

"I do?"

"All these women who put off getting married, who put off having families while they were establishing their careers, suddenly they're our age and they're looking around for eligible guys and there just aren't any." He pointed at me then. "Except for a few guys like you."

"Like me?"

"You're good-looking, not as good-looking as me, but presentable."

"Oh, thanks."

"Plus, you have money. But what makes you a catch is what you don't have. You don't have an ex-wife. You don't have kids. You don't have debts. You don't have a chemical problem. You don't have a criminal record. You're not a jerk. Mac, you don't have baggage. Intelligent, accomplished, independent career women like Kirsten, geez, Mac, they fall all over guys like you. I only wish I was in your place. You are so lucky."

I thought that was pretty funny. Bobby asked me why I was laughing. I flashed on Shelby and his two daughters.

"Because I was going to tell you the same thing."

Merci Cole's last known address was a dilapidated apartment building that looked abandoned except for the silver Lincoln parked in front. Several screens had been punched or kicked out, a few windows were broken, and the sidewalk was littered with broken glass. CRIPS, the name of an L.A. street gang transplanted to the Twin Cities, was written across the sidewalk with red spray paint. A black man dressed in a white silk suit, white silk shirt, and white silk tie moved along the sidewalk, boogeying to some private riff, not a worry in the world, oblivious to everything around him. You'd think a man in his line of work would be more careful.

I once asked Colin Gernes why most pimps are black.

"For the same reason most basketball players are black," he replied, scarcely believing how dumb I was, wondering where the department found so many dumb rookies. "It's an inner city game and there are more blacks in the inner city."

Oh.

I saw no one as I locked my Jeep Cherokee and crossed the street to the apartment building, yet I could feel eyes from at least a dozen windows and I could hear them: *Who is this white man with his expensive sport utility vehicle and what is he doing in our neighborhood?* Good question.

I opened the door to the building and hesitated. There were mailboxes just inside the hallway, all of them jimmied open. The overhead light had been broken recently and shattered slivers of bulb were scattered across the floor. There was enough light from the street to prove that the hallway was empty so I went inside. Most people will do anything to avoid a fight and the fear it produces. I'm one of them. On the other hand, you have to accept a certain amount of risk in everything you do. I started climbing the stairs, touching my hip where my gun would have been if I had thought to bring it.

Along with the camaraderie, you know what else I miss about being a police officer? The backup.

According to Bobby's file, Merci Cole's apartment was on the fourth floor. I never reached it. When I was midway between the third and fourth floors, a well-muscled black man wearing only blue jeans burst from his apartment, an aluminum Lady Thumper softball bat in his hands. He swung at my head and I jumped backward down the stairs, the barrel of the bat missing my chin by inches and smashing a hole into the thin plaster wall. I grabbed for the railing as he swung again. I lost my grip and fell, tumbling down to the third floor landing as his bat bounced off the wall where my head would have been if I had kept my balance.

He followed close behind. I hit the landing with my shoulder, rolled, jumped to my feet. He pulled the bat back. I did a little hop and stomped his knee with the flat of my shoe. He cried out, an animal in pain, and dropped the bat. It rolled down the stairs, going *thump, thump, thump* as it fell to the next landing. He grabbed his knee. I hit him in the face. He threw a long, complicated, and entirely filthy curse at me. I hit him again. As I hit him I thought, *This is what Kirsten must have meant by associating with "wrong people."*

"No more, no more," he moaned, doing a fair impersonation of Roberto Duran. Apparently, he didn't like pain any more than I did.

"Why did you come after me?" I was snorting, my breath coming hard and fast.

"Are you a cop? You look like cop. You a cop you gotta tell me, that's the rules."

"You swung on me because you thought I was a cop? What are you, a moron? The police would've blown your brains out you swing on them like that."

"No, no, man. They got new rules. They can't just shoot people, no more. They gotta bring in counselors and shit. I read 'bout it."

"Hey, pal. Don't believe everything you read. It's healthier that way."

"You're not a cop? You look like a cop."

"Have it your own way. Where's Merci Cole?"

"Hey man, you not a cop? Fuck you, then."

"Wrong answer." I raised my fist menacingly, giving him a good look at it. Normally, I abhor violence, except I had a hard time getting past the fact the sonuvabitch tried to bludgeon me with a woman's softball bat.

He brought his shoulder up to protect his face.

"She's gone, man."

"Gone where?"

"I don't know."

"What do you know?"

"She got outta Shakopee a month ago, longer."

"Okay."

"Right after, she and another bitch come by lookin' for some clothes and stuff she stashed here before she got busted. Then they took off."

"She didn't say where she was goin'?"

"She didn't say nothin' except scream 'cuz most of her shit was gone. What the bitch expect, man?"

"Does she have any friends here?"

"Nobody's got any friends here."

"Where did she hang out before she went inside?"

"Cheney's. When she wasn't workin' she was there. Cheney's, you know, like the vice president."

I was amazed he even knew who the vice president was.

"Tell me about the other woman. What did she look like?"

"A good lookin' piece. Nice ass, tits out to—"

I hit him again.

"What the fuck, man?"

"I don't need an anatomy lesson."

"What you want me to tell ya?"

"What did she look like?"

"White girl, looked like Cole."

"Hair?"

"Real blond, almost white."

"Eyes?"

"Didn't see 'em. She was wearin' shades."

"Height?"

"Same as Cole, man. Look, Cole stashed her stuff in the trunk and they split, that's all I know."

"Tell me about the car."

"It was a Beamer, man. Fuckin' white BMW convertible. Wait, now I remember. James Bond."

"What?"

"Merci called her James, the other one. Called her James and I was thinking what the fuck kinda name is that for a woman. James. Then I see the license plate. It had a JB on it."

"JB what?"

"Just JB, man. You know, one of those vanity plates."

"Thank you, you've been very helpful. Only listen. For what it's worth, I do believe this life doesn't suit you. You should work for the government, work for the state. Get one of those orange vests and walk along the interstate picking up trash. Think of the job security."

"Fuck you."

When I was a kid, the Midway Shopping Center on Snelling and University was just a dinky little thing. It had a Kroger's where my parents bought groceries, a G. C. Murphy's where I bought comic books, and a hobby shop where Bobby and I sometimes raced model cars on Saturday mornings. Now it was a huge, sprawling enterprise saturated with national retailers, grocery chains, and fast food joints that covered several city blocks. About the only thing that remained from the old days was a locksmith. I stopped off there to have copies made of the keys to my lake home. Since I was in the neighborhood, I also picked up a small gift.

I knocked on the front door, opened it, and stuck my head inside.

"Shelby," I called.

"In the kitchen," she called back.

Shelby was about an inch shorter than I was, only you wouldn't have noticed just then because she was bent over a counter wrapping chunks of beef, cubed potatoes, sliced carrots, assorted spices, and a tab of butter with rectangles of pastry.

"Hey, Rushmore. What are you doing here?"

She raised her cheek to me. I kissed it and said, "I brought over the keys."

She straightened and brushed hair the color of butterscotch off her forehead with the back of her hand. Her eyes were the color of rich, green pastures at sunset.

"What keys?"

"For my lake home." I set three keys on the counter in succession. Each was a different color. "Red is for the house, blue is for the boat house, and green is for the garage."

"Why are you giving me your keys?"

"Bobby didn't tell you? He wants to use my lake home after he clears the case he caught."

"He didn't mention it."

"Perhaps he means to surprise you with a weekend of passion."

"That would be a surprise. He hasn't surprised me for almost a month now."

"Okay, that's more information than I need to know." I was embarrassed by her remark and something else—the suggestion that my best friends were having marital problems frightened me.

"Bobby didn't tell you we've been having our ups and downs?"

"There are subjects we don't discuss."

"Politics and religion."

"Actually, we talk about politics and religion all the time. It's what we do in the privacy of our own homes that we tend to keep to ourselves. Ahh"—I raised a finger, anxious to change the subject—"I have a present for you."

I handed her a small gift bag that I had kept hidden when I entered the kitchen. She took it gingerly. "Rush . . . ?"

I flicked my hand at her.

Shelby opened the bag and fished out a plastic snow globe of Mount Rushmore. She laughed, as I had hoped she would. She shook the globe and watched the tiny white specks fall around the plastic monument.

"Whenever I look at it I'll think of you."

"That's the plan. Listen, I have to go. I'm doing a favor for a guy."

"Bobby told me. Don't rush off. Sit down. Talk to me. Better yet, stay for dinner. The girls'll be home from school in a few minutes. God knows when Bobby will be home."

"I can't."

"The girls will be sorry they missed you. You've become their all-time favorite person."

"Seriously?"

"Ever since you announced that they were the heirs to your fortune."

"Someone has to be. Besides, I'm not above buying affection from women."

Shelby held up the snow globe. "I noticed."

"I'll see you later." I kissed her cheek and made my way to the front door. She followed me. When I reached the door and opened it she was standing there, cupping the snow globe in her hands.

"Don't be a stranger," she said.

"Tell me something, Shel." The words spilled out; I'm still not sure where they came from. "Just out of curiosity, if I had been the one who spilled the drink on your dress back when we were in school instead of Bobby, do you think you and I would have been the ones to get involved?"

"We are involved, Rushmore. Don't you know that?"

A moment later I was in the Cherokee. She was still standing in the doorway. I waved to her. She waved back. I slipped the Jeep in gear and drove off even as I screamed at myself. *What's wrong with you, asking a question like that? What were you thinking? She's the wife of your best friend. What a jerk!*

The e-mail from the Department of Motor Vehicles told me the same thing that Bobby had. The only Carlson, Jamie Anne, with a driver's license in the state of Minnesota was a sixteen-year-old brunette living in Minneapolis. I put my four dollars down and requested another search, this time for the owner of a vanity plate with the initials JB.

Just as I hit the "send" button, the telephone rang.

"It's me," Shelby said.

"Hi."

"I want you to know that you are my good friend and I love you, but you shouldn't be asking questions like you asked and you shouldn't be giving me gifts, even goofy little things like the snow globe, except on my birthday and at Christmas."

"I know."

"I'm married."

She's married, she's married, she's married—to your best friend, you moron!

"I know."

"Well, then, I'll be seeing you soon."

"Sure."

She hung up and I told myself: *Don't ever do that again, you dumb schmuck.*

If you believe the crime statistics—and we all know how reliable they are—there are about 150 full-time prostitutes in St. Paul and three times that many in Minneapolis. The bars, saunas, hotels, convention centers, and private parties—where a working girl can get shelter from the rain—belong to women with valid twenty-one-year-old IDs. The streets belong to the children. The average age of a street hooker in the

Twin Cities is sixteen. You see them waving at the cars that cruise Frog-town, a decidedly blue-collar community north of University Avenue and west of the State Capital, and in East St. Paul, especially in the Arcade-Payne Avenue neighborhood where Cheney's is located.

"Are you looking to party?"

Maybe they'll hop in the cars and find an alley somewhere, or take their customers to the hot-bed hotel up the street renting rooms at twenty bucks a half hour. Or maybe they'll walk the john around back, kneeling on the asphalt, slipping the wallet out of the john's sucker pocket while he's slipping it in—what's he going to do, call a cop? A few minutes later they'll be back on the corner, looking for another willing customer with clean blood.

It's a tough way to make a living. Yet while I can sympathize with prostitutes, johns are a mystery to me. I have no idea what motivates them. Especially those who buy young girls off the street, paying forty bucks to abuse a child. I only know that when it comes to prostitution, we usually arrest the wrong people.

It was still early evening when I arrived at the bar. Three hookers sat together at a square table in the back where they could see the comings and goings of all of Cheney's patrons. When they saw me, one of the women said something to the other two and stood. Time to go to work.

The woman, wearing a short, tight, purple skirt and purple blouse with a plunging neckline, intercepted me at the bar.

"You looking to party?" she asked, exuding all the charm of an X-rated movie.

"Damn right," I said, slapping the bar top with my hand. "Innkeeper! I just hit the Pick Three. Gimme the most expensive beer in the house."

The bartender took a Heineken from the cooler and approached with a wary eye.

"Fine establishment you have here," I told him nice and loud in case there was someone in the joint who hadn't already noticed me.

"We like it," he said, placing the bottle and an empty glass in front of me. I poured the beer myself.

"So, honey," I said to the woman hugging my side. "What's your name?"

"What name do you like?"

"Cloris," I told her.

"You're kiddin' me."

"Would I do a thing like that? So listen, Cloris, did you hear the one about the blind man who walks into a bar and starts swinging his dog over his head by its tail? The bartender asks, 'What are you doing?' And the blind man says, 'Just looking around.'"

"Oh, brother."

"I got a million of 'em."

"That's what I'm afraid of. What's your name?"

"What name do you like?"

"You're a real peach, you know that?"

"Peach is good, you can call me 'Peachy.' What are you drinking, Cloris?"

"Rum and coke."

"Innkeeper," I shouted and pointed at the woman. He nodded and moved toward us. "Did you hear about the woman who calls this guy one night? The woman says, 'This is Mary. Remember me? We met at a party two months ago and you said I was a good sport. Well, I'm pregnant and I'm going to jump off the Lake Street Bridge.' And the guy says, 'Gosh, Mary. You are a good sport.'"

It went on like that for a couple of hours, me buying drinks and telling completely tasteless jokes. After a while, the other two hookers joined us. Most of the prostitutes I've met have been very pleasant to talk to and these were no exception. I was actually enjoying myself and the women seemed to appreciate my company as well. Yet they did not let me interfere with business. They worked out a rotation and whenever they spotted a likely looking customer, one of them would leave, do a bit of work, and return. A woman with a tired face that might have been pretty once tried to join the party, but the others chased her off. She was an amateur, one of those women who gave it away, using sex like a prescription drug. It might have been good for what ails her, but bad for a working girl's business.

Not everyone approved of me. Two overweight women and an undernourished man sitting in a booth looked on with genuine disgust. You could bet that if they had hit the number they wouldn't be wasting their winnings on a bunch of barroom layabouts, no siree. As it was, they were busy pulling tabs and discarding the losers in a plastic laundry basket. They had built up a sizable pile. Whenever they ran out of money, one of them would use the cash machine next to the rest rooms—it's illegal in Minnesota to purchase pull tabs or lottery tickets with a personal check, so some joints install ATMs.

All the while, I watched the door, waiting for Merci Cole.

"A priest, a minister, and a rabbi walk into a bar and the bartender says, 'What is this? A joke?'"

I had reached the subbasement of my joke collection and was rooting around for a trap door when Merci arrived. I recognized her by Molly Carlson's description—tall, blond, with green eyes. She had gone to high school with Jamie which made her about twenty-five. But she seemed so much older than that, her cheeks puffy, her eyes flat and lifeless. Still, she was considerably more attractive than the usual prostitute. If you don't believe me, punch up the St. Paul Police Department's Web site. The SPPD regularly posts photographs of the hookers they arrest and you'll never find a less enticing group of women—which is another reason prostitution baffles me. If hookers all looked like Julia Roberts and Laura San Giacomo, that I could understand. But why pay money to have sex with an ugly woman?

I gestured toward Merci. "I want to meet her."

"Are you serious?" Cloris replied. "You would turn me down for her? I was ready to give it up for free."

"Cloris," I said with mock indignation. "I do believe you have mis-understood my intentions."

"Screw you."

"That's what I mean. Where would you get an idea like that?"

Merci Cole sat at the end of the bar, chatting with the bartender. The bartender whispered something to her as I approached.

"Hi," I said.

"Hi, yourself."

"Busy?"

"Depends," she answered in a professional voice, waiting for the magic words that proved I wasn't a cop.

"I'm not a cop."

"If you say so, officer."

I set a fifty-dollar bill on the bar in front of her, a very uncoplike thing to do.

"What do I get for that?"

Satisfied, she went down the menu. "I get ten dollars for a hand job, twenty for a BJ, and forty if you want the motherlode. Anything else is negotiable."

"How 'bout conversation?"

"You want conversation, dial a nine hundred number, two-fifty a minute."

I pushed the fifty closer to her.

"Are you serious?"

"Let's take a walk."

"Why not?" She snapped the bill off the bar.

"Wait."

"What the hell . . . ," she said to my back as I juked and jived to the table where the three hookers sat scanning the crowd. I peeled off three one-hundred-dollar bills and dropped them on the table.

"Ladies, it's been a pleasure," I announced and waved bye-bye. I was about to become a part of hooker folklore. "Did you hear the one about the trick who paid three girls a hundred bucks each just for listening to bad jokes?"

Merci Cole waited at the door, posing more than standing, a puzzled expression on her face. A few moments later we were walking.

"What do you want to talk about?" Merci asked.

"Why did you become a prostitute?"

"What are you, a social worker?"

"No." I held up a second fifty. "But I have another one of these."

Merci reached for it, but I pulled it back.

"You're Merci Cole."

"What about it?"

"I'm looking for Jamie Carlson."

"Who?"

"Right, you never heard of her."

"I haven't seen Jamie in seven years," she told me. If it wasn't for the description given to me by the brother with the Lady Thumper, I might have believed her.

"Then who was the woman who drove you to the apartment on Avon so you could get your stuff?"

"That was someone else."

Calling Merci a liar wasn't going to get me anything, so I decided to cut to the chase. "I need to find Jamie Carlson and I'll pay you to tell me where she is."

"My friends aren't for sale."

"A hooker with a heart of gold."

She went for my face but I grabbed her hands before she could dig her nails into me.

"Let me go," she snarled.

I stepped back, waiting for her to resume the attack. She didn't. Instead she stared at me with eyes wide with hate.

"Merci." I spoke soft and low, trying to sound sincere. What is it they say? Sincerity is everything. If you can fake that, you have it made. "Jamie's parents asked me to bring her home."

"Yeah? Well screw 'em. Like they really care after all these years."

"Stacy is sick. She might die."

"Little Stacy?"

I was astonished by how suddenly her manner changed from contempt to genuine concern. It was like she had flipped a light switch.

"She has leukemia."

"Little Stacy?"

"Her parents want Jamie to come home. They need her to donate her bone marrow. Otherwise, Stacy will probably die."

"Oh, I get it. They want to use her. Yeah, that sounds familiar."

"I don't know why you're angry about this and I don't care. Just tell me where Jamie is."

"No way. I'm not going to tell you about her. I might tell her about you, though, next time I see her."

"Fine, do that." I was getting nowhere fast and arguing would only make it worse. "You don't have to tell me where she is. Just give her this." I gave Merci my card. "Tell her about Stacy. Tell her to call me and I'll explain. No problem. No hassle for anyone."

Merci read the card slowly.

"Will you do that? There's another fifty in it. Make it a hundred."

Merci smiled. And to prove just how concerned she was for Stacy's well-being, she tore the card in half.

3

I hadn't expected Merci to deliver my message, but you never know. Stranger things have happened. While I waited for Jamie to call, I listened to Curtis Mayfield and read the sports page. Jazzman Art Blakey once said, "Music washes away the dust of everyday life." So does sports. I only wish more pro athletes were like trumpeter Freddie Hubbard. He once told an audience, "I want to thank everyone for their support and for helping me make a living," then gave us two and half hours of pure, straight-ahead jazz. Could you see Barry Bonds doing that? Or Randy Moss? Or Shaq?

I rarely eat breakfast—yes, I know it's the most important meal of the day—and by ten-thirty my stomach was grumbling about it. I strolled down to Como and Carter in the heart of St. Anthony Park and had a cherry munkki and cafe mocha at the combination Taste of Scandinavia bakery and Dunn Brothers coffee house. On my way back I waved at a retired gentleman who was watering his lawn a couple blocks from my house. He waved back even though we had never laid eyes on each other before.

I was back in the house by eleven forty-five. There were no messages on my voice mail, so I checked my e-mail. The Department of Motor Vehicles reported that "JB" was the registered license plate of a 2002 white BMW 330 Ci convertible owned by Bruder, David C., of St. Paul. I had heard the name before. It danced in the back of my head for a few moments, but I couldn't place it.

I now had a name and an address but no handle on Jamie. Was she married to this guy? His mistress? Employee? I was guessing wife. To learn for sure I drove to the Ramsey County Court House on Fourth and Wabasha in downtown St. Paul, first floor, room 110.

The clerk there regarded me with practiced indifference. She was one of those faceless foot soldiers often found inside the bureaucracy who struggle above all else to remain anonymous, to avoid the attentions of supervisors, coworkers, and clients, who have no desire to distinguish themselves from their fellows, who are little more than government statistics and like it that way. When I asked about marriage records, she quickly led me to the county ledgers. "No smoking," she said quietly. I thanked her and she moved away just as quickly, relieved that she didn't have to make a decision.

Marriage licenses in Minnesota are not available online. Nor have they as yet been gathered in a central location. Each county keeps its own and possibly some of them even use computers. Ramsey County was still living in the last century. To locate Jamie's marriage license I was required to search several large and unwieldy ledgers—one page at a time. Of course, Jamie could have been married in Hennepin County, Washington County, Dakota County, or any of Minnesota's other eighty-seven counties, for that matter. Only she apparently lived in St. Paul, which is in Ramsey County, so I took a shot. After ninety minutes and two paper cuts I discovered that Bruder, David Christopher had married Kincaid, Jamie Anne, on June 20th two years earlier.

I left the Ramsey County Vital Records feeling pretty smug—Bobby Dunston had nothing on me. I sequestered myself in an old-fashioned telephone booth, the kind superheroes change their clothes in, and searched the St. Paul directory for Bruder's number. I punched it up on my cell phone. A voice as pure as sunlight told me that David and Jamie were unable to come to the phone, but if I was kind enough to leave a message, they would call back. I declined.

I was hungry again when I left the courthouse and I wasn't in the mood to sit alone in a restaurant. Instead I stopped at the gleaming hot dog cart on 4th Street.

The vendor was named Yu, a soft-spoken Korean immigrant, who wore a bright red T-shirt and a tan and black baseball cap with JOE'S DOGS spelled out above the brim. She knew me well enough to wave, but not to give me priority over the customers lined six deep in front of her cart. When it came my turn, she stuffed a Polish sausage into a poppy seed bun and dug out a Dr Pepper from the cooler without waiting to be asked.

"McKenzie," she said in her sweet accent. "Good see you."

"Good to see you, Yu," I said as I handed her a five and told her to keep the change. "How's business?"

"Business good when weather good." She looked up. The sky was a thin blue and empty of clouds. "Good today."

We chatted about the weather for a bit until several other hungry customers took my place in front of the cart. Six bites and a few swigs of pop later I was back in my SUV.

The traffic was light and it took me only ten minutes to reach Highland Park. I drove west on Randolph, missed my turn, and ended up motoring past the sprawling campus of Cretin-Derham Hall, the private high school that was alma mater to Paul Molitor, Steve Walsh, Chris Weinke, Corbin Lacina, Joe Mauer, and several other professional athletes as well as many of St. Paul's movers and shakers. I would have liked to have gone to Cretin, except I didn't have the money and I couldn't hit a breaking ball. I was forced to attend public high school, instead—not that I'm bitter or anything. I flipped an illegal U-turn, back-tracked to Edgecumbe Road and went south into the part of Highland Park that smelled most of money.

A few more turns and I found the Bruder house, a large, brick structure shaded by a balanced mixture of birch and evergreens. In some places it would have been called an estate. The house was perched atop a small hill on a corner lot. I parked in front of a sidewalk that meandered from the curb to the front door. I drove a fully loaded, steel blue Jeep Grand Cherokee 4 X 4 Limited valued at nearly $40,000, yet I was sure if I left it there too long, it would be removed as litter.

I followed the sidewalk to the door. I rang the bell. When no one answered, I circled the house, hoping the Bruders weren't one of those families who believe in keeping off the lawn. As I turned the corner I was confronted by a thick wall of red, pink, and yellow roses, the wall nearly twenty feet high. The "wall" was actually a trellis made of thin wood set hard against the house. The branches of the rose bushes were tied to the latticework with twine. I stopped to admire the handiwork, amazed by the number of flowers that were still blooming this late into September. I wondered how the gardener had managed it—I admire horticulturists, mostly from afar.

I turned another corner and found a long, curving concrete driveway that emptied into an east-west street. A white BMW convertible with license plate JB was parked outside a three-car garage at the top of the driveway. Between the garage and the house was a redwood fence. Inside the fence I found a swimming pool complete with diving board. Next to the pool was a quartet of lawn chairs surrounding a small table with an umbrella protruding through its center. A few feet to the left of that was a more modest trellis of roses. A young woman knelt before the trellis, her knees resting on a foam-rubber pad. She was scratching at the dirt with a three-pronged hand cultivator, pulling weeds and depositing them into a metal pail next to the pad, while she sang in a pleasant voice.

I walked into the soda shop.
There he was, sipping pop.
My heart whirled like a spinning top.
My, oh my, oh my.

He walked on over to my side.
"Be my bride, cherry pie."
Then he looked into my eyes.
"Bananas is my name."

I cleared my throat. Immediately, she stopped singing and swung toward me, her hand shielding her eyes from the sun.

"Bouncy melody," I said, cracking wise. "You can dance to it. I'd give it an eighty-five."

"Who are you?"

"Jamie Carlson?"

The question seemed to startle her even more than my unexpected presence. She stood and backed away from the trellis, giving herself plenty of room to run. She gripped the clawlike garden tool tightly, holding it like a weapon. I wondered why she was so alarmed. Had Merci Cole warned her that I was coming?

I took the photograph from my pocket and looked at it and then back at her. It wasn't a perfect match. A person can change a lot in seven years and I approved of the changes in Jamie. The sun had bleached her hair a lighter shade of gold and the face was thinner—tiny lines at the corners of her eyes and lips suggested she spent a lot of time smiling. Her breasts were full, her waist thin, and her legs were strong, tan, and well turned. She was wearing a white blouse that was tucked into black shorts, no socks or shoes. For a moment my heart raced. At age twenty-five, Jamie had blossomed like one of her roses into a truly stunning creation.

"Ms. Carlson." I returned the photograph to my pocket.

"No. Bruder. Mrs. David Bruder. If you're looking for my husband . . ."

"Mrs. Bruder," I repeated, making sure I got it right. "My name is McKenzie." I held out my hand but she backed away from it. "I was asked by your parents to find you."

"My parents?"

Apparently she was surprised to learn she had a couple.

"It's Stacy. She's very ill. She might die."

"Little Stacy?" She repeated the name exactly as Merci Cole had.

"Yes."

"Little Stacy?"

She dropped the cultivator and moved slowly toward the table in front of the pool. She collapsed in a chair next to the small table and motioned to the chair on the other side. I joined her. There was a baby monitor on the table, the kind that parents use to eavesdrop on their children when they sleep. Jamie looked at a window on the second floor as she moved the monitor closer to her chair.

"Hang on to yourself, Mrs. Bruder." I told her the entire story, including Stacy's visits to the Mayo Clinic and her doctor's assessment of her chances for survival. The story seemed to impress her very deeply. Several times she rubbed tears from her eyes while glancing from the monitor to the second story window.

When I had finished, Jamie said in a sorrowful voice, "The man who said you can never go home again had it wrong. The truth is, you can never entirely leave."

"That's a lot of philosophy," I told her. "Too much for me."

I heard a muffled sigh. It came from the monitor. Jamie looked at the monitor and smiled a small, sad smile.

"I'm told the procedure to determine if you're a compatible donor is very simple."

"Nothing is ever simple, Mr. McKenzie. How did you find me?"

"It's like the poet said, if you want to escape your past, first learn to walk through freshly fallen snow without leaving tracks."

"Now who's being a philosopher? Have you told Richard and Molly that you found me?"

"Not yet," I answered, wondering why children who are on a first-name basis with their parents rarely get along with them.

"Please don't. Not yet. I need time for this. Time to talk to my husband. He knows nothing about my past and I won't get a chance to tell him until later. He's invited a business associate for drinks by the pool."

"He doesn't know you're Jamie Carlson?"

"He thinks I'm Jamie Kincaid. He thinks I'm an orphan."

"How did you meet?"

"I worked as a paralegal for the law firm that handles his business accounts."

"What business is he in?"

"He owns a string of used car dealerships."

That was why his name had seemed so familiar. *Good Deal Dave*, Bruder Motors, four locations throughout the Twin Cities to serve you. Outdoor boards featuring Bruder's sincere smile were everywhere and his TV spots cluttered prime time.

"How did you manage a new name, social security card, driver's license . . . ?"

"There are ways," the young woman advised me.

There certainly are. "Did Merci Cole help?"

"Does it matter?"

"No."

"I don't want you to be here when my husband and his associate arrive."

"I understand." I rose from the table. I gave her my business card after first writing my cell number on back.

"You will call me tomorrow?" I asked.

Jamie set the card on the table.

"If I don't you'll only come back, won't you?"

Was I that obvious?

"One more thing, Mrs. Bruder."

"Yes?"

"Why did you leave home?"

"I hate lies."

"Such as?"

She didn't answer.

"Must have been a whopper," I told her.

I did some tossing and turning in bed. It wasn't like me to fixate on a woman, especially one so young and inaccessible, yet images of Jamie Carlson Bruder kept floating in the darkness behind my closed eyes. I tried hard not to think about her. The harder I tried, the more impossible the task became. She was a beauty, all right, and I imagined her in ways that were not particularly healthy. Or maybe they were healthy. I don't know. What would a therapist say? Perhaps he'd say that my subconscious was telling me to let go of Kirsten and move on. Perhaps he'd say I was a pervert and required about fifty years of therapy. I flipped over my pillow, nestled against the cool side, closed my eyes, and thought of

Shelby. That probably wasn't healthy, either. *She's your best friend's wife! Get over it!* Jamie crowded her out, anyway. It was when I started envisioning doing terrible things to her husband—a damned used car salesman, no less—that I gave it up and padded downstairs to my kitchen. I took milk from the refrigerator and drank from the carton before rooting through my cupboards for Oreos.

I ate a half dozen. While I ate, I rifled my CD collection, discarding the rockers in favor of Etta James, the last of the great jazz divas. I finished the milk and cookies and sprawled out on my sofa, listening to Etta's honey-drenched voice in the dark. That's where I fell asleep.

4

The pounding on my door was loud enough to wake the dead and at 5:10 a.m. by my watch it had to be. I rolled off my sofa and stubbed my toe against the coffee table. Hopping on one foot while trying to massage the other, I cursed my clumsiness. Yet the pain shocked me awake and my first conscious thought was of a common police practice—we often served warrants early in the morning when the miscreants were too groggy with sleep to put up a fuss. Only why would the cops want to arrest an upstanding citizen like me?

I hopped to the window in my living room. The sky was streaked with a hard gray—the sun hadn't yet decided if it wanted to rise—but it was bright enough to reveal a decade-old Buick Regal at rest in front of my house.

Huh, I thought.

Turning my head I was able to see a tall, young black man standing on my porch. He was holding the barrel of a sawed-off shotgun flush against the front door just below the spy hole with one hand while lifting the heavy brass knocker with the other.

Huh, I thought again.

In the time it took him to knock twice more, I bounded up my stairs, went to my room, slipped the 9mm Heckler & Koch from the drawer of the table next to my bed, flew down the stairs again, and snuck out my back door. I circled the house, staying low beneath the lip of the porch, working toward the front steps.

He was still pounding on the door and starting to get anxious about it, scanning the yards of my neighbors, watching for cars on the street. It shouldn't be taking this long. The black man was about six feet, one-eighty-five, in good shape, wearing jeans and a tan jacket. He was still holding the muzzle of the sawed-off hard against the wood door, staring intently at the spy hole, waiting for the shadow of my eye to pass across it.

I made myself clear.

"DROP THE FUCKING GUN!"

He stopped pounding, his head turned abruptly toward my voice. I was behind him about twenty yards and to his left, sighting on his upper torso even as I watched his hands—always watch the hands.

"YOU HAVEN'T GOT A CHANCE, BUT YOU GOT A CHOICE!" I warned him.

He hesitated.

"DROP IT!"

He smiled, an amazing thing to do, and swung the sawed-off in a small arch toward me. I was too good a shot to miss from that distance. *Wham! Wham! Wham!* I hit him three times in the chest. The force of the nine-millimeter slugs lifted and spun him. His legs hit the low, wooden porch railing and he spilled over it into the front yard.

I moved toward him quickly, keeping the gun trained on his chest, my hands shaking slightly, my breath coming fast. I knew right away he was dead. I didn't have to touch him, didn't have to feel for a pulse, didn't have to hold a mirror to his nostrils. He was dead, his leg and arm twisted under his body. He looked like he had fallen from the sky. I watched him for a long time, watched until repulsion over what I had done made me stagger to a corner of my house hidden by an ancient pine tree and throw up.

There are so many emergencies and so few officers to respond, sometimes 911 will ring ten, twenty, thirty times or more before it's answered. Only at five-twenty-five in the morning it was answered on the second ring. I asked for the cops. They routed me to the St. Anthony Village Police Department. Not to be confused with St. Anthony Park, St. Anthony Village is a northern suburb nowhere near Falcon Heights, yet supplies police services for it just the same. I told them a man was dead in my front yard. Then I went upstairs. Three navy blue squad cars with distinctive gray stripes were parked in front of my house by the time I finished buttoning my shirt. I left the Heckler & Koch in the bedroom.

I stepped out of the front door onto the porch, pushing my shirt tails into my pants. All three officers reached for their guns, yet no one pulled. I made sure they saw my empty hands, then did a slow pirouette to prove I had concealed nothing. They kept their hands resting on their gun butts just the same. They were good boys.

"You do this?" one of them asked. His voice was nervous and a little too loud. His name tag read T. JOHNSON. He ran six feet, one-eighty-five, the same size as the dead man.

"Yes."

"Come down."

I descended three of the four steps before he grabbed my shoulder, pulled me off the steps, spun me around, and pushed my face against the low, wooden porch railing. He wound one cuff over my right wrist and brought it down behind my back. He brought my left wrist around and secured it tightly. For good measure he pushed my face into the railing, again.

"Hey, c'mon."

He bounced me off the railing a third time and sat me on the top step.

"This guy is dead," one officer said, his fingers on the black man's carotid artery.

"How?" Johnson asked.

"Asphyxiation," I said.

"There are three bullet holes in his chest," the officer answered.

"That's why he stopped breathing." Sometimes I just can't help myself—we all deal with fear in our own way.

"Shut up." Johnson smacked me on the side of my face.

Two more officers arrived by that time, making five. They all seemed so young. Each took a turn at examining the body. Finally, I yelled, "Hey, you bozos! Didn't anyone ever teach you about maintaining the integrity of a crime scene?"

Johnson didn't like that. He took a few steps toward me and I braced, waiting for another blow. It didn't come. Before he could raise his hand two men drove up in an unmarked car. The driver was white and wore sergeant stripes. The passenger was a big black man, bigger than Johnson by three inches, heavier by forty pounds. He wore plain clothes and an imperious expression.

He looked at the officers one by one, would have looked them each straight in the eye except all but Johnson had bowed their heads, school kids caught playing while their teacher was in the hall. I couldn't help but smile. He was a crime dog. I could see it in his face.

The sergeant went through the crowd of officers, dispersing them. He fit all of Hollywood's criteria of an ideal law enforcement officer— tall, mean, a perpetual squint. I watched from the steps as he examined the body, moving around it like he'd seen dead men before. Finally, he looked up at me.

"You didn't like him at all, did you?"

I almost smiled, probably would have except that was the moment Tiger started yapping from the sidewalk. Tiger was a purebred schnauzer owned by Karl Olson, my next-door neighbor. He was straining at the leash that Karl held tight with his right hand. In his left, Karl carried a small plastic bag containing Tiger's morning deposits. The expression on his face made me think that Karl thought I also belonged in the plastic bag.

"Can we do this inside?" I asked.

The crime dog nodded. He stopped me when I tried to move past him, took my chin in a huge hand, held my face steady so he could get a good look at it.

"There's swelling," he said.

"I must have fallen down the stairs," I told him.

He released my face and we went inside. Johnson held the door open for us. He avoided the crime dog's gaze as we passed.

I led the crime dog to my bedroom and gestured at the nine on the night stand. He retrieved it and sniffed the barrel.

"Oh yeah, she's been working."

"No, I killed him with a slingshot."

Along with fear-induced insolence, I also have a problem with authority. To my mother's great embarrassment, I was thrown out of the Cub Scouts for refusing direction. Not Boy Scouts, mind you. Cub Scouts.

"Tell me about it," he said patiently.

I told him I found the deceased pounding on my door. I told him the deceased was brandishing a sawed-off shotgun. I told him I gave the deceased a choice, but not a chance.

"Hmm," he grunted.

"Chief?" a voice called from downstairs.

"Up here."

A moment later, the sergeant entered my bedroom carrying several plastic bags. He set them all on the mattress, then held them up one at a time.

"Wheel gun. Twenty-two caliber. Choice of professionals everywhere. The bullet doesn't pass through the body. Instead it bounces around inside, nipping at various vital organs. He was carrying it in his waist band."

A second bag.

"Two twelve-gauge shotgun shells. Fits the sawed-off. I left that in the car." While looking at me, the sergeant added, "Apparently he didn't feel the need for a lot of ammo."

A third plastic bag containing a brown wallet.

"Minnesota driver's license in the name of Bradley Young. Photo matches the dead man. Ran the Buick. Also owned by the dead man."

"Ever see him before?" the chief asked.

I shook my head.

The fourth bag held a white number ten envelope.

"Don't have a firm count, but I figure at least three thousand dollars in twenties and fifties."

"This doesn't make sense," I interrupted. "He comes at me like a professional, but using his own car? Carrying his ID? The motive stuffed in his pocket? That's amateur night."

"Not a pro," the chief said softly. "A soldier. A member of the rank and file recruited for this one job."

"A gang-banger?" I asked.

The sergeant referred to his notebook before offering, "No colors, no insignia, no visible tattoos."

"Hmm," the chief grunted again.

"So why would he want to whack you?" the sergeant asked.

It bothers me when people use words like whack, waste, hit, off, do, grease, zap, and burn when they mean kill. It's like they're trying to pretend sudden, violent death isn't such a terrible thing.

"The word is *kill*," I told the sergeant.

He replied angrily, "You don't think I know that?"

Of course he would.

"You still haven't answered the question," the chief reminded me. "Why would he want to *kill* you?"

"I swear to God I don't know."

"Think about it."

"I have. Believe me, I have."

The idea that the murder attempt was somehow connected to my search for Jamie Carlson flared bright. If you found a woman who didn't want to be found and twelve hours later someone tried to assassinate you, what would you think? Only a young woman, married, with a child, living your basic upper-middle-class American dream—I couldn't make it work. I decided to keep my suspicions to myself until I had a chance to see her again. Why drag Jamie into this if she was innocent? She had enough to worry about.

"It doesn't make sense," I said.

"Hmm."

A few minutes later I was on the front porch again. The sergeant was directing a couple of technicians from Ramsey County around the body of Bradley Young. The techs moved quietly, efficiently, with the easy camaraderie of men who share the same profession.

The chief didn't have a crime, he had self-defense. An investigation would be conducted—about twenty percent of all deaths rate an official inquiry, including one hundred percent of all deaths where the victim is shot three times in the chest. Evidence would be presented to a grand jury. In the meantime, I thought it would be wise for me to cooperate completely, so when the chief said, "You're coming down to the house with us, I want a written statement," I nodded my head vigorously.

Besides, I needed to get away from the body of Bradley Young before I again became nauseous over what I had done.

"Johnson. Take off the cuffs."

Johnson moved behind me with his key.

"Do I have to?" he asked.

I gave a formal statement to a neatly pressed stenographer in a white interrogation room in the cleanest police station I had ever seen. The building was one of those flat, ultra-modern, energy-efficient, multipurpose brick jobs that also housed most of the suburb's other facilities—city hall, community center, parks and recreation, water treatment plant. It was next to a sprawling network of baseball diamonds, football and soccer fields, six well-kept tennis courts, and a fenced-in obstacle course where teenage extremists could practice death-defying feats on skateboards. If I had been their age, I probably would have joined them.

After I finished, Officer Johnson sat me in a molded plastic chair outside an oak door. On the door at about eye level if you're six feet was a name plate that read, CHIEF B. CASEY. I made me think of Bernie Casey, who was a wide receiver for the Rams before he became a pretty good actor and painter. Nowadays, anyone who can do two things well is considered a Renaissance man. Three things and you're off the charts, people don't know what to call you.

"What does the 'B' stand for," I asked Johnson.

"Bart. But don't call him that. He doesn't like it."

I could relate to that.

Across from my chair was a glass display case. While I waited, I studied its contents: 9 mm Intratec spring knife, .22 carbine with bayonet, 12-gauge shotgun, nunchucks, timing chain, Louisville Slugger, and a rusted tire iron. A typed index card taped to the outside of the case read:

"Weapons used to attack St. Anthony Village police officers in the month of August." I shuddered, wondering what September would bring.

Some time after noon Chief Casey arrived.

"Inside," he said, hurrying past me.

His office was small and windowless and extremely cluttered. The chief sat behind a dark wood desk that was far too big for the room and motioned me to the only chair that was empty.

The chief read my statement twice. When he finished, he told me to sign it.

I did.

He said, "The assistant county attorney wants to speak with you."

"I bet."

"Don't go anywhere I can't find you."

He had no right to say that. Unless you're actually charged with a crime, you have every legal right to go anywhere you please, even France. Only I didn't argue the point. Where would I go?

"Johnson," he called.

Officer Johnson and I did a dance number in the doorway until we figured a safe way to pass each other. As I left I heard the chief speak sternly to him.

"Johnson, I don't like cops who are loose with their hands."

It took an hour to drive home, feed the ducks, take a shower, get dressed again, and snap a holstered 9 mm Beretta to my belt. The Beretta nine-millimeter is the official sidearm of the United States Armed Forces and is the standard issue of law enforcement agencies throughout the country, including Minneapolis. If the St. Paul cops had used it instead of the Glock 17, my whole life might have been different.

I slipped a black sport coat over the Beretta and stared at myself in the full-length mirror. The gun was properly concealed. No one would know it was there. But I knew.

I hate guns.

The street where Jamie Carlson Bruder lived was empty. No surprise there. You live in a half-million-dollar house, how often would you go outside? And quiet—well, that's why people bought half-million-dollar homes in this neighborhood, because it was quiet. Yet something was terribly wrong. I felt it as I parked my SUV in the same spot as the evening before and walked to Jamie's front door. I knew it in the same way that I knew my mother had died before anyone had the chance to tell me.

I used the doorbell, then knocked loudly. When no one answered, I circled the house, peeking into windows as I went, ignoring this time the trellis of roses. There was no BMW in the driveway, no beautiful blond scratching in the dirt. I pounded hard on the back door. No reply. It was only seventy-five, but it felt a good twenty degrees warmer. I used the back of my hand to wipe sweat off my forehead.

Colin Gernes used to *like* burglars, would speak longingly of the good old days when burglars were gentlemen thieves who gently jimmied windows and doors, who were actually considerate of their victim's possessions, who never carried, never hurt anyone—Gernes's kind of crook. That was before cocaine. That was before junkies gave burglary a bad name by smashing windows with bricks and hammers, beating, raping, and killing anyone unfortunate enough to be inside, running off with the loot to their junkie fence for ten cents on the dollar or a gram of low-grade dope. That's what I was thinking of as I slipped the burglary tools out of my inside jacket pocket—the "new" burglar.

The tools were illegal for me to carry—a stiff "wire" and the pick I made myself, a long, narrow piece of hard metal with a tiny L on one end. I used them to work Bruder's cheap lock, cursing him when it sprang and the door swung open. A five-hundred-thousand-dollar house and a $2.99 lock. "Call this protection?" A pro could have managed the job in less than thirty seconds. It took me about three minutes.

I returned the tools to my pocket and slipped the Beretta from its holster. The weight of it felt comforting.

I forced myself to breathe normally and moved cautiously into the kitchen, telling myself to "see everything." Only there wasn't much to see. No dishes in the sink, no debris on the table, nothing stacked on the counters, everything just so except for a single cabinet drawer open about three inches. I glanced inside without opening it farther. A junk drawer.

The kitchen reminded me of a remodeler's store display. So did the dining room. And the living room. And the family room. And the den. The furniture was all new. Jamie had arranged it for conversation with a nod to her two fireplaces. I didn't see a TV, but I hadn't looked for one that hard. I did find the Bruders' answering machine at the bottom of the staircase leading to the second floor. A red light blinked and a digital display said there were two messages. I pressed the playback bar with my elbow. It wasn't until I heard a male voice say, "David, this is Warren. Something's gone wrong. Better call me ASAP," that I realized what a foolish mistake I had made. I just revealed my presence to anyone lurking in the house. *You're a real pro, McKenzie.* A woman delivered the second message—"Hey, babe, this is Merci. Have you decided what to do about your visitor? Call me."—but I was listening too hard for sounds of movement to pay much attention.

I left the machine to rewind itself and started up the stairs.

My Nikes made no sound on the thick carpet. I stopped at the top step, looked around, listened. Nothing. There were six rooms. I started with the one nearest me. A guest room with private bath. Unoccupied. I slipped into the next. It was a nursery. The crib was empty.

"Mother and child are out running an errand," I told myself. "It's a pleasant afternoon, maybe Jamie took the child to the park." There were dozens of reasons why they weren't home. I couldn't force myself to believe any of them. I kept moving.

The third room was a catchall and contained a locked glass gun cabinet filled with shotguns, hunting rifles, and two handguns; a sewing machine, empty gift boxes, wrapping paper and ribbons, a desk without a chair. The fourth was a bathroom. The fifth was the master bedroom. That's where I found her.

Jamie was on the bed, her wrists tied to a brass and white-enamel headboard, her ankles tied to a matching baseboard—the skin was torn and bloody where she had struggled against the twine. Her mouth was sealed with duct tape. Bruises covered her face and shoulders. Cigarette burns dotted the rest of her nude body. Strips of flesh hung from her breasts where someone had skinned her. There was a steak knife on the mattress next to her and at least eight jagged holes in her stomach—they were hard to count because of the blood. Blood had poured out onto her black shorts and her white blouse, brassiere, and panties, all cut away and lying beneath her. The pubic hair around her vagina was matted with dried fluid. A broom was on the floor next to the bed. The tip of the broom handle was stained red. Jamie's eyes were open, her fists were clenched.

I screamed at the sight of her.

5

Most murders are mistakes. The majority are committed spontaneously by completely rational people who in moments of rage do completely irrational things. A groom kills his best man over the last slice of pizza at a bachelor party. A man kills his wife for switching the channel during the World Series. A young woman kills her landlord for raising the rent. A teenager is shot on an MTC bus because he refuses to lower the volume on his radio. A father is gunned down by his son during an argument over whether an angel or star belongs on top of the Christmas tree. Mistakes. The killers didn't mean to do it. A surprising number of them will confess to that the moment the cops walk through the door. They might as well. Often they're standing there covered with blood or surrounded by witnesses.

Only the killing of Jamie Carlson was not a mistake. It was methodical, well organized, and terribly ferocious. And the killer had no intention of admitting to his crime. Someone would have to catch him.

That's what I was thinking as I sat in my Jeep Cherokee waiting for the police to respond to the call I had placed with my cell phone, refusing to look at the house, knowing what was inside. Two squads arrived within two minutes. I knew the driver of the second car from my time in the department's Central District.

"How you doin', Mac?"

"I've been better."

"Dispatch said you called it in."

"Yeah."

"Show me."

"Wait for the detectives," I told him. "The house is clean. There's no one inside and nothing you can do."

He didn't like my telling him that, but before he could lean on me a team of detectives I didn't know arrived.

"You call it in?" the taller of the two asked after consulting with the uniforms.

"Yeah."

"Show me." He was more forceful than the uniform had been. I blew him off just the same.

"Show yourself." I wasn't trying to be a smartass. I just wasn't going back into that house. I was a civilian now. There were things I shouldn't have to look at. I told the detective where to find Jamie. I told him that there wasn't anyone else in the house. I told him I would wait there. The detective assigned a uniform to make sure I did. He returned twenty minutes later. His cheeks were pale and his breath came hard, yet he spoke steadily.

"Touch anything?"

"Back door handle, in and out."

"Anything else?"

"No."

"Sure?"

"Yes."

"We might take your fingerprints, anyway."

"They're already on file," I told him. That raised an eyebrow until I explained that I used to work the job he was working. Yet I doubt I had done it any better. He took my statement calmly, professionally, leading me through my discovery of the victim.

The victim.

Already Jamie's identity was disappearing under the weight of what she had become. A victim. Her name no longer represented a living, breathing woman. Whatever her history, whatever her accomplishments and failings, Jamie's life would now and forever be defined by one of the worst things that could happen to a human being. She was a victim now. Nothing more. Murder does that.

Someone laughed, a technician. That's when I noticed Bobby Dunston. He glared at the tech like he wanted to destroy him in place and was looking forward to the opportunity. The laughter died in the tech's throat.

By now the brick house was surrounded by trucks and squads, marked and unmarked. They came silently, without siren, without lights. Yet the neighbors heard them just the same. They emerged from their stately homes and watched from their stoops, wondering what evil had invaded their community and threatened their children. A yellow ribbon went up, circling the Bruder house. POLICE LINE DO NOT CROSS. Neighbors who rarely spoke before gathered in small clusters to discuss it—comradeship in the face of adversity. It happens every time there's a heavy storm.

"What does it mean?" they asked, shaking their collective heads at the army of St. Paul police officers and technicians. The residents of Highland Park were already embarrassed and ashamed. They weren't yet sure what had happened, but they all knew that it wasn't supposed to happen there. University-Summit, maybe. Or Frogtown. Or the west side of St. Paul. Not there. Highland Park was a "safe" neighborhood. All the real estate agents said so.

I gave my statement twice more, the second time to Bobby, only I told him things I didn't tell the others.

"I picked the back door lock." I didn't want any scratches I might have left on the metal to confuse his investigation.

"Goddammit, McKenzie."

"Thought you should know."

"What else?"

"I listened to the answering machine. Two messages. The first was from a man named Warren, the second was from Merci Cole."

"I already secured the tape."

I nodded.

"What the hell were you doing here?" he wanted to know.

"This morning I killed a man named Bradley Young." The rest of the story came out in a flood and Bobby forced me to repeat it, slowly.

"What do you think?" I asked after I had finished.

"I don't believe in coincidences."

"Neither do I."

"But, they do happen."

"Yes, they do."

"Know anything about the husband?"

"Good Deal Dave? Do you honestly believe a man could do something like that to his own wife?"

"Christ, Mac. Men do things like that to their wives all the fucking time."

Bobby was trying hard to contain his rage, but it was spilling out in his language. "Where the fuck is he?"

"And the child," I added.

"And the child."

"The killing—it's just like Katherine's, isn't it?"

Bobby rubbed his eyes.

"Maybe it's the guy I killed."

"We should be so lucky."

"Bobby?"

"Yeah?"

"Will you make the call to the Carlsons? I mean, you're gonna have to call them anyway, right?"

"You coward."

Yeah, that's me all right.

"What are you doing here, McKenzie?" It was Deputy Chief Tommy Thompson. Neither Bobby nor I saw him approach. "I'm waiting for an answer."

Thompson often spoke in a very soft monotone and you'd better listen carefully because if you asked, "Huh, what did you say?" he'd turn on you with an angry squint and demand to know why he should waste his breath if you can't even be bothered to pay attention.

"McKenzie discovered the body," Bobby answered for me. "He has an angle on the case."

"I must have missed that memo. The St. Paul Police Department is hiring consultants?"

Bobby rubbed his eyes some more. "He discovered the body."

"I'm listening," Thompson said.

Bobby told him about my mission to find Jamie Carlson and my early morning visitor. Thompson was singularly unimpressed.

"Find the husband," he said and started to move away. He had no intention of entertaining other theories. Find the husband. Case closed.

"Yesterday it was Katherine's boyfriend!" Bobby shouted at his back. "Today it's the husband! Who's it going to be tomorrow?"

Thompson turned. He had one of those who-do-you-think-you're-talking-to expressions on his face. "You are out of line, Detective," he said, his monotone rising several octaves.

Bobby didn't reply and Thompson smirked like he had won some kind of victory. He spun toward the TV crews filming from behind the yellow tape and the news hounds with pens poised over notebooks. Thompson made his way to the waiting reporters. "It's a sad day for St. Paul. . . ."

I tuned him out when Bobby spoke to me. "You're in a restricted police area."

"Excuse me?"

"You're not a cop. You're not even a licensed PI."

"So?"

"So, investigate this Bradley Young 'til hell freezes over, I don't care. That's someone else's problem. But you stay away from this. You don't go near Jamie, or her husband, or her child. . . ."

"Bullshit."

"Serious shit, McKenzie. I have a serial on my hands. You keep your distance, I'm not kidding."

"Bobby, you're forgetting something."

"What am I forgetting?"

"Stacy Carlson, the little girl . . ."

"Dying of leukemia."

"Jamie can't help her now. But maybe Jamie's child can."

"Can children donate bone marrow?"

"I don't know. But . . ."

"But." Bobby glared at me just to prove he was serious. "Do not get in the way. I swear to God I'm not kidding. I'll bust your ass for obstruction."

He might have said more, but we were both distracted by movement at the front door of the house. The wagon boys were bringing Jamie out, her body encased in a bag of black vinyl, the bag zipped shut.

"So many women die in the bedroom," Bobby murmured.

———————

I didn't realize night had fallen until it became impossible to see the wall on the far side of my living room. There was nothing particularly interesting about the wall. I would have been hard pressed to describe it although I had been staring at it since I arrived home. It just happened to be opposite the chair closest to my front door where I had collapsed in a stupor. Nor could I tell you how long I had been looking at it or what I had been thinking of. Perhaps I had fallen asleep, although I don't remember that, either. All I knew is that several hours had passed and even then I couldn't tell you exactly how many.

I roused myself and went from room to room, turning on every light I owned, including the rechargeable flashlight I keep plugged in the socket next to my bed. Soon my house was bathed in the light of several dozen 150-, 100-, and 60-watt bulbs. Probably impressed Xcel Energy but didn't do much for me. You're supposed to feel safe in your own home. Secure. Yet Jamie Carlson Bruder had been murdered in hers and a man I didn't even know had attempted to assassinate me in mine.

It was only then that I had the presence of mind to check my voice mail. The electronic female told me I had two messages. The first was from the guy who cleans my fireplace. "Winter's coming," he warned.

The second was from Chief Casey telling me to call. I punched in the number he left but he had already retired for the day and I didn't feel like leaving a message.

I wondered what he wanted, and thinking about it kicked open the door that I had so carefully and firmly locked when I left Jamie's home. My mind suddenly became a satellite dish, five hundred channels. I surfed through them all, never holding an image for more than a few fleeting moments, each one rated TVMA. I didn't want to think about them. To distract myself, I tried to get involved in the baseball game that was broadcast by one of the so-called superstations, but after three innings I realized I didn't even know who was playing. I went from the TV to *Time* magazine and attempted to read a report on the goings-on in the war zone that is much of Africa. A think-tank expert suggested that the fighting, including the systematic slaughter of count-less innocent civilians, was rooted deep in tribal history and construed by many in the region as a matter of principle and honor. That's when I lost it.

"Lies!" I barked, tossing the magazine aside. There are only two rea-sons people commit murder—love and money. I wondered which motive applied to Jamie Carlson Bruder.

"God," I screamed, using His name like an obscenity. I certainly wasn't calling on Him. I hadn't called on Him since my mother died. I fell to my knees and started shaking when they told me the news. It's the closest I'd come to prayer since. What good would He do me, anyway? Go to confession. Bless me, father, for I have sinned. I broke the biggie. Number five on the Roman Catholic hit parade. Thou Shalt Not Kill. What penance do you get for that? Five Our Fathers? Three Hail Marys? Sure, I dread the loss of heaven and the pain of hell, but you know what? I've done it before. I might do it again.

Besides, I had some serious misgivings about God. Is He really all powerful *and* all loving, both at the same time, like they say? See, I can understand how an all-loving God, one who cares deeply, might not have the power to intervene. But if He's all powerful and still allows innocent people to suffer and die as Jamie and Katherine had suffered and died, wouldn't that make Him one callous sonuvabitch?

I picked up the phone, set it down, picked it up again, hesitated, punched Kirsten Sager Whitson's home number and hung up before it rang.

Call someone else.

Who?

There was no one else.

Shelby?

No. Absolutely not.

I consulted my watch. Nine-forty-one and forty-five seconds. *My, how time flies when you're having fun.*

Work. Fill the hours with work, I told myself. *Concentrate on that.* I sat at the kitchen table and wrote notes to myself. I filled half a yellow tablet, gripping the pen so hard I bent it. I forced myself to record every detail since I met the Carlsons while they were still relatively fresh. I didn't really think remembering would be a problem. Forgetting, now that was a different matter.

I had made Jamie the star of my sexual fantasies, dancing with her in my prepubescent imagination at the same time she was being raped and butchered. How could I get past that?

I took a long hot shower and climbed between my bed sheets. I don't know why I bothered. Sleep was impossible. I gave it an hour before rolling out of bed, pulling on gym shorts and a T-shirt. I grabbed the plastic ice cream bucket filled with dried corn that I keep on my back porch and went to the pond. I called for the ducks. They came to me even in the darkness. I tossed them the corn and they ate happily although the smallest, Maureen, my favorite, insisted on feeding from my hand. That didn't bode well for the long flight south, yet I fed her just the same.

Think, I urged myself. *Think clearly.*

Jamie was murdered just hours after I located her. There had to be a connection—life is a lot less random than we believe. Was Bradley Young the connection? Did he kill Jamie, and Katherine before her? Bobby would find out in a hurry. He was probably already talking to the Ramsey County ME.

Think.

Whether he killed her or not, there had to be a connection. Young came to my house because of Jamie. I knew it. Maybe he didn't kill Jamie, but he tried to kill me *because* of her.

Think.

Bobby wouldn't hesitate for a second to arrest me for obstruction if I even came within shouting distance of his investigation. So, I needed to be careful. But I was going to learn the connection between Young and Jamie. That was my a-gen-da, as Kirsten would put it. That's what I'm going to do, screw Dunston.

And then there was Stacy. Oh God, did she die when Jamie died? *Think.*

Did I have to kill Young? What if I had just stayed in the house and called the cops? What if I had left my gun in the drawer? What if I had been more forceful when I confronted him. What if . . . ?

Kirsten was right. There is so much in my world that's wrong.

"Are you okay?"

I had been concentrating on the ducks and my own thoughts and didn't see her approach.

"Are you okay?" she repeated.

"Margot?"

Her white satin robe gleamed in the moonlight, seemed nearly as bright as the moon. She was standing in bare feet on her side of the pond, her arms folded under her ample bosom. Her reflection shimmering in the water reminded me of Galadriel, the ethereal elf in *The Lord of the Rings.*

"As well as can be expected," I told her.

"I heard what happened. I guess everyone in the neighborhood has heard what happened. Are you sure you're all right?"

"Yes."

"I think you should know, Karl Olson is making noises about getting up a petition to force you to move."

"Throw one dead body on the front yard and the whole place gets paranoid."

"It is the suburbs."

"Just barely," I reminded her.

"I saw you from my bedroom window." She gestured with her head at the large white house behind her. "I thought you might want to talk."

"No. Thank you."

Margot sat on her well-trimmed lawn, hugging her bare legs to her chest. She rested her chin on her knees. She seemed so young, although she was a half decade older than I was.

"How are the ducks?"

"They'll be leaving soon, I think."

"I'll miss them."

"Me, too."

"I never thanked you."

"For what?"

"For the ducks. For the pond. I had my misgivings when your father put it in, but now . . . It's really quite lovely."

"You spent a lot of time with my father when he was digging it. You brought him lemonade."

"I only brought him lemonade once. After that it was Leinies."

"Leinenkugel's, brewed in Wisconsin. To my dad that's an imported beer."

"He liked them."

"Yes, he did."

"Did he ever tell you what we talked about when I brought him the beers?"

"Dad? No. When you told Dad something, that's as far as it went. He was the keeper of everyone's secrets."

"He was very proud of you. He said so. Many times. He thought you were a good man, only he didn't know how to tell you."

"You told me. At the funeral. I've always been grateful to you for that little bit of kindness."

"Your father was kind to me at a time when I needed kindness."

"He was that way."

"He never remarried after your mother died. He never even dated. Did he ever tell you why?"

I shook my head.

"He couldn't. His love for your mother wouldn't allow it. I wish I could find a man to love me that much. I'm three husbands down and I haven't even come close."

"They say the fourth time is the charm."

"They say the third time is the charm, but never mind."

She stood and wrapped her arms around herself like she was suddenly cold.

"Why don't you come up to the house with me? We'll have coffee."

"It's tempting, but . . ."

"It'll be fine."

"I'm afraid I wouldn't be very good company, tonight. I have too much on my mind."

"That's why I'm offering."

"A rain check?"

"Put it somewhere safe, where you won't lose it."

Margot turned then and drifted up her sloping lawn toward her house. I watched her until she disappeared into the darkness.

6

I showered for the third time in twenty-four hours, dressed quickly, fed the ducks again, skipped my own breakfast, and hurried out of the house. I didn't want to hang around. I wanted to be out and doing. Ten minutes later I was standing in the City of St. Anthony Village municipal building—don't ask me why it's called both a *city* and a *village*. I was trying to get through the secured door that led to the cop shop, only the receptionist wouldn't push the button that unlocked it until she was given the high sign by Chief Casey.

"I called," he told me.

"I didn't get the message until late."

"Yesterday you killed a man. Want to know why?"

"You're volunteering?" This was a first for me—a cop besides Bobby Dunston who freely gave me information. *What's the catch?* I wondered.

Casey led me to his small, cluttered office. I told him he could do better but he blew me off. "I have gold braid on my hat. I don't need a corner office with a view."

I liked him more and more.

There was a file folder in the upper corner of his desk under a small trophy with the words TO THE WORLD'S GREATEST DAD etched into its base. Casey sat behind his desk, snagged the folder, and opened it. He began to read.

"Wait, wait," I implored as I took my notebook and pen from my jacket pocket. "Okay."

"Bradley Young, AKA Emilio, AKA Billy the Kid . . ."

"Emilio? Billy?"

"Emilio Estevez starred as Billy the Kid in *Young Guns*. Apparently there was some resemblance."

Casey slid a photograph of the dead man across the desk. I didn't see any similarity between the white actor and black gangster, but I didn't look very hard. I don't like looking at photographs of the recently deceased, never have. I like to think there's a dignity in human beings that transcends the life they live, that gives them value no matter how cheaply they died and you can see none of that in a photo taken at the scene.

The chief kept paraphrasing. I set the photograph aside and wrote quickly, trying to keep up.

"Born and raised in Detroit, Michigan, the only child of father Robert, mother Jo Jo. Both parents killed when the propane tank exploded in their mobile home, cause unknown."

The chief tapped the file.

"This guy's sheet is so long you could wrap it around a jury box, but only one conviction, second-degree burglary in Detroit. I spoke to the arresting officer, an old buddy. Two years ago he nabbed Young as he was entering an apartment building, a video recorder and a boom box under his arms, a pry bar, screwdriver, rubber gloves, and a stethoscope in his pockets. Search warrants were obtained. My guy found sixteen stereos, eight VCRs, eight TVs, eleven ghetto blasters, four bikes, thirteen guns, some jewelry, and thirty-seven pawn shop tickets in Young's crib. Young was arraigned in the Frank B. Murphy Hall of Justice, bail set at twenty thousand, trial date set for mid-October.

"Young couldn't make bail and he didn't want to sit in jail for a couple of months awaiting trial so he cuts a deal with the state attorney. He'll cop to one count of second-degree if he can get help for his drug problem. The prosecutor figures what the hell, first conviction, Young will probably get probation and time served anyway, why waste the taxpayers' money? So he goes for it, you know how it works."

"Yeah."

"Young pleads guilty and a hearing is scheduled, but rather than send him back to jail to await sentencing, the prosecutor asks the judge to release Young to a treatment center. The judge agrees and Young is given conditional release. As long as he reports for treatment he can come and go and . . ."

"I see it coming."

"He boogies. A warrant is issued for his arrest, but c'mon. A property crime? No one exactly broke their hump looking for him."

"How long had he been in Minnesota?"

"DMV issued a driver's license fourteen months ago."

"Where did he live?"

"Nine hundred South Fifth Street in Minneapolis."

"Ahh, Chief. That's the address of the Hubert H. Humphrey Metrodome."

"Hmm," he grunted. "Serves me right for not being a sports fan. But it makes sense. He worked a concession stand at the Metrodome for two months before he was fired for employee theft."

"But not prosecuted. Big surprise."

"There's more, but the way the intel came to me makes me nervous."

"In what way?"

"I was checking on a possible gang connection. Gangs and Guns Unit in Ramsey County, Minneapolis Police Gang Unit, the BCA—no one knew anything. Suddenly, I get a phone call from an officer who works armed robbery in Minneapolis, some guy I never heard of, says he heard about my problem, says I should call ATF."

"Alcohol, Tobacco and Firearms? Why?"

"Why, indeed? But gift horses, right? I call ATF in Minneapolis. The receptionist hands me off to an agent named Bullert."

"Did he know anything?"

"He knew plenty."

"And he told you? When did the ATF become so forthcoming?"

"Since nine-eleven, I guess. Anyway, turns out that Bradley Young was a leading member of a street gang called The Family Boyz."

"Never heard of it."

"According to Bullert, this particular group is very tight, very small, and far less visible than Young Boys, Inc. or Pony Down or the Crips, Bloods, Gangster Disciples, El Rukns, White Knights, Vice Lords, Lower-town Gangstaz, Bogus Boyz—who have I missed?"

"Brown for Life, Vatos Locos, Surenos Thirteen," I offered.

"The new kids on the block. Only these A-holes are much better organized from top to bottom than the other gangs. They operate like a corporation, what we call a CEO—a covert entrepreneurial organization. Very security conscious. They don't wear gold chains or beepers, nothing to draw attention to themselves. More likely they wear ratty clothes and drive beaters. Family Boyz was one of the first gangs to stop wearing colors. They laugh at the gangs that still wear jackets and flags and tattoos. Something else. They have a very limited presence in the drug trade. Drugs fuel nearly every gang in the country, but not these guys."

"What are they into?"

"I don't know."

"What does ATF say?"

"They don't."

"Is ATF investigating them?"

"I asked. Bullert wouldn't confirm."

I had to think about it. When I finished, I said, "If the Family Boyz is active in the Cities, I know a guy who can tell us all about it."

"Cop?"

"Hardly."

"Keep me informed."

"It's the least I can do."

"The very least," the chief said. "There's one thing you should know, however. For what it's worth, Bullert gave me the package like the file was open on his desk and he was waiting for me to call."

I thanked the chief and headed for the door. Before I reached it, he stopped me.

"Are you busy, McKenzie?" Here it comes, I warned myself. The reason he had been so forthcoming. "Have a cup of coffee with me."

To get the coffee, the chief led me through the maze that was the City of St. Anthony Village police department. I had a good look at dispatch, booking, the holding cells, squad room, even the garage, stopping for the coffee at the offices of the investigation unit, then out the back door. It was like he was giving me the grand tour but not once did he introduce me to anyone or say, "Look at this."

Outside, he gestured at the impressive baseball, football, and soccer fields, the skateboard course, the park, the tennis courts, and, up on the hill, the St. Anthony High School and Middle School—all of it in the shadow of a huge, white water tower painted with the community's name and logo.

"Beautiful, isn't it?" he said.

"Bart. It's the suburbs."

"I love this town," Casey said.

"You're from Detroit," I told him. "If I had been from Detroit, I'd love the suburbs, too."

Casey seemed surprised that I knew where he was from.

"Earlier you said Young's arresting officer was an old buddy," I reminded him.

"Very good, McKenzie. Yeah, I'm from Motown, did seventeen years there, six in homicide. After seventeen years, nothing bothered me. Fourteen-year-old boy rapes and kills an eight-year-old girl, then torches her apartment house killing four more. Didn't bother me. We take a drug dealer out of his place, his kids are standing there in diapers that haven't been changed in three days. Didn't bother me. Three black teenagers rape an elderly white woman to death then hire a high-buck activist lawyer to scream racism when we take them down. Didn't bother me. Pretty soon my own kids are in trouble in school and that doesn't bother me. My wife is threatening divorce, that doesn't bother me.

"Then one day I'm doing shooters in this joint near the Renaissance Center and I realize something better start bothering me pretty damn quick or I'm gonna end up flushing my whole life down the toilet. That evening I saw an ad in the trades for a police chief in St. Anthony Village, Minnesota. Never heard of the place, but I apply—anything to get out of Detroit. They jumped me through some hoops, did the dog and pony show for the city council, gave me the job. That was twenty-seven months ago. Now my life is ordinary and predictable. My kids are happy. My wife is happy. And everything bothers me. I'm telling you this because I know you've been there. I checked you out and I know you've been there."

"You checked me out?"

"Of course I did. After the shooting, you know I did. You used to be a pretty good cop."

"Thank you for saying so."

"You should have been promoted to sergeant. You should have been in plain clothes. You would have been, too. You were first in line. Only you killed that kid in the convenience store and that ruined everything. Righteous shoot is what they tell me. The store's security cameras filmed it all. The whole world could see the suspect waving his piece, could see what you did about it. Textbook stuff. Only—shotguns are controversial."

"Tell me about it."

"Shotguns are messy and citizens don't like a mess. There was a lot of loud talk about excessive force that would have been only a whisper if you had used your Glock. Glocks are nice and clean."

"Except I don't like the grip."

"Using the shotgun knocked you to the bottom of the promotion list—SPPD didn't want to look like it was rewarding an officer accused of using excessive force. I'm guessing you figured that your career was over and that's why you took the price on Teachwell."

"Do you have a point here, Chief, or are you just auditioning for Peter Graves's job on *Biography*?"

"Ever think of going back?" he asked.

"Going back?"

"Your arrest record is outstanding. The Ranking Officer's Association made you Police Officer of the Year. You were given the citizen's medal for that Minh Ha thing . . ."

"Are you offering me a job?"

"I have a budget for twenty officers, but I only have fifteen, including a one-man investigative unit that should be as least three, four guys. There hasn't been a single day since I arrived here that I haven't been shorthanded. I hire an officer, he puts in a few years learning the trade, next thing I know he's taking a better paying job in St. Paul or Minneapolis or somewhere else. Small suburban departments like St. Anthony Village have become little more than training grounds for other, wealthier departments. My senior sergeant—you met him yesterday—suddenly he announces he's taking a job in Brainerd, wherever the hell that is."

"Central Minnesota. Great hunting and fishing up there."

"Whatever. I'm having trouble keeping officers. Worse, I'm having trouble keeping veterans. I understand it. There are just so many slots in a small department like this. You could be here for twenty years and not move up. The only chance you have for promotion is if someone retires. Which brings me to you."

"You are offering me a job."

"I would bring you in through a lateral entry program I've installed. Which means you'd get credit for your experience. Eleven years and eight months in St. Paul makes you a sergeant in St. Anthony Village. Something else, and this is between you and me. The lieutenant running my investigative unit assures me he's pulling the pin the day after he puts in his full thirty—at least he had the decency to warn me. If you sign up, I'll give you a shot at the job. Chief of Detectives."

Supervising a unit numbering only four—assuming it was at full strength—wasn't all that impressive. Still, I immediately fell in love with the sound of those three words: Chief of Detectives.

"You don't have to make a decision right away," the chief assured me. "Think about it. We'll have to wait and see what the county attorney does about the Young shooting, anyway—wait to hear what the grand jury has to say. And make no mistake, McKenzie. This isn't a slam-dunk. I insist you go through a mini-academy, make sure the tools are still there. But think about it."

"Okay."

"You'll think about it?"

"I will."

"One more thing. Don't ever call me Bart."

Here I thought I had slipped it by him.

————

I was excited when I returned home. Chief of Detectives. I had considered going back to police work in the past couple years but never with such a grandiose title. I wondered what Bobby would think of it and called to ask, only he wasn't in his office. I thought of calling Kirsten to learn if the new job would change things between us. But I didn't. Never count your chickens, someone had once told me—probably my father, an immensely practical man. I didn't have the job yet. I didn't even know what it paid.

The thought of money made me pause. I didn't know any millionaire cops. I wondered if it would make a difference. I pushed the thought away. Don't buy trouble, I told myself, which was something else Dad used to say.

I decided to quell my anxieties by returning to the problem at hand—finding Jamie's killer. I put Elvis Costello on the CD player and looked to see what the newspapers had.

The St. Paul *Pioneer Press* is trustworthy and rarely emotional. The Minneapolis *Star-Tribune* often seems to be written by closet suspense novelists who just love to tell a crackling good yarn. Naturally, it had the higher circulation of the two. Yet on this day, there seemed to be little difference. Both papers played Jamie Bruder's violent death across the front page. Both used adjectives like "barbarous." Both used the term "serial killer."

I read the articles three times each and to my great relief they didn't mention my name once. Instead, I was referred to as the "friend of the family" who discovered the body. The cops also managed to keep other pertinent details to themselves—that twine was used to tie Jamie to the bed frame, that duct tape was used to seal her mouth, the broom.

The St. Paul paper said, "Bruder died violently," that "she was found nude in the bedroom of her fashionable home," and that "she was stabbed repeatedly." The *Star-Tribune* was considerably more graphic, suggesting that Jamie was "sexually mutilated" and "possibly decapitated, according to a source close to the investigation." I could see Bobby spoon-feeding that last bit to the media to help filter out the whackos who were probably already lining up to confess.

Both papers speculated that Jamie and Katherine Katzmark were killed by the same assailant, but refused to actually come out and say so because the cops refused to actually come out and say so.

Both papers also reported that a massive search for Jamie's husband and son had begun, certainly a reasonable response by the cops, all things considered. But did St. Paul Deputy Chief Thomas Thompson need to claim that Jamie's murder was a "domestic killing," which the newspapers translated to mean Bruder did it? Did the Ramsey County Attorney, an elected official who had never tried a criminal case before a jury in her life, have to support that allegation during a press conference outside the county's domestic abuse office, pledging, as God was her witness, that Good Deal Dave would be brought to justice?

"Don't you think you should prove he did it first?" I shouted at the CA's photograph on page 5A. I admit that Bruder looked good for it, especially if he could be tied to Katherine Katzmark. Only Thompson's and the county attorney's public remarks were unprofessional, gratuitous, and sloppy. A good defense attorney would hurt them with it later.

Along with the lead stories were the inevitable sidebars. Minneapolis ran an interview with a sociologist turned best-selling crime writer who compared Jamie's and Katherine's killer to Ted Bundy and warned readers to be alert. St. Paul ran a story pointing out that late summer was America's "killing season," the time of the year when we murder ourselves with the greatest frequency. Both papers also printed editorials speaking out against violence toward women with headlines like, WE MUST SAY 'NO' TO ABUSE OF WOMEN OR THE TRAGEDIES WILL GO ON AND ON and ABUSERS OF WOMEN: IS THERE A COMMON THREAD AMONG MEN WHO ATTACK?

I looked for my own story and found it in the Minnesota Briefs

column, three paragraphs under the bug with the subhead: MAN SHOT
IN ROBBERY ATTEMPT. It read as I would have predicted:

> A young male was shot and killed early Wednesday morning
> during an armed robbery of the private residence of a former
> St. Paul police officer, St. Anthony Village police reported.
>
> Bradley Young, 23, a reputed member of a local street gang,
> had attempted to rob the house in order to gain money to pay
> for drugs, authorities speculated.
>
> Young had been sought by Michigan authorities for the past
> two years after he failed to show up in court for sentencing
> stemming from a conviction on a charge of burglary in Detroit.

Drugs and street gang. The magic words. Now the world could dis-
miss Young, as if he had never existed. I wish I could do the same.

The phone rang. I picked it up without checking the caller ID. Richard
Carlson. He wasn't happy.

"A man called last night. He said my little girl was . . . Why didn't
you call?"

The answer was simple. I didn't want to be the one to tell the Carlsons
that their child had been killed. It was the hardest thing I had to do
when I was with the cops and I hated it. Suddenly I realized if I put a
badge back on, I'd have to do it again.

"The cops said they'd take care of it. They don't want me involved
anymore." It was only partially a lie, I told myself.

"I know my rights. You're involved if I say you're involved." Carlson
was not crying, but I could hear the grief in his voice. It was hidden
under the anger. "I want to know where we stand. The man, the policeman who called, he said you found Jamie."

"Yes, sir."

"Found her body."

"Yes, sir. I spoke to her Tuesday."

"The day before she was killed? Why didn't you call?"

"Jamie wanted to speak with her husband before she spoke to you. Apparently, he didn't know about her family. Jamie said she would call me later to set up a meeting with you and your wife. When she didn't call I went over and found out why."

"There was something about a child. A son."

"He's missing. Along with Jamie's husband."

"My grandson?"

I didn't reply. After a few seconds, Richard Carlson asked, "Do you know his name? The papers didn't say."

"No, I don't."

"We have to find him."

"Yes, we do."

"I talked to a doctor. He said the child, my grandson could be a bone marrow donor for Stacy."

"I understand."

"Will you find him?"

"The police have a better chance of doing that than I do, but I'll try."

"This husband, this Bruder guy . . ."

"Yes, sir."

"Papers say he did it."

"Papers could be wrong."

"Tell me about him."

"I never met the man. I only know what they said about him in the papers."

"You think maybe when Jamie told him about us, about who she really was . . . ?"

I hadn't thought of that.

"I don't know. The fact he disappeared along with the child makes him look bad, but—I don't know. If Bruder killed Jamie then he also killed another woman, Katherine Katzmark. Bruder could have done it, I suppose. Only it doesn't feel right to me. Plus, there's someone else involved."

"Who?"

"A man named Bradley Young."

"Who's he?"

"A gang-banger who tried to kill me after I found your daughter. He's dead."

"You make 'im dead?"

"Yes, sir."

Carlson paused to think about it.

"McKenzie, can you stay on this for me? Not just because of Stacy, but—I hope Bruder didn't kill my daughter, but if he did I want to make sure he's found and punished. I want to make sure whoever did it is found and punished."

I knew what he was saying.

"I can't be there, Mac. I have another daughter, remember?"

"I remember."

"I want you to act as my representative, make sure the job gets done."

"What job is that?"

I wanted him to say it.

He hesitated yet again, then answered. "I want revenge."

If he had said "justice" I might have told him to go to hell. But revenge, that's something a man can appreciate.

"We'll see," I told him.

"One more thing. Not important."

"Yes?"

"Did you ever find Merci Cole?"

"Yes."

"She's in the Cities?" He seemed excited by the prospect.

"Yes. Why do you ask?"

"Is she okay? Is she—is she okay?"

"Yes." And again I said, "Why do you ask?"

"No reason. Just curious. Is there anything else? Yes, I almost forgot. The body. The medical examiner won't release the body. He said he has to maintain control of the remains until all forensic work is completed. That means he's gonna cut her up, doesn't it?"

"Everyone is being careful. They don't want your daughter's killer to walk away because they weren't careful."

"Whatever it takes. I'm willing to do whatever it takes."

He hung up without saying good-bye. I didn't fault him for that, either. We had been talking for several minutes. That's a long time when you're trying not to cry.

Richard Carlson was the kind of man who preferred to grieve silently. Yet that didn't make his agony any less real than those who beat their chests and tear their clothing. As a culture, we tend to underestimate how deeply and completely people suffer from a tragedy of this proportion. Family and friends will surround us with a cocoon of love and support. They bring us food, they do our errands, they relieve us of our responsibilities. All they ask in return is that we weep loud and long and hard and when we no longer have any tears left to shed, that we return to normal. If we don't give them a public display of grief, they wonder what's wrong. Didn't we care? If we don't return quickly to normal, they become impatient. It's a problem of perspective. Unless you've had prior experience you don't know about acting like a robot, about going through the motions, about washing a dish ten times without realizing it. You don't understand crying jags. You don't understand unfocused anger. You don't understand dependency.

Right now, Richard Carlson was hanging on by his fingernails to the prospect of revenge. Who knew, he might get it. Only it wouldn't change anything. Instead, you change. You invent a new personality, adopt new values. Think about the person involved in a car crash who must now spend the rest of his life in a wheelchair. It's the same with victims of extreme violence. To survive, you stop being the person you were and become someone else. That's the long term. In the short term you grab hold of whatever you can, even the myth of sweet revenge, and hang on.

The busiest intersection in Minnesota is probably Hennepin Avenue at Lake Street, the heart of Uptown, a yuppified district in Minneapolis near Lake Calhoun where you can find designer ice cream, Oriental food for white people, bars with plenty of vegetation growing in them, overpriced arts and crafts, foreign movies, a pretty good comedy club, an overrated rib joint, and plenty of MTV wannabees, young men in fifty-dollar jeans torn at the knees and young women in black lace, the kind of women who carry toothbrushes in their purses.

This was where Chopper told me to meet him, in a fast food joint overlooking Hennepin.

I knew Chopper when he was Thaddeus Coleman and worked Selby and Western, an area of St. Paul that used to be rich with prostitution until patrons became bored with it, as they do with any trendy hot spot, and moved elsewhere. Coleman would put a girl on the street, wait for a john, then rob him, waving a blade at the john or making like he had a gun. That lasted until the pimps calmly explained to him why his behavior was bad for their business. He has two scars on his shoulder as reminders of the conversation.

Afterward, he moved to Fuller and Farrington and sold laundry soap to the suburban kids, soap and Alka Seltzer tablets crushed to resemble rock cocaine. I busted him for that. Representing and selling a substance as a drug—whether it is or not—is a felony. Only the judge dismissed the charge. He took one look at the complaint and announced from the bench, "Boys, we haven't got time for this, not when there are assholes out their selling truckloads of the real thing."

"Nothing personal," Coleman told me when he waltzed out of the courtroom.

I didn't take it personally, but someone else did. Two days later I scooped Coleman off the pavement of a parking lot at Dale and University. A person or persons unknown had put two slugs into his back. I saved his life that night, although the damage to his spine put him in a wheelchair. He refused to ID his assailants. "It musta been an accident," he insisted. "Everyone gives me love."

Yeah, right.

You have to hand it to him, though. Coleman was one tough SOB. Six weeks after the shooting, he wheeled himself out of the hospital in a stolen chair. Couple days later we discovered the bodies of three Red Dragons under the swings at a park near the St. Paul Vo-Tech. They had each been shot numerous times. We never did learn who killed them, but the ME reported that most of the bullet wounds had an upward trajectory, as if whoever fired the shots was sitting down.

Later, Chopper moved his various enterprises across the river into Minneapolis. He was Chopper now because of the chair, which he wheeled about with the reckless abandon of a dirt bike racer.

I found him inside. He was sitting in front of the stainless steel counter wearing a battle-dress uniform and arguing with an older man who was wearing a paper hat and telling Chopper to either order something or wheel his sorry ass out of there. Chopper accused him of violating the Americans with Disabilities Act as I tossed a crumpled twenty on the counter.

"I'll have a Cherry Coke," I said.

Chopper scooped up the bill with an immaculate hand—some people are nuts about shined shoes, with Chopper it's his fingernails.

"Your fries hot, man?" I heard him say as I retreated to a booth. "I ain't buyin' no cold fries."

I sat in the booth and watched a woman stroll casually up and down Hennepin through the window. She could have been a working girl, but in Uptown you never know. Maybe she was just waiting for her boyfriend. Or girlfriend.

"Sex is easy," I said aloud. "It's affection that's hard to come by."

"Huh?" Chopper asked.

He wheeled himself to the front of the booth. The red plastic tray balanced on the arms of his chair was loaded with two Quarter-pounders, two large fries, some kind of apple turnover, four cartons of milk, and a small Cherry Coke. I took the drink.

"Want some fries?"

I shook my head.

He kept the change.

"McKenzie, you look gooder than shit."

"High praise, indeed." Ever since I saved his life, Chopper and I have been pals.

"So how you doin'? Still drivin' that piece of crap SUV?"

"Are you kidding? It's a chick magnet. Soccer moms love it."

"I'll tell ya what them soccer moms love." He was pointing toward his lap but the tray was in the way.

"Are you talking about that Quarter-pounder? You get cheese with that?"

Minute chunks of potato flew from his mouth as he laughed. "You're bad," he told me. "You are soooo bad." Chopper washed the contents of his mouth down with a carton of milk and asked, "So, whaddaya need?"

Most of the informers on television and in the movies are skinny black dudes with an encyclopedic knowledge of the streets and a mortal fear of the cops. I know no such people. Nearly all of the informers I know fall into two categories. There's the professional who trades infor-mation for money or favors and there's the perp looking to score a deal. "Hey, man, get the charge reduced to third degree and maybe we can do some business, whaddaya say?" All of them are more terrified of getting caught by the individuals they inform on than they are of us.

Then there's Chopper, who just likes to show off.

"What can you tell me about the Family Boyz?"

"The Boyz on your ass, McKenzie? Cuz if they are, you got trouble."

"You know them?"

Chopper smiled and shook his head like I had just asked who was Michael Jordan. "Everyone knows 'em."

"The authorities don't."

"Authorities." He said the word like it was a punchline.

Chopper set down his sandwich and wiped his fingernails with a napkin. He took another sip of milk and started talking before he swal-lowed it all.

"Family Boyz, they weird, man. Blew in from Detroit City, dealin' shit all over the place, good shit, too, Acapulco Gold just like the old days, straight from Mexico they say, undercuttin' the competition with lower prices. There was some dust-ups with the Bloods and El Rukns, but that went away cuz the Boyz, all they doin' is dealin' grass and ain't no one wants to go to war over that. Then all a sudden it's like one of them stealth bombers, man, they off the radar, still dealin' MJ but the volume way down, like they was runnin' one of them hobby farms, you know, doin' it for the fun. Last couple of years you hardly know they're there, keepin' a low profile, just goin' about their business."

"What business is that if not drugs?"

"I don't know."

"Protection?"

"I don't know."

"I thought you knew everything."

"I know enough not t' go messin' with the Boyz. A Disciple tried to put down a Family member a few months ago, somethin' t' do with some pussy—shit, these guys fightin' over pussy, you believe that?—and the Boyz blew the flag right off his head, blue bandanna, all fuckin' red now. I'm figurin' it's war, we're gonna have a war, no fuckin' shit, only it don't happen."

"Why not?"

" 'Cause the Boyz, man, they pack some heavy ordnance, that's why. They got machine guns. M-60s. German MG-42s. The Disciples are totally whacked, but they ain't so stupid t' go against that kind of firepower."

The weapons might explain the ATF's interest, I figured. Chopper ate some more of his sandwich. I thought of Good Deal Dave and took a shot.

"Know of any white guys running with the Boyz?"

"Fuck, McKenzie. You think the Boyz is like some kinda equal opportunity employer? Man, with the Boyz you gotta be family, man, *real* family, that's how they git their name. You look at a guy you say, 'that's my bro, that's my cousin, that's my *blood.*' That's how you git to be in the Family Boyz, man."

"Know where I can find them?"

"You're shittin' me, right? You ain't lookin' for no Boyz, right?"

"You don't have to go with me, Chopper."

"Damn right I ain't goin' with you."

"So where are they?"

Chopper gave me an address of an apartment building in Richfield near the Minneapolis-St. Paul International Airport.

I thanked him.

"So you got any next a kin, Mac? Got an address? I want t' know where to send flowers."

"You're a funny man, Chopper."

I slid out of the booth, said I had to leave. Chopper said he had to scoot, too, and followed me out of the restaurant, one hand working his chair and the other balancing a carton of milk and an envelope of fries. I exited in front of him, holding the door open. That's when I saw the black teenager striding toward me, walking with purpose, his hands wrapped around a twelve-gauge Mossberg pump gun with pistol grip.

You feel it in your stomach before you understand it in your head, the animal-like mixture of fear and confusion that makes you flinch, then freezes you in place until the brain has a chance to analyze the danger. If the brain takes too long, you'll stand there, paralyzed with uncertainty, until the danger overwhelms you, like a deer in the headlights. But if the brain is well trained, with plenty of experience, you just might have enough time . . .

I dove headlong between two cars parked side by side in the lot. A shotgun blast took out a chunk of headlight. Another smashed a windshield. I ran forward in a crouch, fumbling for my Beretta, trying to get it out from under my jacket. A third blast sprang the trunk as I swung behind the far vehicle. I came up with the Beretta in both hands. The shooter was facing me, pointing the pump gun at me, yet he was looking at Chopper through the window of the restaurant door, Chopper just sitting there munching fries, watching.

I fired three times, hitting the teenager in the chest. Dead center.

I moved slowly toward his fallen body, breathing hard, my gun trained on his chest, my hands trembling slightly, waiting for him to move. He didn't. I had won again. Yet you can't win them all. Just ask the kid lying flat on his back, his right hand still clutching the pistol grip of the Mossberg.

Chopper pushed through the door. Now he was sipping from his carton of milk.

"Holy shit," he said.

I bent over the teenager and put two fingers on his carotid artery.

Blood was forming a puddle under his body, spreading across the asphalt, but none was pumping through his neck. I felt nauseous and faint, like I hadn't eaten in three days. I moved to the back of the parked car, set my gun on the trunk lid and leaned against the fender, sucking air through my mouth. I had managed to go all those years since the convenience store shooting without pointing a gun at anyone. What tough work was necessary I was able to perform with my hands. Now I'd killed two men in two days.

The air was loud with sirens as I emptied my insides onto the dirty asphalt.

7

I gave my statement six times, starting with the officers at the scene and ending with Minneapolis Police Lieutenant Clayton Rask and the assistant county attorney at about nine p.m. Everyone wanted to know what I had against Cleave Benjamn. That was the kid's name, Cleave Benjamn.

The final statement was made in front of a videotape camera in room 108, the Minneapolis Police Department's homicide office located in the "Pink Palace," the city building noted for its gothic architecture and pink granite facade. For some reason the camera made me nervous. And humiliated. Still, I tried as best I could to sit up straight and look directly into the lens when I answered Rask's questions.

"No, I didn't know him."

"No, I never saw him before."

"No, he didn't say anything."

"Yes, he was awfully young."

"No, I didn't see anyone else."

"No, I don't know why he was shooting at me."

"No, I don't know why he would want to do that."

"Yes, I have a permit to carry a concealed weapon."

"No, I don't believe it's a license to kill."

The carry permit seemed to irritate them more than the shooting. It was issued to me by the sheriff of Itasca County. Itasca County is where my lake home is located. I had once done a favor for the sheriff.

"Goddamn rurals hand these out like they were party favors," Rask told the ACA. The ACA agreed.

"McKenzie, listen to me." Lieutenant Rask was smiling like we were pals, a very scary sight. "If you talk to me, maybe I can help you get through this."

It wasn't the first time I considered lawyering up.

"I've told you everything I know, LT." I was smiling, too. "Check with the witnesses. Uptown early on a Thursday afternoon, there must have been a hundred people saw what happened, easy."

"Are you telling me how to do my job, McKenzie?"

"Of course not."

Rask told me he was asking the questions. He told me to shut up unless I wanted to spend the night in a holding cell. Then he asked me if I had anything to say that might make things easier on me.

I assumed we weren't friends anymore.

Merci Cole was waiting for me on the porch of my house, standing exactly where Bradley Young stood before I killed him. I was still jazzed from my encounter with Benjamn and my first impulse was to reach for the Beretta, only Lieutenant Rask had confiscated it—I was running out of guns, probably for the best. I parked the Cherokee at the curb and walked to the front door like I owned the place.

"I'm glad you're here," I told her. "It saves me the trouble of finding you."

Merci responded by taking a small automatic from her purse and pointing it at my heart. I stopped and stared at the gun. It was too far away to do much about, so I took a chance and ignored it. I stepped past her. She held the gun steady. I unlocked the front door.

"Want a sno-cone?" I asked, stepping inside. She followed. I snapped on a light.

"A sno-cone?"

"Yeah. Before you shoot me. You are going to shoot me, aren't you?"

She moved forward, her arm extended, until the muzzle of the gun was six inches from my face and pointed between my eyes.

"Yes," she said.

It was a mistake moving that close. To prove it, I shifted my head out of the line of fire, knocked the gun up and away with my left hand. I held tight to her wrist as I cocked my right and punched her in the stomach just as hard as I could. She dropped the gun and crumpled to the hardwood floor, rasping for breath. I retrieved the handgun and unloaded it. It was a Ruger .22 with nine rounds in the magazine and a live one in the chamber. The bullet bounced and rolled across the floor when I ejected it. I lost sight of it, decided to forget it.

Merci was in pretty rough shape on the floor, still doubled over, holding her stomach, coughing to regain her breath.

"Forget the sno-cone," I told her. "How 'bout a beer?"

I went into the kitchen and leaned against the refrigerator door while I tried to steady my nerves.

"What next?"

A few minutes later, Merci Cole stumbled into the kitchen and sat at the table. I left an open bottle of Summit Ale for her—good, old-fashioned sipping beer brewed in St. Paul, my hometown.

"I didn't kill Jamie," I told her. When she didn't reply, I added, "Isn't that what you came here to find out?"

Merci picked up the beer. "I guess," she said, and chugged half of it.

"I found her body. It wasn't pleasant. I want to do something about it if I can."

After a few moments of reflection, she took the beer by the throat, killing it.

I perched on the chair across the table from her, setting the Ruger in front of me. Suddenly, Merci bowed her head, covered her face with her hands and wept. Her shoulders shuddered and her chest heaved with every sob. I leaned back in the chair and sipped my beer. A woman cries and most men become uncomfortable. A man cries and they become downright claustrophobic. Not me. I don't trust tears. I know people who can cry at Laurel and Hardy shorts and Merci's grief noises didn't sound even remotely genuine. In any case, she didn't grieve long.

"I'm all right," she told me, dabbing at her eyes with a balled-up paper napkin she took from the dispenser on the table. I had no reason to doubt her.

"Want another beer?"

She nodded too quickly, like a saleswoman anticipating a big commission.

I went to the refrigerator.

She went for the Ruger.

I took the Summit from the refrigerator and returned to the table, once again ignoring the gun. I couldn't believe I was wasting my good beer on her.

She snarled and pointed the Ruger at my chest.

"It requires these." I fished nine bullets from my pocket and held them out to her.

She slammed the Ruger down on the table and I dropped the .22s back into my pocket. Merci grabbed the beer from my hand and took another long swallow.

"I didn't kill Jamie," I repeated.

"Who did?"

"Her husband."

"No."

"I only know what I read in the papers."

"No," she repeated, adding a head shake.

"What makes you so sure? Have you seen him? Do you know where he is?"

"If I did, I sure as hell wouldn't tell you."

"Not even if he killed Jamie?"

"He didn't!"

"Well, if he did, he's going down for it. It's not easy to hide these days, especially with a baby, especially if you're Good Deal Dave and your face is plastered all over billboards. On the other hand, if he didn't do it, maybe I can find out who did. You can help. You did come here to avenge your friend, right?"

"Something like that."

"Not very smart," I told her. "There's no such thing as getting even—trust me on this. Besides, think how bad you would have felt when you discovered I was innocent."

"I would have gotten over it."

In about thirty seconds, I figured. I swallowed some more Summit Ale.

"There's something else. Jamie's child."

"Thomas Christopher," Merci said. "They call him TC."

"TC might be able to donate his bone marrow. He might be able to save Stacy's life."

"I hadn't thought of that," Merci said. "Are you sure? He's so small."

"That's what I've been told."

"By who?"

"Richard Carlson."

"That bastard. Yeah, he cares about Stacy, but fuck everyone else."

"He asked about you."

"Sure he did."

"He seemed genuinely pleased when I told him you were all right."

"What else did you tell him about me?"

"Nothing."

She hit the beer again, then said, "Yeah. Good."

"You hooked up with Jamie after you were released from Shakopee," I said.

"She let me stay at her place for a couple of weeks."

"How did they seem to you, Jamie and David?"

"Fine. They were okay. We didn't spend much time with David. Mostly he played with the kid while Jamie and I talked."

"What did you talk about?"

"Jamie was trying to get me to change my ways. Like I haven't tried. Only it seems every time I make an effort, there's a man standing there with money in his hand."

"Did you talk to Jamie after you met me?"

"No."

I remembered the message she left on Jamie's answering machine.

"We'll get along so much better if you don't lie to me."

"I'm not," she began, stopped, thought about it. "After *you* found Jamie, *Jamie* called me. She said she was going to tell her husband every-thing, said she was going back to Grand Rapids to help little Stacy."

"What was Bruder's reaction, I wonder."

"He said he was fine with it, said he was looking forward to meeting his in-laws."

He said?

"Do you know where David Bruder is?" I asked again.

"No. How many times do I have to say it?"

I finished my Summit Ale and went for another bottle. When I returned I asked Merci to tell me about Jamie. "Start with when she left Grand Rapids."

"Why should I?"

The average person is so unaccustomed to sudden pain that one quick, violent thrust is enough to leave them shaky, nauseous, and immensely cooperative for a week or more. Only Merci Cole had been hit before and she wasn't afraid of being hit again. No threat was going to persuade her to do my bidding. So I gave Merci the truth. "It might help me find Jamie's killer."

"Like you care."

"I do care. I care very much."

Merci studied me over the mouth of her beer bottle for a moment. Then she began to talk.

Merci claimed she hadn't encouraged Jamie to leave home, hadn't invited her to her fleabag apartment on Franklin Avenue in Minneapolis. Yet one day there she was, suitcase in hand. Of course Merci took her in.

"Why did Jamie leave home?"

"What did she tell you?"

"She said she was tired of the lies."

"Aren't we all."

"What lies?"

"Ask Richard."

"Something happened between her and Mr. Carlson?"

"What's it they say? 'It's always something.' I don't want to talk about it."

I did. But I was afraid I might lose her if I kept pushing, so I changed the subject.

"Her new ID. Jamie Kincaid? Did you manage it?"

"ID? Yeah. I knew a couple of guys that helped us out—for a price. We furnished Jamie with a new name, driver's license, social security number, the works. We even forged some transcripts to get her into community college. She worked as a receptionist during the day, went to school to be a paralegal at night."

"She worked for a law firm," I added.

"In Arden Hills."

"That's where she met Bruder?"

"Uh huh. He took one look at her and, well, you saw how pretty she was."

"She was beautiful."

Merci nodded and bowed her head. This time the tears that formed in her eyes were as real as life and death. She brushed them away and took another swallow of beer.

"I tried to talk her out of it, the marriage I mean." Merci's voice was suddenly drenched in regret. "It was selfish of me. I was afraid of being alone again. You gotta know, when we went out together, it was pretty amazing the sensation we caused. Guys would line up three deep to buy us drinks, buy us dinner, buy us all kinds of things. Jamie didn't like it, though. She thought by accepting gifts we were entering into some kinda—what did she call it—'implied contract.' I guess she learned that in school. She said the guys now had the right to expect something in return and she wasn't willing to reciprocate, which is another legal word. You believe that? I told her to loosen up, only she never did. Then when David came around—Mr. Nice Suit, Nice Manners, Money-in-the-Bank—well, I guess that's what she was looking for. Jamie earned her diploma but she didn't use it long. They were married like three months later and that was that."

"What about you?" I asked.

"I was Jamie's maid of honor. Isn't that a laugh? Maid of Honor.

Me? After the wedding, you knew Jamie wasn't going bar hopping anymore. That left me by myself and I started to get into some—unsavory situations."

"Prostitution?"

"I got screwed over so often I figured maybe I should make some money at it."

"Drugs?"

"That was a bum rap. I wasn't dealing, not really. Sometimes I help a guy I know, that's all. Anyway, I'm on the bus and I asked these black dudes if they want a taste and all of a sudden a guy's got his arm on my shoulder. I didn't know they had bus police, guys who ride undercover on the MTC. I didn't know that. My PD, he says cop a plea and I'll get probation, it's my first felony so I'll get probation, maybe some community service, but no time. So I cop. Wham, the judge gives me eighteen months, no probation. Don't ever listen to no overworked public defender, that's what I learned.

"So now I'm in Shakopee. People say Shakopee is like a summer camp or something. No fences and you're allowed to walk around during the day and there are crab-apple trees and a wishing well and inside there's a gymnasium with a weight room, and a dark room, and a pottery kiln, and a bowling alley. Only it's no summer camp, no way. The first day I'm there, I'm trying to call Jamie, and this big bull dyke swings a twenty-four-pound fire extinguisher at my head cuz she wanted to use the phone. It was crazy. I decided right then I was going to keep a low profile. I was going to mind my own business and do my time and get the hell outta there and never go back. Jamie was a big help. She would visit and we would talk. Mostly she would talk and I would listen. Jamie was going to straighten me out. I was going to let her."

The tears returned, flowed freely. This time Merci made no attempt to brush them away. I moved to her side and covered her hand with mine. She surprised me by not pulling away. Instead she rested her forehead on top of it, her hair spilling across the table. I guess neither of us was as tough as we pretended to be. A moment later, I felt her body shudder. She jerked back her head abruptly, angry at her weakness and quickly brushed the tears from her eyes with the heel of her palm.

"Anyway, it's like I always say. Live fast, die young, leave a beautiful corpse."

"That's original."

"Oh? Has it been done before?"

I wanted to talk more about Jamie, only Merci had tired of the subject.

"This is a nice house," she told me. "You live alone?"

"Yes."

"How come a bachelor lives in such a big house?"

"Just lucky, I guess."

I finished my beer and went for another. I felt light when I moved. I hadn't eaten and what little had been in my stomach had been washed off the fast-food joint's asphalt parking lot with a hose. The alcohol was taking effect.

"You don't talk much," Merci observed.

"On the contrary," I answered. "I can be a regular chatterbox."

"I don't see it."

"Right now I need information. You never learn anything while talking."

"You're trying to learn stuff from me?"

"I want to find Jamie's killer."

"Why?"

"It's what I do." It's what I've always done, I reminded myself. I concentrate on other people's problems to keep from facing my own. It's a form of cowardice, I know. At least I admit it. Every day I learn something new about myself, gain a little maturity. At this rate, I figure by the time I hit eighty I'll be a full-grown adult.

"You remind me of a cop," she told me.

"I was a cop."

"Did you like it?"

"I loved it."

"How come you're not a cop now?"

"I quit."

"Why?"

"It seemed like the thing to do at the time."

"You're doing it again."

"Doing what?"

"Talking without saying anything."

"It's a gift."

Merci actually smiled at me. "I like you."

I wondered if she liked all men who punched her in the stomach.

"I like you because when you look at me, your eyes don't look away much. Most men, I can spend an entire evening with them and they won't know the color of my eyes. You know the color of my eyes."

"They're green," I said, proving it. Someone much wiser than I once said that the eyes were windows to the soul. He never looked into Merci Cole's eyes. They were as hard as marbles and revealed nothing of what was behind them.

"We'd be awfully good together," Merci volunteered.

The remark surprised me, put me on the defensive. "I don't sleep with hookers," I said too abruptly.

Merci looked at me with an expression that could peel paint. "I tried brain surgery but I couldn't hack the hours, too much time on my feet."

"As opposed to your back."

"I actually spend very little time on my back."

"Your knees then."

I didn't mean to be insulting. The remark had just slipped out—blame the beer. Merci took it like she had heard it before. She smiled a joyless smile and said, "All we need is a blackboard and some chalk. I'll write down my personal history and you can tell me where I went bad. Then I pay you a hundred bucks and we schedule another session for next week."

"You don't have to be a prostitute."

"You don't have to be a sanctimonious sonuvabitch."

Touché.

Merci finished her beer and gathered up her belongings. She reached for her Ruger, but I pulled it away.

"Can I have my gun, please?"

"You might hurt somebody."

Merci made a face, a little girl's face with her tongue protruding between her lips, and I found myself chuckling. Still, I kept the gun. She went to the front door. I followed her. She opened the door and stood gazing into the night. Without turning around, she asked, "What are you going to do now?"

"Damned if I know."

8

It was cold Friday morning. Not heroic cold, not national news cold, not even local news cold, just plain middle of September in Minnesota winter's coming cold, which is nothing to complain about, only something to get through. I powered up the windows on my Cherokee, closed the sun roof and actually flirted with the idea of activating the heater, but declined. In Minnesota, the longer you can go without heat, the more manly you are. Ask anyone.

The traffic was heavy as I caught I-35W south. Used to be "rush hour" was confined to seven to nine a.m. and four to six p.m., only that changed dramatically in just the past few years. A growing population and subsequent urban sprawl—and our ponderous mass transit system— have given the Twin Cities rush hour traffic around the clock. The worst of it probably can be found at the bottleneck known as the 35W-Crosstown Interchange, where a four-lane freeway suddenly narrows to three lanes and then splits off in three separate directions.

Traffic heading into it began to slow at 38th Street. By 48th it was stop and go.

As I drove I listened to Minnesota Public Radio. *"In local news, the massive manhunt for suspected killer David C. Bruder and his infant son continues . . . Elsewhere, authorities believe that the shooting in the Uptown area of Minneapolis late Thursday afternoon that left one man dead, is indicative of the escalating gang violence in the city . . . "* Unlike the newspapers, MPR didn't mention my name and I made a silent vow to increase my contribution during its next membership drive. Yet when it segued into a liberal discussion about the appropriateness of making inmates in the county jail pay for their keep, I put Bonnie Tyler on my CD system and cranked the volume.

I drove east on Highway 62, leaving the bottleneck behind and increasing my speed to a brisk forty miles per hour—don't you just adore freeway driving—until I caught the Portland Avenue exit. I went south, east, south, then east again, driving deep into the suburb of Richfield, until I reached the address Chopper had given me.

It was a three-story, white-brick apartment building set a respectful distance from the look-alike split-levels located on either side and across the street. I guessed six units to each floor, maybe another six in the basement. On the left side of the building was a parking lot filled with a half dozen older vehicles and two identical, brand-spanking-new black Chevy vans. Behind it there was an empty, unkempt field that extended a good hundred yards before butting up against a cyclone fence. There was a hole cut into the fence. A narrow path beaten into the ground ran the distance from the fence to the street.

The apartment building seemed to be in direct line with one of the runways at the Minneapolis-St. Paul International Airport about a mile to the east. Planes flew so low over the neighborhood you could smell the fumes from their exhaust. They took off at thirty-second intervals. You could set your watch by them. The noise was so loud you felt it in your teeth and I wondered what fool would build an apartment building there and what moron would live in it.

I parked down the street where I could watch the front and side of the building. There was a black man in the foyer leaning against a bank of mailboxes and watching out the glass door. A sentry. I took a pair of Bushnell 7 X 25 binoculars I keep in my glove compartment and gave him a hard look. He was cradling what seemed to be—"Geezus"—a Romanian AKM assault rifle. You could tell by the distinctive pistol grips, one behind the banana magazine and one forward. *Where the hell did he get that?* I asked myself. A moment later, he was joined by another brother who was also carrying an automatic rifle, this one an East German MPiKM. Warsaw Pact ordnance.

Chopper was right about the firepower. The Family Boyz were packed to the max, as the kids would say. I unholstered my last handgun, a Model 85 Beretta .380 with walnut grips and a single line eight-round magazine, and set it on the seat next to me. It didn't make me feel any safer.

The brothers didn't seem to have much to say to each other and a few minutes later the East German moved out of sight and the Romanian resumed his vigil. I turned on the AM/FM and tuned it to a classic rock and roll station. Joe Cocker was playing so I cranked it. He was followed by Bob Seger and I left the volume up. Next came a group called Tears for Fears. I turned the radio off. The noise was worse than the jet engines.

I watched the apartment building for another hour, only crime when it's well run is boring and besides, the airplane noise was really starting to annoy me. "Why would anyone live in Richfield?" I asked myself as I fired up my Cherokee and headed home.

There were no messages on my voice mail so I got right to it, activating my PC and accessing my Internet provider. I have broadband so it didn't take long.

Few government agencies in Minnesota post public records online. A notable exception is Hennepin County, which posts property information. I accessed its Web site. The home page offered several options. I clicked on *Property Address (Quick Search)*. A new screen appeared, offering me a box in which I typed the Family Boyz's Richfield address. Execute. The next screen provided me with the apartment building's property identification number. Execute. I scrolled down the screen and discovered the building's school, watershed, and sewer district numbers, construction year, tax parcel description, current market value, the date the building was last purchased and for how much, and an updated tax summary. I was also given the name of the building's fee owner.

David C. Bruder.

My telephone rang.

"Yes?" I answered automatically, not taking my eyes from the computer screen.

"Are you deliberately trying to make this difficult?"

"Hi, Chief."

"This kid you killed, Cleave Benjamn."

"I had no choice."

"I appreciate that, McKenzie, but it makes you a hard sell. The mayor and city council, they're pretty open-minded folks—they hired a black police chief for a white community, didn't they? Only a cop with three killings to his name? I don't know."

"Don't put yourself out, Chief," I told him, sadly accepting my fate. "I know how it works. A cop gets so much political capital to work with and no more. Don't waste it on me. You might need it some day."

"I didn't say it couldn't be done."

"Even I wouldn't hire me now."

"Don't say that. We'll see what happens. By the time this gets to the grand jury—Christ, two grand juries now—you might be hailed as a hero."

"How could I not be?"

"Just do me a favor, will you? Stay home and play with your damn ducks."

"I'll try," I told him and he hung up.

How did he know about the ducks?

Bobby Dunston sat on a bench in Rice Park in downtown St. Paul, eating the chili dog I bought for him from the vendor who worked the corner of 5th and Market. Unlike Yu, I didn't know him by name.

"What's so damned important?" Bobby wanted to know.

"I'll show you mine if you show me yours."

"I'm really not in the mood, McKenzie."

I told him what I had discovered. He stopped chewing and slowly dabbed the corners of his lips with a napkin—Bobby could be so dainty.

"Landlord to the Boyz," he said at last.

"How 'bout that?"

"I don't suppose you saw anyone matching Bruder's description in or around the premises in question?"

"I'd be happy to say I did if it'll help you get a warrant, but you won't need my statement for that. Just surveil the joint for about ten minutes and you'll see enough to satisfy any judge. It's a stash pad if I've ever seen one and I've seen plenty."

"What do the Family Boyz have to do with this?" he asked himself. He seemed surprised when I answered.

"I find Jamie. Jamie's husband's hooked up with the Family Boyz. The Family Boyz try to kill me—twice. Obvious progression."

"So obvious I can't see it. Why would Bruder send the Boyz after you?"

"Because I found Jamie," I repeated.

"So?"

"I don't know." I was just throwing spaghetti at the wall now, seeing if anything stuck.

"You're making this more complicated than it needs to be. There's no doubt that Katherine and Jamie were killed by the same man. I don't have a formal protocol yet, but more and more it looks like Bruder."

"Not Bradley Young?"

"Young was right-handed. The killer was a southpaw. Also, the ME vacuumed the bodies of both victims and found head and pubic hairs. He put 'em through a full SEM analysis. Thickness and length suggest a male, but not Bradley. Something else. There was no trace of semen inside or outside the body of either victim, but we did recover the remains of a cigarette at both scenes, what he used to burn them with. Saliva on the filters indicate a group A secretor. Bradley Young was not group A. Nor were the victims. But I checked with David Bruder's doctor. Guess what?"

"He's group A."

"Move the man to the front row. When Bruder is found, the ME said he'll go for a genetic fingerprint. He said that like it's the most fun a forensic pathologist can have."

"Huh."

"Is that all you have to say? Huh?"

"Can you connect him to Katherine?"

"Yep. Turns out they were both members of the same club, the Northern Lights Entrepreneur's Club."

"Interesting."

"Oh, it gets better. We've interviewed Bruder's secretary, his employees, his friends, we checked his appointment calendar and his credit card receipts. It looks like our boy's been having an extramarital affair for at least the past six weeks."

"With who?"

"We don't know, but Jeannie . . ."

"Your young, beautiful, and smart as hell partner that you haven't introduced me to yet."

"Is flashing Katherine's photograph in the restaurants and hotels listed in Bruder's credit card records to see if we can find a witness who saw the two of them together."

"Fingerprints?"

"Everything has to be perfect with you, McKenzie. Yeah, we lifted latents in Katherine's bedroom that match latents lifted in Jamie's. We don't know yet if they're Bruder's. That's something else we'll find out when we take him. The point is, there's plenty of probable cause to arrest Bruder, but I don't see where Young and the Family Boyz enter into it."

"Maybe they're hiding him."

"Maybe they are. But why try to kill you?"

"Because I found Jamie."

"You keep saying that."

"It's all I have."

Bobby finished his chili dog.

I finished mine.

"Did you get a line on Bruder's business associate?" I asked. "The one who was stopping for drinks the day Jamie was killed?"

"Napoleon Cook. He owns Bloomington Alarms out on the strip. He's also a member of the Entrepreneur's Club. He said he spent a half hour, maybe forty-five minutes at Bruder's house, just enough time for a drink and to discuss The Entrepreneur's Club Ball. He said everyone was healthy and happy when he left and we have no reason to doubt him."

"The Entrepreneur's Club Ball?"

"Each year the club throws a formal ball over at the Minnesota Club, invites a slew of young entrepreneurs like themselves. Getting an invitation is supposed to be quite an achievement. I'm surprised a rich fella like yourself hasn't been invited."

"Makes you wonder, doesn't it?"

"Wonder what?"

"When Chief Casey described the Family Boyz to me, he called the gang a 'covert entrepreneurial organization.'"

"McKenzie, a lot of these rich guys own property they've never even seen. They hire agents to take care of it for them. Bruder probably doesn't even know who his tenants are."

"He's landlord to the Boyz. That can't be a coincidence."

"Ahh, hell."

Bobby slapped his napkin and chili dog wrapper into my hand and marched briskly from the park more or less in the direction of the police building a half mile away. He didn't look back.

Napoleon Cook danced in front of his audience like one of those crazed infomercial hosts you see on TV, except his stage was a large meeting room in the Creekside Community Center on Penn Avenue and West 98th Street about a mile north of the City of Bloomington government offices. I had been directed there by a sign attached to the door of his business: BECAUSE OF INCREASED DEMAND, BLOOMINGTON ALARMS FREE SECURITY SEMINAR HAS BEEN RELOCATED . . .

Cook was all smiles and positive energy—I could feel it even where I sat way in the back of the room. From his unrelenting upbeat delivery, you'd think he was selling a food processor or a set of Ginsu steak knives instead of alarm systems designed to keep you or your loved ones from being raped and murdered in bed. "It's something I wish there was no market for," he claimed. "But today we need the Bloomington Alarm's comprehensive emergency-alert system more than ever." Not once did he refer to Katherine Katzmark or Jamie Carlson Bruder by name, yet from the way his audience nodded its collective heads, I guessed the murders were foremost in their minds. Probably the reason for the "increased demand" from customers, I concluded.

Nor did Cook linger over the cost of his toys, which started at $799—a small price to pay for peace of mind in a dangerous world, Cook insisted. Given the quality of his products, I figured his customers would be better off keeping geese, only no one asked for my expert opinion and I didn't offer it.

As advertised, the seminar was free. However, the audience was encouraged to sign up afterward with Cook's "lovely assistant Meredith" for a fifty-dollar home security assessment and at least half of the people who crowded into the room queued up in front of her. While they waited in line Cook kept selling. He shook hands, listened patiently to tales of property theft and other outrages, and offered advice, which nearly always consisted of arranging an appointment with one of his highly qualified security agents.

I sat in the back and waited. Cook noticed me and several times glanced my way. When the last customer left he moved quickly to my side, extended his hand. "Napoleon Cook. Can I be of assistance?" He probably thought I was a big fish in a pond of guppies, the manager of a large apartment complex, perhaps.

I shook his hand and said, "McKenzie."

Cook's body stiffened and the pupils of his eyes grew wide at the sound of my name. He knew who I was and the knowledge frightened him. Lovely assistant Meredith came up from behind. "Is there anything else, Napoleon?"

She had to ask twice before Cook answered, "No, Meredith, thanks."

"Okay, see ya Monday," she replied in a pleasant sing-song voice.

I watched her go through the doors of the meeting room. "Pretty," I said.

"Huh? Yeah. Sure, she is." I had been holding Cook's hand all that time and he pulled it away. "Very pretty." And winked. "Very athletic, too, if you know what I mean."

He smiled mightily, selling me like he did the rest of the crowd.

"Oh, does she play tennis?"

"Tennis?" Cook started to laugh. He patted my shoulder. "Tennis?" he said. "Yeah, you should see her serve."

We were pals now, talking dirty in the locker room.

"How can I help you?"

"I'm investigating the murder of Jamie Bruder," I told him.

"Unbelievable, isn't it? Such a lovely woman. Terribly tragic."

"Good for business, though."

"Sad, but true. I thought I would take some of my profits and start up a memorial in her name, something like that. Such a lovely woman."

"You were there the evening she was killed." I made it sound like an accusation.

The smile froze on his face and he brushed a hand through his hair. It was hard hair, not a strand moved out of place. "No."

"No?"

"I was invited for drinks, but I stayed for only a few minutes."

I stared at him without blinking, waiting for him to blink, which he did several times before looking away altogether.

"You're not with the police," he reminded himself more than me.

"I'm doing a favor for the family."

"Family?" The word seemed to frighten him more than my name did.

"Jamie's family," I clarified. "Were you thinking I meant the Family Boyz?"

Cook lost his smile completely. He began flexing the fingers of his hands without purpose. "Family Boyz? What are you talking about?"

I was on to something and kept pressing. "I'm talking about conspiracy, murder, drugs, guns . . ." On the word "guns" Cook's eyelids began to flicker.

"I have nothing to do with any of that," he insisted.

"Aren't you and Bruder and the Boyz all members of the Northern Lights Entrepreneur's Club—same as Katherine Katzmark?"

"Katherine," he whispered, like it was the first time he had heard the name. Cook moved quickly away from me. I thought he was going to make a break for it, but he stopped at the door and spun to face me.

"I'm very upset about Katherine and Jamie." My take was that he was telling the truth. "But I can't help you. I've already told the police everything I know."

"Of course, you did. Thank you for your time, Mr. Cook." I extended my empty hand. He shook it vigorously like he was relieved about something.

Quickly, I slapped my left hand over the back of his right, making sure my thumb was over his wrist and my fingers underneath. I stepped in with my left foot and brought his hand up in a counterclockwise motion over his head. I pivoted my body in a complete circle, locking his shoulder. I let go with my left hand, clutched his elbow at the point and pulled up hard, arching his back. And that, boys and girls, is how you execute a shoulder-lock come-along.

"Stop it, that hurts," Cook bellowed.

"No doubt about it," I said, giving the hold a little extra pressure. I walked him face first into the wall. I bounced him a few more times before releasing him and pushing him away. I pointed an accusing finger at him.

"You and the Family Boyz killed Jamie and tried to kill me," I hissed through my teeth. "I'm going to get you for it."

Cook shouldn't have even known who I was, yet he was afraid of me. I had decided to use that, accuse him, muss him up some, then sit back and watch what he did. If he was completely honest and totally innocent, he'd scream bloody murder, maybe even call the cops. If he wasn't, his outrage would be overshadowed by fear—a fear he might want to share with whoever else was involved. When he did, I would be there.

Napoleon Cook rubbed his wrist vigorously. "You're making a big mistake," he told me as I went through the door.

It wouldn't be the first time.

I left the parking lot but didn't go far, idling on Penn Avenue where I could get a clear view of the front door to the community center with my binoculars. Cook didn't come out right away and I speculated that he was making a phone call. Despite the cool air, the sun beat hard through my windows and I began to feel sweat on my back.

At about six-thirty-five, Napoleon Cook left the building and walked to his own car, a black Porsche. The vanity license plate read IMCUKN. It took me a while to figure it out. *I'm Cookin'? He paid an extra hundred bucks for that?* Still, I admired the vehicle. I followed it onto I-494, staying eight lengths back and to his right as we went east toward St. Paul at ten miles above the speed limit. We followed I-494 until it became West 7th Street, continued east to Lexington, went north, turned east on Summit, then north again on Dale Street, stopping for a light at Selby Avenue, not far from a restaurant where August Wilson wrote some of his plays and a bar where Scott and Zelda used to party. We hung a right. Too many turns, I told myself. Cook should have made me long ago, but apparently he wasn't paying attention.

Cook drove Selby until he reached the parking lot adjacent to Rickie's, a jazz club that was developing a nice reputation for displaying gifted performers on their way up—Diana Krall had played there early in her career, but I had missed it. Minneapolis may have had the best rock, but by far St. Paul had the best jazz in the Twin Cities—Artists' Quarter, Brilliant Corners, Blues Saloon, a new joint called Fhima's. I had frequented them all, yet I had neglected Rickie's because the name reminded me of Rick's Café Americain in the movie *Casablanca*. I'm not a big fan of retro.

I gave Cook a two-minute head start and followed him inside. Rickie's was lightly populated—I had caught the seam between the one-drink-before-I-go-home and the let's-get-dressed-and-go-out-tonight crowds. When I didn't see him downstairs, I went upstairs. A dozen steps past the door, a spiral staircase with red carpet and a shiny brass railing led to a comfortable second-floor dining and performance area. I peeked just above the landing. An elevated stage was set against the far wall, a baby grand and several microphone stands sitting unattended in the center. A couple dozen small, round tables were arranged immediately in front of the stage and a second ring of larger square tables covered with white linen and set for dinner were strategically placed beyond them. About a dozen booths and another bar lined the remaining three walls. Cook was leaning into a booth in the corner, bussing the cheek of a woman with raven hair. Even from a distance the woman looked expensive. I retreated downstairs.

To my delight, the decor was about as far away from *Casablanca* as it could get. In fact, the first floor of Rickie's reminded me of a coffee house. A large number of comfortable sofas and stuffed chairs were mixed among the tables and booths. A small stage big enough for one or two performers was erected near a fireplace. There was even a large espresso machine behind the bar. The sound system played Hoagy Carmichael and Cole Porter. There wasn't a TV in sight.

I made a quick pit stop at the men's room—I didn't know when I would have another opportunity. Afterward, I found a spot at the far end of the bar where I could watch the staircase and front door without seeming conspicuous. The bartender was busy serving a woman who ordered a champagne cocktail in a pleasant, somewhat aristocratic voice. The bartender refused to serve her. "Do you have an ID?"

"What?"

"An ID? A driver's license?"

"Are you kidding?" asked the woman. "I'm over twenty-one."

"Yeah, yeah, I've heard it before. C'mon, let's see it."

The woman tried to act indignant but couldn't quite pull it off. She unfolded her wallet and flashed her license at the bartender. He studied the photograph on the license, glanced at the woman, went back to the photograph and said, "Yeah, right. Tell your big sister I said, 'Hi.'" He made the drink and served the woman. The woman left a bill on the bar and drifted to the table where her friends sat. "You're not going to believe this," she told them, a happy grin on her face. The bartender pocketed the bill and came over to me. I ordered a Grain Belt and club sandwich.

"Hey," I said as the bartender moved away.

"Something else?"

"How much did the woman give you?"

"A ten."

"How much was the drink?"

"Four-fifty."

"Nice."

The sandwich was served by a handsome woman with the most startling silver-blue eyes I had ever seen, made even more luminous by the short jet black hair that framed them. She reminded me of the actress Meg Foster. You know who I mean. She did *The Scarlet Letter* on PBS a while back as well as *The Osterman Weekend* and *Leviathan,* been on TV a hundred times.

Just in case Cook started to move, I told the server I wanted to pay my tab right away. She seemed to read my mind.

"Whatever you say, shamus."

"Shamus?"

"Isn't that what they call private eyes these days?"

I didn't think they ever called detectives that except in the movies. "What makes you think I'm a detective?"

"I saw you come in, saw you follow a man upstairs, saw you watch him over the railing while trying not to be seen yourself, and now you're sitting here, a little mouse in the corner, paying up front in case you need to make a quick getaway."

"Amazing."

"Yes, I am," she told me, her silver eyes twinkling mischievously.

"Why not a cop?"

She pointed at the Grain Belt.

"Cops don't drink on the job—well, most of them don't."

"Amazing," I repeated.

"Besides, I figured someone like you would be along sooner or later."

"Someone like me?"

"The woman that met the man you're following? She's married. Wears a ring the size of a grade AA jumbo egg. Yet she comes in once, twice, sometimes three times a week, sits alone in the same booth and waits for a man to meet her. Rarely the same man twice. None of them her husband."

I didn't ask her if she was sure. Why insult the woman? Instead, I asked, "What's her name?"

"She doesn't pay, the man always pays, so I've never seen her name on a check or credit card. But she reserves the table under the name Hester, just Hester, no last name. I figure it's a private joke."

"Why?"

"Hester Prynne."

I shook my head.

"The adulteress in *The Scarlet Letter*."

"Oh, okay, sure. Say, has anyone ever told you that you have eyes just like Meg Foster?"

"Who's she?"

"A pretty good actress."

The woman shook her head.

"Never mind."

"So, are you working for the woman's husband or what?"

"I'm following the man. I don't know anything about the woman."

"Why?"

"Why what?"

"Following the man."

"It's a complicated story."

She leaned an elbow on the bar. "That's what bartenders are for, to listen to complicated stories."

"Who are you?"

"I own the place."

"You're Rickie?"

"Nina. Nina Truhler." She offered to shake hands, her grip was firm. "Rickie's my daughter, also known as Erica."

"McKenzie." I didn't tell her I wasn't a private investigator. Why ruin the illusion?

"Pleasure."

"Where's the namesake?"

Nina looked at her watch and said, "Erica should just be getting home from dance class now. She'll read my note telling her to eat a decent meal, ignore it, grab some Lucky Charms and eat them dry from the box like peanuts while she decides if she'll go cruising with her friends tonight or simply curl up with a good book. I'd say it was fifty-fifty."

"No gentlemen callers?"

"She's fourteen. Boys bore her."

"Boys bored me when I was fourteen, too."

"Are you gay?"

"No," I said way too loud. "I was just making a joke."

"Oh, funny." She rolled her eyes and moved down the bar.

I liked her. I liked everything about her. I liked the way her movements were smooth and effortless when she served her other customers—a dancer who knows all the steps. I liked her clear, unaffected voice and the way she spoke as if she was in the habit of speaking up for herself. I liked it that her high cheekbones, narrow nose, and generous mouth required little makeup. I liked her outfit—a brandy colored turtleneck sweater under a matching long-sleeve cardigan, the sleeves pushed up, and a pleated, charcoal gray skirt. I even liked it that she was ten pounds over what the New York fashion designers decreed was her ideal weight—a woman who cared about her appearance but who wasn't going to starve herself over it.

"Okay, good, not gay," she said when she returned. "Are you married?"

"No."

"Divorced?"

"No."

"Children?"

"No."

I was beginning to think Bobby was on to something. Maybe I was a catch.

"How about you?" I asked.

"Divorced."

"Happily?"

Nina chuckled. "Very."

"Rickie your only offspring?"

"Yes, thankfully."

"Thankfully?"

"Believe me, Erica is enough to keep both hands full."

"And all this," I said, gesturing at the club.

"The business is starting to run itself, now. I could probably even sneak away on a Saturday night and not be missed."

"Is that a proposition?"

Nina blushed, something rarely seen in a mature woman. I found it entrancing. She glanced away, looked back.

"Try me."

I think maybe we should start seeing other people. It seemed to me I heard someone say that not too long ago.

"Ms. Truhler, I would be delighted if . . ."

"Call me Nina."

"Nina, I would be . . . Damn!"

Napoleon Cook was coming down the staircase.

I pretended I was a photograph on the wall. Nina did an interesting thing. She positioned her body to conceal me from Cook as Cook swept the room with his eyes. How could I not like her?

When Cook reached the bottom step, he shot an impatient glance upward. Hester had halted halfway down the staircase and leaned against the shiny brass railing, posing like a model in a Victoria's Secret catalogue, looking just as alluring, just as inviting as any of the women you'll find there. Cook watched her. I watched her. Nina watched her. The bartender watched her. So did everyone else. Now I know what is meant when they say, "A hush fell . . ."

Hester's hair was long and black, blacker than Nina's if that was possible. Her eyes were the color of flawless jade. She wore an oriental-style jacket, carefully fitted at the waist, with a floral tapestry on a hunter green background, a high mandarin collar, antique gold buttons, and slightly raised shoulder pads. Below the jacket was a very short, very tight black skirt—it could have been painted on—and black hose and heels. The ensemble didn't look like something you ordered from Spiegel.

Hester glided—I'm not exaggerating—to the bottom of the staircase. Cook said something to her. She grinned at him. Cook moved to the door. I swear she winked at the room before following him out. I waited a few beats and followed, too. I covered half the distance before turning back. Impulsively, I told Nina, "I'll call you when I can."

"Please do."

The way she said that made *me* blush.

Cook and Hester went to Cook's Porsche. I headed for the Jeep Cherokee. Cook didn't notice me two rows back. I guessed he had something else on his mind. He started the Porsche, went west out of the parking lot. I gave him a reasonable head start.

I began to think about the woman. I placed her in the midtwenties, five feet eight or nine inches tall, one hundred twenty pounds, with the kind of face and figure usually featured on the cover of women's magazines found at supermarket checkout lines. The way she had moved—if Merci Cole could move like that she'd be rich.

The Porsche went north on Dale to I-94, followed the freeway west two miles, took the Snelling Avenue exit and headed north again. I followed, punching it through the yellow on University Avenue to keep up. We went north past Hamline University, past Midway Stadium where the St. Paul Saints play, past the state fairgrounds, to a low-slung motel with green neon flashing the name PARADISE between two pink flamingos. The Paradise was what they used to call a "motor lodge," with a dozen or more rooms each facing an asphalt parking lot. A man in shirtsleeves was busy hosing down the driveway. He waved as the Porsche passed him and parked at the far side of the lot in front of the last room. I hid my face as I drove past, stopping down the street.

Cook left the car and walked toward the office—walked like he was trying hard not to run. Hester waited in the Porsche. Shirtsleeves decided he had given the asphalt enough water, shut off the hose, pulled it to the side and, wiping his hands on his trousers, followed Cook into the office. A few minutes later, Cook worked the lock of the room directly in front of the Porsche. Hester stayed in the car until the door was opened. The light did not go on until both were safely inside. It stayed on for only a few moments.

I glanced at my watch. Seven-thirty-three.

I flipped a U and parked the SUV in the street next to the motel parking lot. I turned on the radio and worked the tuner until I found WCCO-AM, joining the game in progress. The Rangers were shredding the Minnesota Twins' pitching staff, knocking out a long reliever I hadn't even heard of with three singles, a double, and back-to-back dingers justlikethat. The Twins were forced to bring in a third pitcher and it was only the bottom of the second. Damn. It looked like the eight-game winning streak was about to end. Still, the team had a sixteen-game lead over the Chicago White Sox in the American League Central and were cruising into the playoffs. It was just like the glory days of Puckett, Hrbek, Gagne, Gladden, Bush, Newman, and Larkin—the seven players who were on both the 1987 and '91 World Series championship teams. I found myself humming the Twins' fight song.

In the top of the fourth the door to Cook's room swung open. He and Hester stepped out, looking no worse for wear. They wasted little time climbing into the Porsche. I glanced at my watch. Eight-oh-two? You're kidding me? They had been in the room only twenty-nine minutes? I guess passion does burn fast.

The Porsche went south on Snelling. So did I. They made me almost immediately. Cook sped up and slowed down and sped up again. He watched his mirror. Hester turned around to look at me twice. At University Avenue they hung a left, Cook accelerating through the turn. I went straight, hoping he and Hester now felt silly over their unfounded suspicions. I caught I-94 again, exited at Dale and about a mile later parked on the street across from Rickie's parking lot. I didn't have to wait long. The Porsche, coming from the opposite direction, soon pulled into the lot and sat idling, its headlights on.

Hester's door opened. By the interior light I could see her smile seductively at Cook as she slid her fingers across his cheek. She leaned toward him like she was going to kiss him, but didn't, laughing in his face instead and swinging her legs up and out of the Porsche. She yanked down the hem of her short skirt, then extended her hands high above and behind her head, stretching like she had just awakened from an afternoon nap. The silhouette she created was inviting indeed. In fact, I found the entire performance quite exciting. I especially liked the part where she closed the car door with a bump of her hip—I gave it two thumbs up. Cook apparently disagreed, burning a couple of inches of rubber as he drove off, leaving Hester standing alone in the parking lot. He didn't even bother to wait until she had unlocked the door to her silver Audi and was safely inside. Miss Manners would have been appalled.

I stayed with Cook. He must have assumed I was a figment of his guilty imagination because he was paying no attention now to what was behind him. He went north on Dale again and west on I-94, crossing the Mississippi River and driving toward downtown Minneapolis. He caught the Fifth Street exit, but stopped midway on the ramp, swinging off into an "accident reduction area," a kind of wayside rest where accident victims can threaten each other with lawyers without blocking freeway traffic. I was forced to drive past him. Fortunately, there was a meter at the bottom of the ramp and I parked there. My first thought was that Cook had made me again. After a few minutes I realized he was waiting for someone. Perhaps that was why he had been in such a hurry at the motel—he was late for an appointment.

At exactly eight-thirty a black Chevy van pulled up next to Cook's Porsche. It was identical to the pair parked next to the apartment building the Family Boyz were renting from David Bruder.

What was it Bobby told me? *You're making this more complicated than it needs to be.* Right.

Neither driver got out. The vehicles stayed side by side for about five minutes and then the van departed, driving the rest of the way down the ramp. I ducked when the van sped past me. I was tempted to follow it. Instead, I stayed with Cook. He fired up the Porsche and followed 5th Street around the Hubert H. Humphrey Metrodome. After a succession of rights and lefts, he pulled into the underground garage of a thirty-floor tower of apartments and condos overlooking the Mississippi River. I parked on the street and made my way into the well-lit foyer. According to the directory, Cook had a place on the twenty-seventh floor.

I thought of returning to Rickie's, but decided against it. I'd had enough excitement for the day.

9

Wondering what Napoleon Cook and the Family Boyz had to discuss kept me up much of the night. However, the next morning the answer seemed clear. They were talking about me. I came to this conclusion because the black van Cook had met was now outside *my* house, parked across the street and one block down with an unobstructed view of my front door. I noticed it when I bopped outside to get my newspapers.

Bradley Young, Merci Cole, and now this. Why do so many people know where I live? Foolish question. In the computer age, nothing is private.

I was so pumped with adrenaline I could have beaten Carl Lewis in the sprint of his choice, yet I forced myself to stroll—*stroll, dammit!*—back into my house. Once inside, I locked the door. Like that was going to keep me safe. Like the ordnance the Boyz packed couldn't reduce my place to a box of toothpicks.

"Okay, okay. Relax. They came at you before and things worked out. So, relax, wouldja! Besides, they had plenty of chances to kill you already and they haven't. Which means they have something else in mind. What would that be? How the hell should I know? I don't even know why they wanted to kill me in the first place. Okay, relax. Think. You could ask them what they want. Sure. Just walk up and say, 'Hi, guys.' Where do you get these ideas, anyway? HBO? Think. What do they want? They want to watch me, follow me, find out where I go and who I talk to. Why? How the hell should I know why? Think . . ."

It's a bad sign when you start talking out loud to yourself.

While I was talking, I went upstairs and took the Beretta from the table next to my bed. Gun in hand, I went through every room in my sparsely furnished house—including rooms I hadn't entered in months— peeking through window blinds and around curtains, my CD player off so I could listen for any unusual noises. There were plenty of them in that old house. I found myself jumping at every creak. I really should renovate. Maybe put in bulletproof glass and armor plate.

"This is ridiculous," I told myself as I descended the staircase for the third time. "Show a little backbone, geez."

It's easier to be calm when you have a plan, so I sat on my soft leather sofa and made one up. After a few deep breathing exercises—I think I might have cleansed my karma, too—I picked up the phone and punched 911.

"I need the police. Yes, it's an emergency. There's a van parked outside my house. A black van. And there's a, a, a *Negro* sitting in it. Maybe a whole bunch of, of *Negroes*. They've been there for hours. Maybe all night. No, I don't know who they are. I think they're criminals, why else would *Negroes* be in a white neighborhood. I want protection. That's what we're paying you people for." I gave the operator the street location but not the address. "My name? I don't want to get involved."

I hung up the phone, watched and waited. I felt kind of crummy about the Negro BS and declared to the ceiling that I wasn't a racist, I only play one on the telephone. It didn't help, but you have to admit, these days anything with racial connotations gets immediate action. Four minutes, count 'em, four minutes after I called, two squad cars painted navy blue and gray bracketed the van like parentheses, one front, one back.

I strolled—strolled, mind you—to my garage, started up the Jeep Cherokee and drove away, using a remote control to close the garage door behind me. The cops had two black men, one sporting a mustache, leaning on the hood of the van when I shot past, picking up speed, although I had nowhere important to go.

"Napoleon Cook is dead," Bobby Dunston said.

"Someone killed him Friday night," Clayton Rask added.

"Whoever it was threw him off the balcony of his apartment in downtown Minneapolis," Bobby continued.

"Twenty-seven floors," said Rask.

"Straight down," Bobby added.

They were beginning to sound like a vaudeville team.

"Perhaps he jumped," I offered.

"If he did, he cut off his genitals first and stuffed them in his mouth."

"Ouch."

So that's why two homicide cops were standing in my living room on a Saturday evening. Uninvited. When their knock first sounded on my front door I jumped three feet, instantly flashing on the black van. I had searched carefully when I arrived home—trust me on this—only it was not to be found, neither the van nor any other out-of-place vehicles. Beretta in hand, I carefully made my way to the door. Some might have accused me of being paranoid.

"Can I offer you anything?" I asked them. "Coffee? A beer?"

They shook their heads. Rask glanced around the living room. It contained only two chairs and Bobby slumped into one of them. I had eight rooms excluding bathrooms, but only four were furnished—my bedroom, the room my father slept in, my kitchen and the "family room," which contained my large-screen TV and about a hundred video tapes and DVDs, my CD player with over six hundred discs, and my PC. Months earlier Shelby had toured the place. "Congratulations, Mac," she had told me then. "You've taken a three-hundred-thousand-dollar house and turned it into an efficiency apartment."

"How 'bout a sno-cone?" I asked.

"Sno-cone?" said Bobby.

"Nobody wants a damn sno-cone," Rask barked. He would have said more but he was distracted by the music on my speakers—I had at least two in every room.

"What is that?"

"The Benedictine Monks of Santo Domingo de Silos."

"It's the most depressing thing I've ever heard."

"Who asked you?"

"Have you done something that's tugging on your conscience, McKenzie? Is that why you're listening to this crap?"

"Do you think I killed Cook?" I asked.

"If I could prove it, you'd be in cuffs."

"Then why are you here?"

"You followed Cook to Rickie's last night," Bobby reminded me. "You followed him when he left."

Nina, I told myself. *And after all we've meant to each other.*

"We have video taken by a security camera of you checking Cook's address in the foyer of his building," Rask added. "Nice, crisp images."

"Doesn't mean I did it."

"Doesn't mean you didn't," Rask replied.

Bobby said, "You've been known to manufacture a little justice of your own from time to time, Mac."

"Not like that."

"So you say," Rask told me.

"Screw you."

"Now, Mac . . ."

"You too, Bobby. You guys come into *my* house accusing *me* of murder—I offered you sno-cones!"

Rask took a small, thin plastic bag from his suit pocket. Inside the bag was a business card. My business card. With my cell number written on back. He waved it under my nose and my first thought was that he shouldn't be handling evidence that way—the bag should have been logged in at the cop shop.

"Talk to me, McKenzie. Talk fast."

I told when and where I met Cook and I told him what he spoke about. I omitted the part about slamming his face into the wall.

"You followed him," Bobby said sharply. "Why?"

"To see where he went and who he talked to, why'd you think?"

"Why would he go anywhere or talk to anyone that would interest you?"

I didn't answer.

Rask crossed his arms and shook his head like he was disappointed in me. "Keep talking."

"I can't believe you guys are accusing me of murder."

"No one's accusing you," Bobby assured me.

"Keep talking," said Rask.

"The last time I saw Cook was around nine last night when he drove his car into the underground garage of his apartment building. Just before that, at exactly eight-thirty, he met with some people in a black van. It was the same van I saw parked outside David Bruder's apartment building in Richfield. The one he's renting to the Family Boyz."

"Who are the Family Boyz?" Rask asked.

"Not that again," said Bobby.

I told Rask everything I knew about the Boyz, then I spun around to face Bobby.

"Did you get a search warrant like I suggested?"

"Tommy Thompson killed the request."

"Well, gee whiz!"

"Any other startling news you'd care to impart at this time?" Rask asked, sounding like a wise guy.

"Yeah. I never gave Cook my business card." I pointed at the plastic bag he still held in his hand. "That's the card I gave Jamie Bruder."

There were many more questions. Most centered around the relationship between the Family Boyz, Bruder, and Cook, and their possible involvement in Jamie Carlson's death. They were questions without answers. Rask wasn't satisfied until I announced, "You now know everything I know."

"Isn't that a pity. We'll be speaking, again." He went for the door, reached it, spun toward me. "McKenzie, your fingerprints are on dead bodies all over the Twin Cities." It was a statement of fact, yet sounded like a threat just the same.

After Rask left, Bobby relaxed his head against the back cushion of the soft leather chair and closed his eyes the way people do when they're trying hard not to fall asleep. He looked tired and I told him so.

"I am tired."

"Tired people make mistakes."

He didn't reply.

After a few moments, he opened his eyes and said, "I don't think you killed Cook, just in case you're wondering. When I learned he was dead I called Rask and told him Cook might be connected to my case and one thing led to another."

"How did you know I followed Cook to Rickie's Friday night?"

"The owner told us."

"How did you know to ask?"

"Jeannie went there to check on Bruder—oh, you'll love this. I said before that Bruder seemed to be having an affair. He was. With his wife."

"Jamie?"

"They would meet at hotels and out-of-the-way restaurants. Meet like lovers instead of married people. Sometimes couples that have just had children do stuff like that. It's kinda romantic when you think about it."

"Did you and Shelby ever do anything like that?"

"No."

"Romantic love. Doesn't exactly fit the profile of a serial killer, does it?"

"Maybe, maybe not. His absolute last credit card purchase was for dinner at Rickie's on the evening Jamie was killed. He dined with a woman who was obviously not his wife."

"Who?"

"The woman Nina Truhler calls Hester Prynne."

"The same woman who met Napoleon Cook."

"We're going to have to find her."

"Does the ME have a firm time of death?"

"Between eight and midnight. We know Bruder was at Rickie's at seven forty-five. That's the time that was recorded on his receipt. But we don't know where he went after that. That's why we would need to find the woman."

"So, it's possible that Bruder not only killed Jamie, he cheated on her, too."

"We don't know for sure that he was cheating."

"I've seen the woman. He was cheating."

"If you say so."

Bobby closed his eyes again. While his eyes were closed, he said, "I wish you hadn't given your keys to Shelby."

"To my lake home? Why wouldn't I?"

He didn't reply.

"Bobby?"

He still didn't answer and in a flash it all seemed perfectly clear to me.

"You sonuvabitch."

That got him to open his eyes.

"You weren't going to take Shelby up north. You were going to take someone else. Who?"

"Mac . . ."

"Your young, beautiful, and smart as hell partner? Dammit, Bobby. You were going to cheat on your wife—on Shelby—at my lake home."

"You're obsessed with cheating, you know that? You have cheating on the brain."

"Tell me it's not true."

"It's not true."

"Don't lie to me, you sonuvabitch."

"McKenzie, you don't know anything about it."

"Go 'head. Enlighten me."

"I've been married for twelve years. Twelve years with the same woman, while you were always with somebody different."

"Somebody, but never someone."

"Oh, please. Make me feel sorry for you. Poor little rich boy. You don't have a clue, McKenzie. You don't know anything about it."

"I know this. You're going to ruin your life because you're bored. Why don't you do what Bruder did if you want adventure. Meet Shelby in hotels and out of the way restaurants. Have sex on the fifth hole of the Como Park golf course like you did with what's-her-name when we were kids."

"That wasn't me," Bobby shouted. "That was you! It was always you. You talk about adventures, but they're your adventures."

"And now you want to know what you're missing."

"Something like that."

"Give me back my keys."

"C'mon."

"You're going to do what you want to do and I'm not going to stop you or dime you out to Shelby, either. Only I'm not going to help. So, give me my keys back."

"Fine," he said, but I noticed he didn't reach into his pocket.

"I'll tell you something else. When this goes bad, and it will, and I have to choose between friends, I'm going with Shelby and the girls."

"Oh, I've never doubted that. Not for a second."

"What's that supposed to mean?"

"C'mon, McKenzie. You've been in love with Shelby since the day you met her. Do you think I don't know that?"

"So, I'm in love with Shelby. You have a problem with that?"

"You're damn right I have a problem with that. She's my wife!"

"That's right. She's your wife. She chose you. She could have had me. She chose you. She married you. She had your children. She keeps your house. She loves you. Not me. She wouldn't go near me to save her life. Or any other man. It's you. It's always been you. And now you're going to cheat on her if you haven't already."

"I haven't and I never said I was going to."

"But you're thinking about it."

"There's thinking and there's doing."

"Well, don't do it."

"Fine."

"Fine."

"Okay."

"Okay, then."

"Happy now, McKenzie?"

"You want a sno-cone?"

"You really have a sno-cone machine?"

"Sure."

"Where did you get a sno-cone machine?"

"Remember Tommy Baumgartner from high school?"

"Kid who broke his collarbone playing basketball?"

"He owns a bunch of sno-cone concessions at the Minnesota State Fair now. He helped me get one."

And so we had sno-cones. The machine was probably too big—it was designed for amusement parks and will shave over five hundred pounds of ice in an hour, but I liked its antique charm. Bobby watched intently as I loaded the machine with about two and a half pounds of ice cubes and shaved enough of it for two large cones. I flavored mine with cherry syrup. He took grape.

"This is pretty good," he told me. "But about that music . . ."

I replaced the monks with *The Very Best of Aretha Franklin, Vol. 1.*

Bobby liked the first sno-cone so much he had a second. While he was eating it he said, "You're the best friend I'll ever have."

"You don't get out much at all, do you?" I told him, keeping it light.

"Where in hell is Bruder?"

The Sunday newspapers speculated that Good Deal Dave was no longer in the state. I know I wouldn't be. 'Course, there are plenty of places in the Twin Cities where a man could hide. Places that deal in cash only, where they don't want to know who you are or see a credit card or a personal check or any form of ID, where they don't want to know what kind of car you drive or what your license plate number is. The question was, how would a yuppie from Highland Park know where to find those places?

And another question.

"How did Cook get my business card?"

"It's a mystery to me," Bobby said.

When he left a short time later, we shook hands.

10

Molly Carlson called early Monday morning and requested that I meet her at a funeral home on Snelling near where it intersected with Randolph, about a mile from where Jamie was killed. I could see a bar at the intersection from where I stood speaking with her in the parking lot and wished I was in it.

"My father died when I was eleven years old," Molly told me. "That was what? Forty years ago? I thought I was over it but I'm not. Sometimes I'll hear a laugh that is the same or a song he used to sing or see a man who resembles him and suddenly I'm a child again, holding my mother's hand, asking her if Daddy's gone to heaven. That's what happened just now. The funeral director, he looked like my father, the same height, the same color hair, and when he came close I could smell his aftershave. It was Old Spice just like Daddy used to wear and I started crying and I couldn't stop. He thought it was because of Jamie." Molly dabbed her eyes with a wadded-up tissue, not concerned at all that so many strangers could see her tears. "I'm sorry I called you."

"That's all right."

"I wish Daddy were here now."

"What about your husband?"

The ME hadn't yet released Jamie's remains but he promised that he would soon. Molly Carlson had driven the two hundred miles from Grand Rapids to arrange to have them sent home when he did. She didn't want to use the telephone for this. She had come alone.

"Richard doesn't understand," Molly said. "It's only been a few days since—since the policeman called, and he thinks I should be over it by now. We haven't seen Jamie for seven years so he says I should be over it by now. Maybe he needs me to be over it so he can get over it, but I can't get over losing a child in less than a week. And Stacy. Oh, Stacy, Stacy—what about Stacy? We're going to lose her, too. How can Richard get over that in less than a week? How is that possible?"

"People heal in their own time, you can't hurry it," I said, repeating a line that someone once told me. I was trying to be a comfort to her and not doing a very good job of it. That's why she called. She needed comfort. She had been crying uncontrollably in the funeral director's office. He asked her if there was anyone he could call. Only she didn't have family or friends in the Cities. All she had was my business card.

"I've been having this dream every night, a recurring dream," Molly said. "In the dream everything is back to normal and Jamie is seven years old. She's sitting in the backyard, feeding tea and cookies to her dolls. She's happy and she's smiling. Then there's the sound of heavy footsteps and the footsteps grow louder and louder until Jamie looks up, only it isn't Jamie, it's Stacy, and a shadow covers her face and she screams and I wake up and start crying. The first time Richard held me in his arms and told me it was just a bad dream. Now he pretends to be asleep."

"Maybe the two of you need to see a counselor."

"Maybe. After Stacy—you will find Jamie's son, won't you? Richard said you would."

"I'm trying."

Molly unlocked her car door, but she didn't get in.

"Do you want to hear something funny? The funeral director told me that when you ship a body home by plane or train, you have to purchase a ticket for it just like it was a living person. Can you imagine that?" She started to laugh. The laughter soon turned to more tears, torrents of them.

I took her in my arms and held her tight.

"I wonder if Jamie has ever been on a plane before," she said, weeping into my shirt collar.

I rocked her gently back and forth and thought about Richard Carlson, that big, proud man. I doubted he could appreciate the dark irony of buying an airline ticket for a dead woman. If the flight was overbooked, could she be bumped? Did she get frequent flyer mileage?

We stood like that for a long time, crying over the ticket that would take Jamie home, the one-way ticket that waits for all of us, like the one that took my mother and father to Turtle Bay, the bay on the lake where I built my lake home. My father had had my mother cremated. He stored her ashes in an urn that he kept in a box on the top shelf of his closet. He never opened the box as far as I knew. When he died, I had him cremated, too, and mixed their ashes together and scattered them on the bay and sat drifting in a canoe until the moon was high and the water was black.

If we're lucky, our ticket isn't collected until we're old and gray and dying is as easy as closing our eyes and whispering good-bye. If we aren't—but what does it matter? When it's time for our tickets to get punched, it's time. Neither when nor where nor why nor how many people mourn our passing nor the quality of their tears will make a bit of difference. The conductor simply punches our ticket and sends us home.

I broke my rule against drinking in the morning, stopping at Plum's just down the street. I had a CB and water, but it didn't do me any good so I had another. After the third drink I decided I had had enough.

A half hour later I was home. I wrote a detailed report on my PC that explained what I knew, what I thought I knew, and what I was going to do about it. I printed four copies and sealed each in an envelope along with disks containing copies of my notes. I addressed the envelopes to Bobby Dunston, Clayton Rask, Chief Casey, and Richard Carlson and left them in the center of my desk. Just in case.

Embedded in the floor of my basement is a safe. It's where I keep my guns. I opened the safe and withdrew an extra magazine for the Beretta .380. I also pulled out a hand grenade, circa 1945, with ridges cut deep into the heavy metal to make fragmentation easier. It had been given to me a year earlier by a World War II vet I once did a favor for, a guy who was at the Battle of the Bulge and Remagen Bridge and who now lives in Hibbing. After all this time, neither of us knew if the grenade would still work.

"Let's hope we don't find out," I told myself as I slipped it into the pocket of my Minnesota Timberwolves sport jacket. The .380 was on my hip.

I drove past the apartment building in Richfield, turned around, and drove past it again. A sleek Jaguar XJ6 was parked in the lot next to the two black Chevy vans—who says crime doesn't pay? I turned south on the next street and followed it to the hole in the chain-link fence behind the apartment building. The empty field between the hole and the rear of the building made me nervous. I would be so exposed. Then there was the thick glass in the back door—easy to see through, easy to shoot through. That made me nervous, too. I couldn't see a sentry with my binoculars but that didn't mean he wasn't there. I'd certainly station one at the back entrance, wouldn't you? I hesitated for a few minutes, told myself, *A guy in a T'wolves jacket cutting across a vacant lot, why would anyone get excited about that?* I took a deep breath.

"Nothing ventured, nothing gained," I muttered to myself, which was something my father probably would have said if he had been around. Either that or "When the going gets tough, the tough get going." He had a cliché for every occasion. For a long time I thought he made them up as he went along.

I left the car, squeezed through the hole in the fence, and quickly followed the path to the rear of the apartment building. I watched the door as I went. Saw no one. I paused outside the door. Through the glass I could see the corridor that ran the length of the building. Two black men holding automatic rifles were clearly visible just inside the front entrance. They were talking, their backs to me. Several large packing crates were stacked along the corridor walls between me and them. They looked like the boxes refrigerators came in. I took several more deep breaths, slipped the Beretta from its holster and activated it. *Quitters never win and winners never quit.* I went inside. In retrospect, it was one of the dumbest things I have ever done. Also the most amazing. I have no idea who I was pretending to be.

"What are you doing?" a voice called out.

"Oh oh." I flattened against a refrigerator box, hiding.

"You're supposed to be at the *back* door," the voice screamed.

"Chill, man, I'm watchin'. I's just talkin' to my bro."

"Don't give me that shit, man. You suppose to be guardin' the back door."

"Ain't no thing."

"Tell that to Stalin. Now git your black ass back where you belong 'fore he see you. Move now."

I listened as two sets of footsteps approached my hiding place. They were hard to hear on the carpet over the loud and imaginative curses the screamer was laying on the guard who'd neglected his post. The cursing continued as they passed me.

"Don't move," I said. I was trying to sound forceful but I doubt my words came out that way.

The two black men were startled. They swiveled their heads to look behind them. I made sure they saw the gun I held with two hands at eye level.

"Don't talk. Don't think. Just get against the wall. Do it now."

They did what I told them.

"Set the rifle on the floor. Do it now."

The guard thought about it. "I've already killed two of you," I hissed. That convinced him. He dropped the rifle and the two men assumed the position without my telling them to.

"You dead, man," the screamer told me.

I ignored the remark. "Call your friend."

"Fuck you."

I poked the muzzle of the gun into his eye. He cried out in pain.

A voice from down the hall. "What is it?"

"Call him," I hissed.

"Get down here," the screamer yelled.

"What for?"

"Get your ass down here."

The other sentry came running.

"Drop the gun. Up against the wall."

He looked at me, looked at his friends.

"Do it now."

"Stalin ain't gonna like this."

"No lie," the second guard replied.

The sentry dropped his rifle, assumed the position next to his friends.

I slipped the grenade from my pocket with my left hand, pressing the lever hard against the body. It felt like it weighed fifty pounds. I thrust it to the screamer.

"Whoa!"

"Pull the pin."

"No fuckin' way."

I shoved the muzzle of the Beretta close to his eye and repeated my instructions. His finger trembled as he hooked it through the ring. He pulled. The pin slipped out far too easily for my peace of mind. I pressed the lever hard against the grenade body.

"Are we having fun yet?" I asked.

The three brothers didn't think so. Truth be told, neither did I. I told the screamer to slip the pin into my left jacket pocket. He did it without taking his eyes off the grenade.

"Now," I said. "Let's go see Stalin."

Stalin's apartment was on the third floor. His corridor, like the others, was littered with crates that apparently contained major appliances. The word BELLOTI was stenciled on the larger crates and WORLDWARE, MELLGREN'S, and CK COMPUTERS were stamped on the smaller boxes. The four of us juked and jived around them, me in the rear, my heart pounding like I was running the Twin Cities marathon.

Through the door I could hear a man shouting. "I don't believe it!" He repeated the phrase three times.

"What now?" a second voice responded without rancor.

"Stems and seeds. I'm standing here with a baggie full of fucking stems and seeds."

"You the one insists we cut back on distribution, git outta the trade."

"And you the one insists we keep our hand in. So how come I'm standin' here with a bag of stems and seeds?"

I gestured for the screamer to open the door. He did and the four of us poured into the room. Two men turned to look at us. One was sitting in a brown vinyl lounge chair, a ledger book balanced on his knee. The other was standing in front of him, gripping what remained of a nickel bag of grass. The man with the bag was tall and thin, his eyes glistened with fury and his mouth was frozen in a vicious snarl.

"How many times I gotta tell you all to knock!"

"Stalin," the screamer said quietly.

That's when Stalin noticed me standing behind the three brothers.

"Who're you?" he asked.

I pointed the Beretta at his face.

"McKenzie."

Stalin didn't seem too impressed. He glanced down at the man in the faux leather chair and said, "Who in charge of security 'round here?"

"You are."

"I gotta do everything. . . ." Then to me, "How come you still alive, McKenzie?"

"Clean living."

"Man, you drive an SUV."

"So now you know I have nothing to lose."

Stalin grinned brightly.

"Last mother point a gun at me, know what I did to 'im? I wired his johnson to a car battery. That got 'im up." He chuckled at his own joke. The screamer and two guards chuckled, too, but you could tell their hearts weren't in it.

"Was it a Die Hard?" I asked.

"A Die Hard?" Stalin laughed harder. "A Die Hard battery, that's funny. You're a funny guy, McKenzie."

"You're a real humorist yourself." I was trying to sound confident. I doubt I looked it. Especially after I heard the voice to my right.

"Shhhheeeeeeettt," it said, drawing the word out. I took my eyes off

Stalin only long enough for a glance. Two men were standing in the doorway of what looked to be a bedroom. One was sporting a mustache. The other was clean-shaven. The same guys the cops rousted outside my house Saturday. The one with the mustache was hefting a Soviet-made RPK light machine gun with forty-round magazine—our equivalent to the BAR. He was pointing it at me.

Where were they getting this stuff?

The man without the mustache said, "This is McKenzie, man."

"No shit. You just tune in?" Stalin asked calmly. "Git with the program."

"You're dead, McKenzie," said the one with the mustache as he sighted down the barrel of the machine gun. My three companions became anxious and started to slip away.

"Nobody moves," I told them and they froze in place around me, my bodyguard.

Stalin seemed almost amused. "What's the matter with you three? Get outta the way."

I kept pointing the Beretta at Stalin. He didn't seem to mind.

"Well?" he asked.

I brought my left hand up from behind the screamer's back and let Stalin get a good look at what I was holding.

"Fuckin' A!" He said it like an actor trying to reach the upper balcony. "What up with that shit?" He looked at Mr. Mustache with the light machine gun then back at my companions at the door. He was staring directly into the screamer's eyes when he said, "I am really, really, really unhappy 'bout this."

"It weren't me," the screamer told him. "Damon here left his post."

Stalin looked at Damon. The guard shifted his weight from one foot to the other, looked at me, looked at the closed door behind us, wishing he was out the door and down the street.

The room fell silent. Somewhere a TV played loudly—a game show host was telling a disappointed contestant that there were parting gifts waiting backstage.

From his chair the man with the ledger told Stalin calmly, "Ax him what he want."

"So why the fuck you here, white meat?"

"I thought we'd get together and chat, seeing how we have so many friends in common."

"What friends?"

"Bradley Young and Cleave Benjamn for two."

"Let me smoke 'im!" shouted the man with the machine gun. "Let 'em put 'im down. You say the word, he gone."

The shout jolted me and for a moment I thought I saw a train conductor coming my way with a paper punch in his hand. Only Stalin was on top of it.

"Chill!" he shouted, then added in a calmer voice, "Slack off but don't back off."

Mr. Mustache allowed the muzzle of the light machine gun to dip slightly—instead of my head he was now aiming at my chest, not much of an improvement.

Stalin crossed his arms like he didn't have a care in the world.

"Why you comin' like this, McKenzie? You erase two a my family then you come to my house playin' fuckin' GI Joe. What up with that?"

"Like I said, I want to talk."

"So talk."

"Crowds make me nervous. Everyone out except you. And tell this moron to put the machine gun away."

"Or what?"

I waved the grenade.

"You ain't got the size," Stalin told me.

"Tell it to Young and Benjamn."

Stalin walked right up to me—didn't seem to mind at all that the muzzle of the Beretta was now pressed against his chest. He stuck his face an inch from mine and gave me the mad dog. I could smell his breath. Peppermint.

"You make me mad, I'll be makin' you sad," he hissed. Then, "Everyone out. Me and McKenzie gonna discuss his life 'spectancy."

The room cleared slowly. Mr. Mustache leaned in close when he passed me. "You think you're large, you think you're bad," he hissed. "Later for you, my man."

He was followed by the man in the imitation leather chair moving at his leisure. "We ain't got time for this, Raymond," he said. "We got business can't wait."

"I know, I know."

"Raymond?" I asked when we were alone.

"Name's Stalin. It's Russian. It means steel."

"Did the name come with the machine gun?"

"That why you come to my house? Talk 'bout my name?"

"I want to know why you're trying to kill me."

"You keep comin' at me, bitch. You want my ass cuz me and mine are gettin' and niggers ain't supposed to get."

"You don't mean shit to me," I told him. "I didn't want your ass until you started comin' after mine. Tell me why?"

"I was told you're bad for business."

"Who told you?"

No reply.

"Was it Napoleon Cook?"

"Could be." Stalin kept smiling. I've seen sociopaths like him before. They frighten me.

"Why did you kill Cook?"

"If'n I done Cook and I'm not sayin' I did, it woulda been cuz he be bad for business, too."

"What business are you in?"

Stalin glanced around the apartment. I followed his eyes and got part of an answer. The apartment was loaded with hard goods and appliances—copy machines, stereo receivers, TVs, VCRs, CD players, answering machines, fax machines, microwaves, an electric range, clothes hanging from racks like a department store, about a dozen PCs. The floor sagged from the weight of it all. Most of the merchandise was still in boxes, much of it was covered with dust.

You have to understand, a player doesn't care about owning things, or using things, only about his ability to *buy* things. His life is centered on money, nothing else. The women, the cars, the clothes, the merchandise he piles up—that's just for show. What matters is the money he holds in his hands, he measures his self-worth in cash. That's why he never pays for anything with a check or credit card. He wants to see your face when he digs the bills out of his pocket, he needs to see the envy in your eyes when he presses them into your hand.

"Why did you kill Jamie Bruder and Katherine Katzmark?"

For the first time Stalin's eyes displayed a genuine emotion: outrage.

"Don't be blamin' that shit on me. I ain't had nothin' to do with that, man. You gotta be crazy to do like that."

"If not you, who?"

"Bruder, man."

"How do you know?"

"What the paper says."

"Where is Bruder?"

"How should I know?"

"You and him are tight, aren't you?"

"That's business, man. I don't 'sociate with them exceptin' for business."

"Them. The Entrepreneurs, you mean?" When he didn't reply I asked, "What business do you have with them?"

He didn't say. I glanced over the apartment again. What was I missing?

I looked back at Stalin. His smile had returned. I was tempted to wipe it off his face. At the same time I realized that he was probably telling the truth, that he had nothing to do with Jamie's and Katherine's murders. I could see him raping both women before killing them. Raping them and then bragging on what a fine lover he was. But the rest? You don't do that in front of an audience and I couldn't imagine Stalin doing anything without a chorus applauding him.

I also realized that I wasn't going to get any more from him—I had learned precious little considering the huge risk I was running.

"We're leaving," I said.

"We?"

I gestured at the door. He went to open it. I shoved the muzzle of the Beretta against his spine.

"It's real simple," I said. "If anyone does anything foolish, I'll kill you."

"And then you die."

"Do you really want to trade your life for mine?"

"You gonna go down, McKenzie. You gonna die."

"Just not today."

"Day ain't over yet, man."

Stalin opened the doors. The guards had retrieved their weapons and the machine gunner still had his. They pointed them at us. Stalin smiled.

"Me and McKenzie goin' for a walk. I don't come back you kill him, you kill his momma, his old man, his brother and sister and aunts and uncles and cousins—you kill everyone he ever knew."

"It's done," said Mr. Mustache with the machine gun.

Satisfied, Stalin led us out the door, along the corridor, down the stairs, out the back, and across the field. His people watched but didn't interfere. When we were on the other side of the hole in the fence, I told Stalin to remove the pin from my pocket. He did. I told him to slip it back into the grenade. He didn't like that plan at all but the Beretta convinced him. I was pleased to see his hands shake as he carefully shoved the pin through one side of the firing mechanism and out the other. I smiled at him then and tossed the grenade through the open window of my Cherokee. It landed on the passenger seat, bounced off and rattled on the floor.

"You nuts, man," Stalin said.

He heard no argument from me.

Stalin was breathing hard now and looked sweaty and tired—he burned energy like a highway flare. I fought the impulse to blow his brains out.

"Next time," I said.

"Next time gonna be *real* soon."

I shifted the gun to my left hand, opened my car door, and slid behind the wheel while making sure the Beretta was pointed at Stalin through the open window. I closed the door and started the car.

"The Jag in the parking lot. The XJ6. That yours?"

"Cost fifty K," he announced proudly.

"Just the kind of car you'd expect a Motor City pimp to drive."

The remark seemed to disturb him more than the grenade.

"I ain't no pimp," he yelled at me as I drove off.

I went north, then west, then south, then west again, then north, then east, then south, making sure I wasn't followed until I was completely lost. My hands were shaking so badly I could barely control the Cherokee—it was like the lug nuts had fallen off and all four wheels were wobbling. Finally, I pulled over and shut down the engine. I had intended to stir the pot and see what surfaced. Yeah, I stirred it, all right. What was I thinking of, letting Molly Carlson's tears move me to such a risk? Or was it Bobby and Clayton Rask accusing me of murder? My hands shook and my legs shook and my stomach churned with fear. I was perfectly calm in the apartment, almost arrogant, thank God. Only now I just wanted to go home. *You're gonna die.* The words echoed through my brain. How do I get myself into these situations?

I was nearly thirty-seven. In medieval times I'd be considered ancient. In ancient times I'd most likely be dead of old age by now. In this century I was merely stupid.

I leaned back against the seat and closed my eyes, waiting for my nerves to quiet themselves, breathing deep, exhaling slowly. Eva Cassidy was on the CD player. I thought her exquisite voice would help. It took both her and Ella Fitzgerald.

11

"You don't look like a detective," the old man told me. I hadn't told him I was one. Like Nina Truhler, he connected his own dots.

"Who does?" He gave me a little head shake, suddenly embarrassed, so I answered for him. "James Garner? Tom Selleck?"

"Robert Mitchum," the old man said. "And Bogart. He was good."

"I always liked Alan Ladd. Remember *This Gun for Hire?*"

"He was a bad guy in that one. A hit man. 'Sides, Ladd, he was a pretty boy. And short. They made all his leading ladies stand in slit trenches."

"Well, you can't judge a book by its cover," I said, which was another of Dad's favorite clichés.

"No, I s'pose not," the old man said, smiling slightly and patting his ample stomach. The old man was the proprietor of the Paradise Motel, the one I saw watering the asphalt a couple evenings earlier. After sitting in my car for an hour I decided the best thing I could do for my nerves was to get back to work.

I asked about Napoleon Cook. He spoke about the woman.

"The dark-haired lady, she comes in plenty, but I ain't hardly never got no up-close look at her, if you know what I mean. She always parks at the far end, in front of sixteen. I keep the room empty for her cuz I know it's her favorite."

"She comes in often?"

"Couple times a week usually, never no trouble. Sends the man in for the key and to pay up. 'Course it ain't always the same joe. This guy you're askin' about, this Cook fella, I seen him maybe two, three times, no more than that. What I figure, I figure the lady, she must rotate 'em. Like tires."

I pulled a newspaper clipping out of my pocket, one that featured a photograph of David Bruder, and showed it to the man.

"Have you ever seen him?"

"Could be, can't say for sure. He looks familiar but after a while, don't they all sorta look alike?"

I folded the clipping and returned it to my pocket.

"How long has the woman been coming here?"

"A year, maybe. Good customer. Hardly ever messes the room. I figure she's one of those nymphomaniacs you hear tell of. 'Course I don't know nothin' 'bout that except what I see on them there adult movies— we have adult movies here, you know."

I wasn't surprised.

"She probably ain't right in the head," the man offered. "But her money is healthy."

I gave the man my card and told him to call me the next time the woman came in.

"You don't have to wait for no call," he said. "You want to see her, come by t'night or tomorrow 'round eight, eight-thirty. She's due."

"You don't look so hot," Nina Truhler said when I sidled up to her at the downstairs bar in Rickie's. She was shuffling through a deck of time cards, a large calendar turned to the month of October set before her.

"How do you know?" I asked her. "I might never have looked better."

"In that case, medical science has failed you."

She had a point. It was just past noon, yet I felt like I had been up for three days and probably looked it. Nina, on the other hand, was stunning in a violet shirt and a steel-colored one-button jacket with matching trousers that set off her magnificent eyes.

"I'm sorry." She set her cards down on the calendar. "I'm not usually such a smart aleck."

"I've been known to bring out the best in people."

Her mouth worked like it wanted to say something, but only "Arrrggg" came out. Nina pronounced it like a word.

"Nice command of the English language."

"I'm frustrated," she said.

"Emotionally? Physically? There's a cure for all that which has nothing to do with medical science."

"Are you flirting with me?"

"Are you flirting with me?" I asked.

"I'm trying to but it's coming out wrong."

"You should practice more." I made a production out of adjusting my sports coat, shaking my head, flexing my shoulders and smoothing my hair. "Okay, I'm ready. Give me your best shot."

"Hi, honey. Come here often?"

"Puhleez."

"Baby, I've been looking for a man like you all my life."

"Like I haven't heard that a hundred times before. C'mon, make an effort. You meet me in a bar and you want to take me home. What do you say?"

"Nice butt."

"Very good. That works with me."

"It does?"

"Every time. So, your place or mine?"

"Depends. What do you think of children?"

"I'd like to try dating adults, first. See how that works."

Nina laughed, which was my intention. Afterward she leaned in closer and said, "Seriously. What do you think of dating a woman with children?"

"I don't understand the question."

"I have a daughter. I told you."

"Erica, a.k.a. Rickie—boys bore her."

"Most men, you tell them you have a child, a family, and they run the other way, guys who'd be all over me otherwise. I learned that the hard way. Now I'm right up front with it. I let them know before date one I have a daughter so not to waste my time."

"Wise decision."

"Well?"

"It doesn't bother me that you have a daughter. I'd like to meet her. If she's as pretty as her mother she must be beautiful indeed."

Nina took a deep breath and said, "I told them you were here the other night, that you were following Napoleon Cook—that's his name, isn't it?" with the exhale.

"Yes."

"Did you get into trouble?"

"No more than usual, but thank you for asking."

"I'm sorry."

"Don't be sorry. You did the right thing. I would have done the same."

"I'm sorry anyway. I wanted you to know in case this goes any further."

"Since we're being honest here, I should tell you that I'm coming off a relationship and I don't know how I feel about that yet."

"You're afraid of getting involved again?"

"I'm afraid of getting involved with the wrong woman again."

Nina cupped her chin in her hand and leaned toward me. I cupped my chin in my hand and leaned toward her. We were close enough to kiss. I should have kissed her. I don't know why I didn't. Instead, I told her, "I need a favor."

"Oh." She sounded disappointed.

"I want you to call me the next time Hester comes in. I need to find out about her."

Nina pushed herself off the bar. "I can do that. But I also promised I'd call the cops."

"Who?" I was thinking it was Bobby.

"Policewoman named Jean Something."

"Oh."

"Know her?"

"I'm told she's young, beautiful, and smart as hell."

She wagged her hand like she wasn't sure she agreed.

"I don't want to get you into trouble, Nina." She opened both eyes wide in feigned shock. "I mean with the cops."

"I promised to call when Hester came in. I didn't promise I wouldn't call you, too."

"Thank you."

"Don't mention it."

I slid off the stool.

"But what if she doesn't come in again?" Nina asked.

"Then I'll call you."

Nina smiled bright and beautiful. "What does the telephone company say? 'Reach out and touch someone'?"

I went home, checked my mail, checked my telephone messages, and made a pot of coffee—hazelnut, ground from fresh beans purchased from the Cameron Coffee Company of Hayward, Wisconsin. While it brewed I stretched out on my sofa, Fleetwood Mac on the CD player singing "Then Play On." I didn't know which was more exhausting, my encounter with the Boyz or all that heavy flirting with Nina Truhler. I closed my eyes, which was a mistake. I didn't open them again until the ringing telephone woke me about an hour later. I debated not answering it, coming up with five, six, seven good reasons to pretend I wasn't home. Only the challenge of the unknown was too great. After all, it could be Dick Clark and Ed McMahon arranging to give me a cardboard check the size of my mattress.

"Mr. McKenzie, I need your help," a voice told me instead of "Hello."

"Who are you?"

"Dave Bruder."

Bruder wanted to call the shots. I let him. That was my first mistake. But all I could think about was the look on Bobby's face when I brought him in—the look on his face *and* Tommy Thompson's.

Bruder wanted to come in, too—he was tired of running, of hiding. Only he was frightened.

"I need protection."

"This isn't East L.A., pal," I told him. "The St. Paul cops aren't going to beat on you with sticks."

"It's not just them."

"Who else? The Family Boyz?"

"I'm afraid."

Who could blame him?

"Why are you calling me?"

"I'm told you can be trusted."

"Whoever gave you that idea?"

"Friends."

"What friends?"

"Will you help me?"

I thought about it for maybe, oh, three seconds.

"What do you want me to do?"

"Meet me. Come with me to the police station."

I could do that.

"Do you promise not to call the police?"

"Yes."

That was my second mistake.

A half hour later I was sitting at a small table hard against the railing of the third floor food court of the City Center, looking down into the courtyard below. The City Center is a combination shopping mall and office building in downtown Minneapolis. Bruder insisted on meeting in Minneapolis. He figured the cops weren't looking for him there. I should have set him straight, but I didn't.

I watched him ride the escalator up. He was wearing a Pierre Cardin suit with sharp creases, black wing tips shined to a high gloss, a freshly pressed white cotton dress shirt and a perfectly knotted power tie. His face was clean shaven, his hair neatly parted. I didn't know where he had been the past week, but he had taken good care of himself. He stopped in the center of the food court and glanced about. I recognized him, but he didn't know me from the kid at the Orange Julius stand. I gave him a little wave and he came over.

"So, Mr. Bruder. Where have you been keeping yourself?"

He hushed me—"Don't use my name"—and glanced around nervously before sitting.

"Seriously," I told him. "You look nice. Why is that?"

He had no idea what I was talking about.

"I didn't kill my wife," he announced.

You sure look good for it, I thought but didn't say.

"I didn't," Bruder insisted, as if he had read my mind.

"Okay."

"Everyone thinks I did."

"Do you blame them?"

He didn't say if he did or didn't.

"Mr. Bruder, where's your son?"

"He's safe."

"Listen to me. I don't give a shit about you. But your son, Jamie's son, is a different matter. . . ."

"All you care about is Jamie's sister." Bruder sounded disappointed.

"That's why I'm involved. Now tell me where he is."

"With friends."

"What friends?"

"When I'm safe, I'll tell you. But only after I'm safe."

"Is he with the same friends who said you could trust me?"

No answer.

Since Bruder refused to confide in me, I decided to tell him a thing or two.

"You had dinner with a woman at Rickie's the evening your wife was slaughtered."

That brought a high color to his face.

"You know about that?"

"Me and the woman on the psychic hotline. We know everything. What happened afterwards?"

"I went home and I saw, I saw what they had done to her. I took TC—he was asleep in his crib, thank God—and I ran."

"What *they* had done to her. Who is *they*?"

"I won't talk now."

"No?"

"When I'm safe I'll tell you everything."

I was wondering what it would take to make him change his mind.

He added, "This is—this is much bigger and more dangerous than you can possibly imagine."

"I don't know. I can imagine a lot."

"I need to talk to the FBI."

"Federal Building is only a few blocks away."

"Should I go there or to St. Paul, first?"

"St. Paul," I told him. Bobby was in St. Paul.

Young, beautiful, and smart as hell Jeannie took the call. Bobby was in a meeting with Tommy Thompson and couldn't be disturbed.

I told her, "When he's finished with his important meeting tell him that McKenzie called. Tell him I have David Bruder. . . ."

"What? How?"

"Tell him to meet me at the Tenth Street entrance next to the garage in fifteen minutes."

"McKenzie?"

I deactivated my cell phone. This was going to be fun, I told myself.

While riding the escalator to the ground floor, I asked Bruder if he had a lawyer.

"I have a friend, Warren Casselman."

The name triggered my memory's replay button. *David, this is Warren. Something's gone wrong. Better call me ASAP.* The message on Bruder's telephone answering machine.

"Is he any good?"

"He makes a lot of money," Bruder replied. I had to shake my head at that. Judging people by the money they make is like judging them by their height. I didn't tell him so, of course. Bruder had enough problems.

"Here's some advice, for what it's worth," I said. "When we get to the cop shop, don't say a word. Don't say yes, don't say no, don't say your name, don't say anything. Just call your lawyer friend and keep your mouth shut until he arrives."

Bruder nodded. I could feel his muscles tense where I held his arm. He was scared. I didn't blame him.

"Why did you call me, really?" I asked.

"I ran out of options."

Whatever that meant.

We exited through the door on Hennepin Avenue, emerging into bright afternoon sunlight. My SUV was parked in the lot across the street. To get there, we followed the wide sidewalk to the 5th Street intersection. While we waited for a green light, a black Chevy van peeled round the corner at 6th Street and accelerated hard toward us. The cargo door was open.

"Down!" I yelled.

Bruder didn't move. He seemed transfixed by the rapid *bam, bam, bam* the heavy gun made just inside the door.

I dove to the pavement, landed hard on my shoulder, and rolled to the curb, finding cover in the gutter.

Explosions splattered on the sidewalk like large rain drops.

The heavy gun kept firing even as the van accelerated through the intersection against the light.

The street began to fill with screams. I shouted Bruder's name over them. He didn't hear me.

12

"Two dead, three wounded," Clayton Rask said sadly.

I winced at his accounting of the casualties.

"Did you hear that? Did you hear that, McKenzie? Because of you, McKenzie. Two dead, three wounded because of you!"

Thomas Thompson stalked the Homicide Unit's conference room inside the Pink Palace. There were five others in the room—Bobby Dunston, Rask, an assistant Hennepin County attorney, an Assistant Ramsey County Attorney and a lieutenant wearing the uniform of the Minneapolis Police Department who wanted to know what story his chief should tell the media. Thompson was by far the most vocal. Bobby simply sat with his hands folded on the table before him, staring at nothing. Rask was pacing, too, but quietly.

"What should I have done differently?" I asked. The look on Bobby's face, he knew the answer as well as I did—I should have called the cops.

Thompson threatened to send me to Oak Park Heights for ten thousand years.

The unidentified lieutenant said, "This isn't getting us anywhere."

"Two dead and three wounded," Thompson shouted. "He's responsible."

I felt like crying. Only what good would that do? It wasn't going to bring back Bruder. Or the mother of three who had been standing next to him. It wasn't going to heal the wounds of the businessman directly behind her, the one who caught it in the gut. Or the bicycle courier. Or the secretary.

"What do we know about these Family Boyz?" the lieutenant asked.

"They don't exist!" Thompson shouted. "They're a figment of McKenzie's warped imagination."

"My chief wants . . ."

"I don't work for your chief."

The lieutenant wasn't impressed by Thompson's outburst. Calmly, but firmly, he said, "You are a guest of the Minneapolis Police Department. You are in our house now. If you do not behave I will ask you to leave."

"Who do you think you're talking to, Lieutenant?" Thompson said the word "lieutenant" like it was the medical term for a social disease.

The lieutenant rose from his place at the conference table and went to the closed door. He opened it. "Thank you for coming, *Deputy* Chief Thompson."

Thompson didn't say a word, nor did he make a move toward the open door. After a tense couple of moments the lieutenant shut the door firmly and returned to his seat.

"Tell us again what happened, Mr. McKenzie."

I told my story for the fifth time.

"And you're sure it was the Family Boyz?"

"I can't identify the assailants," I confessed. "I only saw the black van, but yeah, I'm sure. The machine gun . . ."

"We found shell casings," Rask interjected. "Seven-point-ninety-two millimeter. Czechoslovakian made."

"They carry a lot of heavy stuff," I added.

"How does this tie into your investigation of Bruder?" This time it was the assistant Hennepin County attorney who asked the question. He was talking to Bobby.

"It doesn't," Thompson told him. "We believe this—assault—wasn't meant for Bruder but for McKenzie."

"Do you agree with that, Mr. McKenzie?"

"I don't know."

"You don't know," Thompson snorted. "Our chief suspect in two brutal murders is dead and you don't know."

"I wonder," Bobby said softly.

All eyes turned to him.

"Now that we have him, there are tests we can perform to determine whether or not Bruder did, in fact, kill his wife and Katherine Katzmark. What interests me is his reference to *they*. When McKenzie mentioned the Family Boyz, Bruder didn't do the one thing everyone else has done."

"Which is what?" Thompson wanted to know.

"He didn't ask, 'who?'"

"We may never know," Thompson insisted. "Two dead and three wounded." He said it just that once too often.

"Excuse me." I was up and moving quickly toward the door. "I need to use the rest room."

I squatted before the porcelain toilet, expecting to vomit. But the gesture alone seemed to quiet my stomach. After a few minutes of unproductive hacking, I left the stall. Rask was waiting for me.

"You better wash," he said, gesturing to the dried blood on my hands and the red swipe on my forehead. I did what he suggested. The blood mixing with the liquid soap created a sickly pink color in the sink and again I felt like throwing up.

I dried my hands, looked at myself in the mirror. I didn't like what I saw. The sight of my own drawn and haggard face made me back away until I was hard against the far wall. I slid down the wall until I was sitting at its base, my legs drawn up, and hugging my knees.

"God help me."

Rask grinned. "Nothing like catastrophe to separate the true atheists from the whiners."

"Do you believe in God, LT?"

"Yes."

"After everything you've seen on the job?"

"Especially after what I've seen."

"I stopped believing."

"No you didn't. You just found an excuse to stop praying."

"I wasn't looking for a sermon."

"No, only absolution. Can't help you there, my friend."

I didn't suppose he could. After a few more minutes of feeling sorry for myself, I used the wall to climb onto my unsteady legs.

"What's going to happen to me?"

"You didn't do anything illegal, McKenzie. You didn't do anything wrong."

"Two dead and three wounded," I said. "And the child still missing."

"It's not your fault."

"It feels like my fault. I had to be a hero. I had to show everyone how clever I was."

"C'mon," he said, putting a comforting hand on my shoulder. "Thompson will think you're making a break for it."

Suddenly, there were ten people in the conference room, including the Minneapolis police chief. None of them were sitting. Instead they were gathered in a knot at the far end of the room around a tall man wearing a dark blue suit with black hair slicked back like the movie star Alec Baldwin. Standing next to him was a smaller man—thin, grizzled, brown suit—who looked like he'd lived three lifetimes already and was working on his fourth. He reminded me of Harry Dean Stanton, one of my favorite character actors. Alec was doing most of the talking, with Harry adding the occasional comment.

Bobby excused himself from the group and approached us as if he had been waiting impatiently for our arrival. "They want you," he told Rask. I made a move to join the group but Dunston put a hand on my chest to keep me in place.

"Who are those guys, Bobby?"

"Tall man in blue is ATF. Small man in brown is FBI."

"What's going on?"

"Listen to me. Are you listening to me, McKenzie? Don't say a word, not to anyone. Don't ask questions. Just go home."

"What are you talking about?"

"Go home."

"Just like that?"

"Exactly like that."

"Bobby?"

"I can't tell you anything. In a couple of days, maybe. Right now you have to leave."

"By whose order? The Department of Justice?"

"Remember what I said Saturday night? About you being the best friend I'll ever have? Well, right now I'm the best friend you'll ever have. Do what I say. Don't make a fuss. Just go home."

I looked past him at the knot of men, picking out Thompson's face. The way he glared at me, it was like he was daring me to do something, anything.

"Ever have the feeling you've been invited for drinks but everyone else is staying for dinner?"

"Frequently," Bobby told me.

I turned to leave. Bobby laid a gentle hand on my arm. "When you get home, stay there."

"Why?"

"Because honest to God, McKenzie, you're in way over your head this time and you're probably going to get yourself killed."

Several hours later the chief of the Minneapolis Police Department, dressed in full regalia, stood before a phalanx of reporters, Thomas Thompson at his side. He calmly told them that David Christopher Bruder, a suspect in the brutal murders of two women in St. Paul, had been shot and killed in downtown Minneapolis earlier that afternoon by persons or person unknown, along with a Golden Valley woman who was unfortunate enough to be standing next to him at the stoplight. Three others were wounded, he added, one in critical condition at the Hennepin County Medical Center, names were being withheld pending notification of family members. A full-scale investigation into the shooting had been mounted and certain suspects had been identified, although the chief declined to identify them at this time. As for the Bruder murder investigation, additional information, such as the whereabouts of Bruder's infant son, Thomas Christopher, would be released by the St. Paul Police Department as soon as it was confirmed.

A reporter asked if the shooting was gang related.

The chief would not speculate at this time.

The reporter persisted, suggesting that "a drive-by shooting" would seem to indicate gang violence.

Again the chief refused to speculate.

What other possibilities existed?

The chief wouldn't say.

Next it was Thompson's turn, acting for the St. Paul Police Department. Only one station carried the news conference live but Thompson acted as if he had an audience of millions. There were a lot of "I"s in his address. Yet despite the fact that his statement was twice as long, in the end he had nothing more to add to what the chief had already said. The only favorable comment I could make about his performance was that he didn't once mention my name.

I lay on my sofa and listened as Cecilia Bartoli sang eighteenth-century Italian songs. Cecilia's magnificent voice climbed to a ridiculously high note, danced on top of it for a while, and then slid effortlessly down the other side. One song in particular—a simple, straightforward aria by Alessandro Parisotti—aroused my interest enough to check the English translation in the liner notes:

> *I no longer feel*
> *the sparkle of youth in my heart*

"Ain't that the truth," I told the empty room.

I closed my eyes.

A sense of unfinished business fell about me like a heavy shroud that provides no warmth. It had been a long, emotionally exhausting day. I just wanted it to end. I should have been so lucky. At seven-thirty-five p.m. the telephone rang.

"The eagle has landed," a woman said.

"Excuse me?" I was groggy from my nap and the reference went right over my head.

"This is Nina."

"Oh, hi."

"Hester is here."

That woke me up.

"Is she?"

"Yes, and if you want to catch her you'd better hurry. She and her date have already ordered dinner and I suspect they'll be going somewhere else for dessert."

It took me fifteen minutes to reach Rickie's. Nina was starting down the staircase as I was starting up. We met in the middle and she took my arm, leading me to the downstairs bar. She was excited.

"Same table in the corner. Hester is wearing mallard blue tonight. The gentleman is wearing tweed—a little more tony than her usual date. They asked for their check as soon as dinner was served. Good Lord, you look worse than you did this morning."

"Thank you for noticing."

"Is that blood?" she asked, noticing the stain on my sleeve—I had changed my jacket but not my shirt.

I nodded.

"You might find this hard to believe since I'm a saloon keeper, but I never encourage customers to drink alcohol. However, in your case . . ."

"I could use a drink," I admitted.

She poured one for me on the house. Booker's neat. The shot was like a cold shower, it jolted my senses, making me more alert. Or maybe it was Nina's brilliant silver-blue eyes, the way they kind of flickered at me, demanding my attention. The second shot she poured had nearly the opposite effect, quieting my nerves, warming me like the blaze from a fireplace. A feeling of perfect comfort and ease settled over me—the way it does when you unexpectedly find yourself somewhere familiar and safe. But again, I don't think it was the high-priced bourbon, as delicious as it was. It was Nina. There was an expression of concern on her face that went well beyond caring about my appearance. Suddenly, inexplicably, I felt as if I had known her since the beginning of time.

I asked for a third shot.

Nina refused. "Two ounces of alcohol acts as a stimulant, three is a depressant."

She would know, I decided. After all, she was a professional.

"How are you doing, McKenzie?" she asked with all sincerity.

"I am so glad to see you," I blurted out.

"Where did that come from?" The smile on her face told me she didn't mind my declaration at all.

"This has been one of the hardest days of my life. Yet seeing you tonight makes it all seem—easy."

"That might be the finest compliment anyone has ever given me. Must be the bourbon talking."

"It's not, Nina. Truly it's not. Believe me, please."

"I do, McKenzie. Thank you. It's just that I'm thirty-seven years old now and when I hear a compliment I tend to look to see what's beneath it."

"We'll have to work on that," I told her.

"First we'll have to work on your timing." She moved to shield me from view. I peeked around her at the staircase. Now I knew what mallard blue looked like.

Hester was wearing an ankle-length silk dress that clung to her devious curves like plastic wrap. It was the bluest blue I had ever seen and if the dress had a button, zipper, or snap, I couldn't find it anywhere—and believe me, I looked hard. Nina gave me a "Hrumph" as I slid off my stool.

"Strictly business," I promised her.

I feared that Hester might be more alert than Cook had been and search for a tail so I decided to make my move before she and her date made theirs. I brushed past them just outside the door. I gave Hester a hard look but she must have been used to stares from strange men and didn't acknowledge it. Her date didn't notice me, either. I went to the Cherokee, which I had parked in the stall directly behind her Audi—her license plate number was already in my notebook. I was on my way to the Paradise Motel before they unlocked the doors of Mr. Tweed's Volvo.

I parked in the Paradise Motel lot in front of Bungalow Seven and waited. I didn't wait long. Less than five minutes after I arrived, the Volvo turned in and drove directly to the stall in front of number sixteen. Mr. Tweed walked across the lot to the office. I watched him as he went past. About thirty-five. Sandy-blond hair. Carried himself like he had done this sort of thing before. I waited until they were both inside the bungalow and then jotted down the Volvo's license plate number. Twelve minutes later I was in the parking lot adjacent to Rickie's.

I thought about going in for another Booker's but decided Nina would be too much of a distraction. Besides, I was afraid of bumping into young, beautiful, and smart as hell Jeannie. Nina had promised to call her. Instead I turned on my CD player and listened to some early Johnny Cash while I waited. I should have gone inside. It was almost ninety minutes before Hester and her date returned. Well, at least this one got his money's worth.

Mr. Tweed opened the passenger door for Hester, walked her to the Audi, borrowed her keys to unlock it, then held the door open as she slid inside. He leaned in and kissed her. She smiled at him. He closed the door, waved as he went back to his car. He started up, but didn't leave the lot until Hester was under way. Chivalry lives, I told myself.

They both drove west on Selby Avenue but at Dale Hester went north toward the freeway while Mr. Tweed turned south. I followed

Hester. A few blocks later she caught I-94 and headed west toward Minneapolis. I replaced the Man in Black with the Brian Setzer Orchestra on the CD player and cranked the volume—a little traveling music.

I stayed five car lengths behind her as she sped past the downtown exits, drove through the Lowry Hill Tunnel, crossed over to I-394, and left the city behind. We stayed on the freeway for over twenty miles, cruising through Golden Valley, St. Louis Park, Hopkins, and Minnetonka, passing such landmarks as Theodore Wirth Park, General Mills, Ridgedale Shopping Mall, and the Carlson Companies' twin office towers, as well as a dozen strip malls featuring generic restaurants and shoe box theaters. The farther west we traveled, the more exclusive the neighborhoods became until we crossed over into Wayzata. Hester left the highway and led me through a maze of twisting streets with barely enough room for two cars to pass, streets with names that ended in Pointe, Wood, View, and Dale. I lost track of the names. It was all I could do to keep up with her. She drove like she had just stolen the car.

We were circling Lake Minnetonka now. The lake is the semi-exclusive province of bankers, corporate raiders, department store owners, and professional athletes with guaranteed contracts. I say semi-exclusive because on any given day the public landings are choked with all manner of pleasure craft brought in by less than well-to-do boat owners who, for an afternoon at least, can get a taste of the good life, their Lund Americans bobbing in the wake of yachts and cigarettes. The swells who actually reside on the lake once demanded an ordinance that would limit access. They wanted to restrict the number of "nonresident" boats allowed, citing noise pollution among other things. The result was a flood of letters to newspapers and local politicians, protest marches, signs that read, "Lake Minnetonka—Please Wipe Your Feet," and even more boats. Personally, I didn't see the attraction. There's no fish in the damn thing.

Finally, we reached a stand of ten mailboxes at the mouth of a gravel road. Hester turned onto the road. A sign just inside warned, DEAD END.

I took a chance and kept following. We passed nine driveways. A brick and metal arch spanned the entrance to the tenth. There was a name written in the metalwork across the top of the arch that I couldn't read in the dark. Hester swung the Audi under it, setting off a succession of motion detectors as she went—spotlights flicked on one by one, following her all the way to a four-car garage about seventy-five yards from the gravel. I went straight, stopping my car at a black-and-white striped traffic barrier. Real inconspicuous. A concerned citizen probably had started dialing 911 before I turned the engine off. "Officer, there's a strange vehicle on my private road and I'm sure it's more than two years old."

I ran back up the road, gravel crunching under my Nikes. The moon was hidden behind a bank of slow-moving clouds but with all the lights, it could have been Yankee Stadium. I watched Hester move to the front door. More lights went on. She unlocked the door and went quickly inside, leaving the door open. It took a few seconds before she returned to close it. Must've punched a code into an alarm system, I reasoned. An inside light went on. And off. I waited a few moments and ran across the lawn toward the house. I gambled that anyone alerted by the lights would have stopped watching once they had identified Hester.

Just as I reached the structure, still another indoor light flicked on. I moved toward it. The moth and the flame. The light shone through a kitchen window. I peeked above the sill. Large kitchen—white walls, counters, cabinets, appliances, and tile floor. Hester was standing at the center island, a brilliant blue flame surrounded by all that whiteness, her profile to me, removing silver earrings. Suddenly, a man appeared, darkness behind him—I have no idea where he came from. The man was dressed in pale green briefs and nothing more. He was tall and strong, muscles rippled as he moved. I ducked down. He didn't see me, but then, he only had eyes for Hester.

The man came up behind her. She didn't turn to look at him, didn't acknowledge his presence at all until he wrapped his powerful arms around her, cupping her breasts through the silk of her dress. Hester arched her back and he kissed her neck as he slowly worked the dress up and off her. Her lace brassiere was the color of her dress and barely contained her. Her matching panties had less material than my handkerchief. He popped her breasts out of the cups and caressed them with one hand. With the other he firmly stroked the front of her panties. She turned in his arms and kissed him hard, opening her mouth to him. He held her tight, but not so tight that she couldn't wriggle free and kiss his neck, his chest, his stomach, his waist. She lowered herself to the floor and, kneeling before him, hooked her fingers over the elastic of his briefs while he played with her hair. I could hear their sharp, erratic breathing through the closed window as the briefs came down. Or maybe it was my own breathing.

The yard lights behind me flicked off one by one. I couldn't tell you how long they had been set for. Could've been ten minutes. Could've been three days. I had lost all track of time as I squatted at the windowsill. I felt considerably safer spying on Hester from the darkness, yet it also made me feel creepy. Time to leave, I decided. If I wanted to see more I could always surf the Internet. I turned my back to the window and dashed across the lawn, setting off the lights again as I made my way to the SUV. I doubted Hester and her friend noticed.

13

They buried Napoleon Cook in a hurry. Dead Friday night, in the ground Tuesday morning. Apparently, the Hennepin County ME didn't see any reason to keep his remains, what was left of them after his twenty-seven-floor swan dive. I would have missed the funeral altogether if I hadn't read the brief notice next to the story about Bruder's murder—bless them, neither the *Star-Tribune* or *Pioneer Press* mentioned my name. I doubted the powers gave it to them. I wondered about that as I drove to the cemetery off Highway 36 in Minneapolis, across from the Francis A. Gross Golf Course.

Cook's funeral, like most funerals I've attended, was a quiet, tedious affair attended by people who would rather have been somewhere else. There was a large crowd in attendance—Cook had considerably more friends than I had supposed—yet no one seemed to be genuinely grief-stricken over his demise. For the most part, the mourners were impassive, merely going through the motions, fulfilling an obligation. That included the Roman Catholic priest who officiated. True, he spoke impressively about Cook's generosity and his concern for others. Still, it was obvious he had never actually met the man and didn't feel any regret about putting him into the ground. The only time his words actually seemed to touch the crowd was when he mentioned that although circumstances forbade Cook from attending, the annual Northern Lights Entrepreneur's Club Ball would proceed as scheduled and we could all rest assured that he would be there in spirit.

"It's going to be one helluva party," a mourner said to no one in particular.

The priest stood behind Cook's coffin, which was carefully set on a platform in front of the grave. Behind him stood four of Cook's pallbearers, each of them dressed in identical black suits and wearing white gloves. They stood soldier-fashion shoulder to shoulder like backup singers waiting for their cue. The other pallbearers and the rest of the mourners had fanned out in a semicircle around the graveside. Alone at one end of the arch stood the woman who had given Cook his last glimpse of Paradise. Despite her sunglasses and large floppy hat there was no mistaking Hester. She looked like a fashion model pushing funeral attire.

"Astonishing, isn't she?" a voice said. The voice belonged to a woman, about five-foot-nothing with a small face, mostly eyes, and a pleasant mouth that smiled as if it had had a lot of practice. She had strawberry hair, a petite figure, short legs and, in keeping with the occasion, she wore black.

"A true freak of nature," she added.

"Who?"

"The woman you've been staring at for the past five minutes?"

"She reminds me of someone I know."

"Your kid sister, no doubt," she said and giggled. The nearest mourners looked at her with barely disguised contempt. Imagine, laughing at a funeral?

"I'm Charlotte Belloti," she announced.

The name was familiar, yet I couldn't place it. She extended a gloved hand. I took it. Her grip was surprisingly firm.

"Don't even think of calling me Charlie," she said.

"Never."

"The woman you're staring at is Lila Casselman. She's married. Not that she lets it interfere with her dating, if you're interested. Rumor has it she was spending quality time with the dearly departed. Were you a friend of Napoleon's?"

"We were acquainted. You?"

"Napoleon was primeval slime and I hope he rots in hell." Strong words, yet delivered with a surprising lack of rancor.

"I take it you were close."

"He was my husband's friend. Personally, I don't know what Geno saw in him. Napoleon was a rutting pig, one of those guys who never leaves the house without a condom in his wallet because he always feels lucky. He tried so hard to get me into bed you'd think he sold mattresses. He and Lila were made for each other."

"She doesn't seem too distraught."

"Who knows? Behind those big sunglasses she might be crying real tears—not!"

"Do you think her husband knows about her and Cook?"

"Warren?" She gestured toward the quartet backing up the preacher. "That's him, third from the left, with the rest of the Entrepreneurs. What's left of them anyway. Can you believe it? They're dropping like flies. Poor Jamie. And Katherine. And Napoleon. And yesterday it was David's turn. It's getting kinda scary."

While she spoke, I studied Warren Casselman. He was five-ten and looked like someone who played racquetball twice a month and figured that was enough. He had sandy hair cut short, thin features, and eyes of indeterminate color. While the rest of the mourners bowed their heads to receive the priest's blessing, he kept his straight and level, staring at something over the priest's shoulder.

"Warren probably knows about Lila's extracurriculars but pretends he doesn't," Charlotte continued. "If he ever admitted he knows, he'd have to do something about it, wouldn't he? It's not about love or honor or jealousy or even pride of possession. Somebody messes with your wife, you're supposed to do something about it. It's expected. Am I right?"

"A man's gotta do what a man's gotta do," I told her.

"Precisely. So he pretends he doesn't know so he doesn't have to do anything. I guess I can understand. Him and Napoleon and the rest of the Entrepreneurs have been together since, God, since school. It's tough to throw away that kind of friendship, even for your wife."

"No, it's not."

Charlotte smiled broadly. The smile turned into laughter and drew even more disapproving stares.

"You're cute," she told me.

"Why? Because I don't wink at adultery?"

"That, too. Who are you, anyway?"

I hesitated, remembering the effect my name had on Cook.

"I'm McKenzie."

"Are you one of the associate members of the club?"

"No."

"Another plus," Charlotte said, padding my account.

"Tell me about the club."

"The Northern Lights Entrepreneurs? Nothing much to tell. I think there's like three hundred associate members now. The founders, all eight of them, went to college together, became successful in their various pursuits at about the same time, and then decided they were important."

"But who are they?"

Charlotte sighed like it was a topic she had grown tired of long ago. "Do you really want to know these people?"

"I'd like to know about them. I might do some business with them."

"Besides my husband, there's Warren, of course. You know Warren."

"No, I don't."

"You never heard of Warren Casselman? To hear him talk about it, you'd think he's the most famous attorney in Minnesota."

I shook my head.

"Well, first of all, he's the attorney for all of the Entrepreneurs, the founders I mean—handles their personal legal stuff. But his big claim to fame is that he keeps suing all those corporations. You must have read about it. What he does, he waits until there's bad news in the press about a company—an announcement over a big loss in earnings, something that causes their stock prices to fall. Then he sues the company on behalf of the shareholders. He says where there's smoke, there's usually fire. So he sues the company, saying the corporation's executive officers made misleading statements or failed to disclose important information and thereby defrauded investors. He uses the lawsuit to gain access to the company's documents and he searches through them until he finds something he can use in court. Geno says the first few times Warren filed a suit, the companies fought him and lost big. Now when Warren files, the companies usually settle out of court and when they do he gets a third off the top. We're talking millions of dollars here. Personally, I think it's a lot like extortion."

"An awful lot. How about the others?"

"Standing to Warren's right is Brian Mellgren."

If Casselman seemed soft, Mellgren looked as hard as fired brick. Lean features, his eyes squinting in the light even though the sun was behind him—he looked like a guy who hated baby ducks, slow dances, and first kisses. His suit jacket was too tight across his chest and I noticed the slight bulge under his left armpit. He was packing.

"He owns all those home stores—you've heard of them," Charlotte added. "Sells appliances and stuff. Refrigerators. Microwaves. All sorts of stuff. Sells it at a discount. Makes a ton."

Why would a man bring a concealed weapon to a funeral? I asked myself. *Because three of his friends have been murdered within a week.* Oh, yeah. Then I remembered that I was armed, too, and pushed the question from my head.

"Next to Brian is Collin Kamp," Charlotte said. Like Casselman, Kamp was in shape once and could be again if he made the effort before too much more time had passed. "CK Computers."

"I heard of them."

"The stores are everywhere. Collin sells at a discount, too. They all sell at a discount. Even John Whelpley . . ."

I eyed the fourth man. He wore a full beard flecked with gray. Compensating for the lack of hair on his head, I reasoned.

"He sells top-of-the-line fashions from Europe at real low prices. Some of it is awfully chic, too. I often wonder how he does it. Then there was poor Katherine Katzmark. She sold discount kitchenware. And David Bruder sold used cars."

"What about your husband?" I asked.

"Geno? Geno owns an export packaging company," she answered proudly. "He'll pack anything for shipment anywhere in the world and back again—pack it to withstand all conditions, from Minnesota winters to Saudi summers, the vibration of airplanes, the rolling of ships, that sort of thing. It was his company that brought the window-washing equipment over from Germany that they put on top of the IDS Tower. You should have seen it, with the helicopters and everything. It was on the news."

"I remember that," I lied.

"He's also an expert with documentation, making sure everything gets through customs without a problem. Every country has its own rules, you know."

"Is your husband here, Charlotte?"

"No. He flew out to Leningrad yesterday morning. Well, I guess they call it St. Petersburg now."

"When's he due back?"

"Tomorrow. He hopes to make the ball, but we'll see. Why? You're not going to pull a Napoleon Cook on me, are you? Take advantage of a defenseless woman all alone in the hour of her grief?"

"I wouldn't think of it."

"Well, think of it," Charlotte said and started giggling again, prompting even more horrified glances.

When the priest finished, the mourners who had gathered around Napoleon Cook's coffin began drifting toward their cars. Charlotte shook my hand and said, "Seriously, it was a pleasure meeting you."

"The pleasure was mine."

"You're just saying that because it's true." She giggled some more. "Am I going to see you at the ball tomorrow night?"

"Probably not," I told her.

"I wish I could skip it, too, but Geno says—anyway, I gotta go."

"Take care," I told her and watched her stroll toward the cars that lined the cemetery's narrow street, swinging her purse from the strap like a little girl. *I like her,* I told myself. *Talks too much, though.*

I searched the dispersing crowd and found the Casselmans. Warren was shaking hands with a man I didn't recognize. Lila, the dutiful wife, stood at his side. After Warren and the companion said their good-byes, Warren nudged Lila toward a black limousine. A man dressed in a chauffeur's uniform appeared and quickly opened the back door and held it until first Lila and then Warren slid inside. Him I recognized immediately, even fully clothed. It was the man in the pale green briefs who had greeted Lila so warmly the evening before.

And people claim daytime soaps are exaggerated.

"What have you seen that I missed?"

Bobby Dunston was resting against the front fender of my Jeep Cherokee when I returned from the graveside.

"What are you doing here?" I asked.

"Same as you. Eyeballing the mourners to see if the killer pays his respects."

"Unfortunately, the Family Boyz didn't show."

"Did you think they would?"

"Should we be talking, Bobby? What would the ATF, FBI, and all the other justice boys say?"

"You sound bitter."

"I am bitter."

"You shouldn't be. They got you out of a jam, whether you admit it or not."

Bobby gestured to the big Oldsmobile parked directly behind my Cherokee. Alec Baldwin was behind the wheel. He wiggled the fingers of his right hand in greeting.

"I see you brought a date."

"He brought me."

My eyes swept from Bobby to Alec and back again. Something wasn't right. The way Bobby held his arms across his chest in a defensive posture, the way Alec waited patiently in the car . . .

"What's going on, Bobby?"

"There's something I was asked to tell you."

"Asked or told?"

"David Bruder was right-handed."

I recalled immediately what Bobby had told me in Rice Park: *The killer was a southpaw.*

"See you around, McKenzie," Bobby said abruptly. He retreated to the Oldsmobile and climbed inside. He never once looked back at me. That should have told me something. But it didn't.

The maniac who slaughtered Jamie and Katherine Katzmark was left-handed. Bruder was right-handed. Ergo, Bruder was innocent. Fine. Glad to hear it. Only why would Justice feel the need to share that information with me? It didn't make sense and thinking about it caused me enough confusion that I nearly sideswiped a minivan when I took the 10th Street exit into downtown St. Paul. I decided to forget about it and instead concentrate on the task at hand, specifically finding an open parking meter within hiking distance of the Minnesota Department of Motor Vehicles.

I ran the plates on the black Volvo I had followed the previous evening and was disappointed by the result. The car was owned by Geno Belloti, who apparently left for St. Petersburg on a much later flight than his wife had been told. I wondered if Charlotte knew that Lila had gotten to him, too.

"I'm sorry, Charlotte," I said out loud. So much betrayal.

Next I ran the Audi's plates. No surprise. The car was owned by Lila's husband, Warren Casselman.

Only the very rich name their houses as if they were pets. The Cassel-man house was called "Birchwood." It said so on the iron arch that straddled the driveway. I drove under the arch and along the curving concrete driveway to the four-stall garage. The door to the second stall was up, revealing the limousine. The man who drove the limo and gave

Lila her late night snack was now driving a lawn tractor around a clump of maple trees. There were maple, ash, and fir trees scattered all over the property, but no birch. Go figure.

When the driver noticed me he steered the tractor in my direction, coming fast, cutting a swath through the tall grass. He was wearing khaki pants and sneakers, no shirt, taking advantage of the unseasonably warm September day. Twenty yards out he hit the kill switch and the tractor shuddered to a halt. He dismounted and moved closer. He was tall and rough looking—dirty blond hair cut short, sweat glistening on taut muscle. As he closed the distance between us I made the gold earring. Closer still and I could see the terrible scar tissue on his shoulder and stomach. I took a deep breath.

"I don't need this," I told myself as I watched the driver approach. "I really don't."

"You want something, asshole?" he asked.

"I take it you're not with Welcome Wagon."

"We don't like peddlers here."

"Too bad. If I sell enough magazine subscriptions . . ."

He threw a left. I ducked under it. Only he was quick. Before I could step away he set a headlock with his left arm and pulled up. I brought my right hand up under his chin and pushed his head to the left, forcing him to release his grip. I slipped out of the headlock and reversed the move, moving my right hand down and around so that my forearm was under his chin. I drilled an elbow just inside his right shoulder blade, putting him down. It should have been enough. It wasn't. He came up with a left to my head. I blocked it with my right forearm. He followed with a right to my stomach. My right arm swept counterclockwise across my body for another block. Then I uncurled a vicious back fist into his jaw and followed with a four-knuckle punch to his solar plexus. He backed away and grinned at me, a wicked, yellow-tooth grin. Yeah, this sure beats the hell out of cutting grass.

"Pussy," he hissed.

"Chauffeur," I hissed back. It wasn't much of an insult but I felt I had to say something.

He moved closer than I wanted him to be. I could smell his breath—he needed a mint. Yet it was his eyes that got me. Everything you wanted to know was in those eyes. Eyes from a black-and-white movie, the color sucked out. Eyes that said he didn't care if he lived or died.

I reached for my gun.

"Devanter! Devanter, what the hell!"

I heard the voice and footsteps before I saw the man. It was Casselman. He grabbed Devanter's shoulder, the one with the scar. "Are you crazy?"

Devanter pushed Casselman back. "Don't touch me!" he snarled.

Casselman backed away. Suddenly he was a five-year-old losing a battle with an ice cream cone on a hot summer day. Yet at the same time he was used to giving orders and having them obeyed.

"Don't talk to me that way," he said evenly. "You will treat my guests with respect."

Devanter smirked. I didn't think Casselman sounded convincing, either.

"Don't you have work to do?" Casselman asked.

Devanter grunted and then deposited a gob of spit next to my shoe before shooting me a mocking "next-time" glance. *Not if I can help it, pal.* As he restarted the lawn tractor Casselman took my arm and shouted above the noise, "Are you all right?"

I shouted back, "I heard good help is hard to find."

"Devanter is one of my wife's reclamation projects from the VA. She says he's harmless."

"She's wrong."

"He's a great gardener—all my friends use him," he added as if he felt obligated to explain Devanter's presence. Didn't surprise me at all that the guy worked in dirt.

Casselman gave me a grand tour of his home by way of apologizing for Devanter's treatment, and with each wondrous sight I heard Bette Davis speak her most famous line as clearly as when she did it in the movie: *What a dump.*

The outside of the Casselmans' house was strictly English Tudor, with stone walls and high gables and so many windows you wondered why they didn't just build the damn thing out of glass. Yet the inside had no particular period. It was all white with vaulted ceilings and arched passageways, ceramic tiles and hardwood floors. It looked like it was thrown together by someone who knew nothing about interior design, but damn well knew what he liked. What Casselman liked was stenciled wallpaper, small bronzes by Rodin, Chinese porcelains, neoclassic chairs, gilded antique tables, numerous jade statues and figurines, and handmade Persian throw rugs that I found myself stepping over and around.

The place reminded me of an exhibit at the Minneapolis Institute of Art and I could well imagine how the plush surroundings might intimidate visitors unused to such opulence—provided they didn't take time to notice the dust bunnies peering out from under the love seat and the hairline fracture that ran the length of the dining room ceiling. I make a point of searching out such imperfections. I find them comforting. Still, it was a grand house and I told Casselman so.

He seemed pleased that I was pleased.

Casselman was dressed casually. He had changed from his somber black funeral suit to little-worn blue jeans and a soft-blue knit shirt with the scales of justice embossed above the breast pocket, the kind of shirt you'd get at LawCamp, where yuppie kids can spend their summers studying torts, trial advocacy, evidence, and how to master the LSAT for a thousand bucks a week. He spoke openly with me like we were friends, like I was no threat to him at all.

"Can I get you anything? A drink?" he asked, a gracious host quite at home in a house that had its own name.

"I'll have a beer if you'll join me."

"Agreed." He guided me to the kitchen. It seemed bigger than I remembered. I purposely avoided the spot where Lila and Devanter exchanged pleasantries the evening before while Casselman took two Amstel Lights from the refrigerator, handing me one.

"This okay?"

"Excellent."

Casselman took a long pull from the bottle, no glass for him, and smiled. "So tell me. Who are you exactly and why are you here?" The question seemed silly after all the time we had already spent together.

"My name's McKenzie." I watched Casselman's face carefully to see if he'd react to my name the way Cook had, but he gave me nothing. I could have been the meter reader. On the other hand, I suspected he knew who I was from the moment he found me in his driveway—why else would he be so gracious?

"I represent Jamie Bruder's family," I added. "They asked me to look into her murder."

"I thought David Bruder did it."

"He didn't."

"No?"

"It's been proven."

Casselman quickly turned away, yet I saw enough of his eyes to know that the remark had unsettled him. Like most attorneys, Casselman preferred to ask only those questions he already knew the answer to, and apparently, he thought he had known the answer to that one.

"Are you sure?" he asked.

"Quite sure. The police will probably make an announcement about it soon."

"Do they know who did kill Jamie and Katherine?"

"Not yet."

"My wife is quite shaken by all this. First Katherine, then Jamie. Now Napoleon and David. She feels like we're being targeted."

"The Entrepreneurs?"

"Yes. It's as if someone is after us."

"Is someone after you?"

He paused for a moment while he considered his answer. "I can't imagine why."

I took a sip of the Amstel, made him wait for my next question. "You were David Bruder's lawyer, weren't you?"

"Who told you that?"

"Bruder."

"You talked to David?"

"I was with him when he was killed."

Casselman moved smoothly to the refrigerator, opened it, rummaged through its contents for one, two, three, four, five, six, seven, eight, nine, ten seconds and closed it again, taking nothing out. I smiled at his back. At heart, everyone is a mystery—the mind, however, is a different matter. I knew what Casselman was thinking even before he did. He was thinking that Bruder had put him on the spot.

"What did David say?" he asked.

"He said you were his lawyer."

"What else?"

"This and that."

"It's true, of course. His business affairs were handled by a firm in Arden Hills—I believe that's where he met his wife. However, I was his personal attorney."

"The night he disappeared you called him. You left a message on his answering machine. 'Something's gone wrong. Better call me ASAP.'"

"The police already asked about that."

"And?"

"It was about the ball, the Entrepreneur's Club Ball to be held tomorrow evening. We were having trouble with one of the bands, but it was straightened out."

"So, your call had nothing to do with the Family Boyz."

"The Family Boyz? What's that? A rock band?"

"A street gang, a little more interesting than most."

"I know nothing about them." Casselman looked me straight in the eye, not daring even to blink. I took it as proof he was lying.

"Bruder had dealings with them. So did Cook."

"I don't believe that."

"Don't believe it or don't want to?"

"I can't imagine what kind of business dealings David and Napoleon would have had with such people."

"You were their lawyer."

"But not their keeper."

"Nonetheless."

"Do you have any proof of their involvement? Any evidence that would stand up to scrutiny?"

"In court, you mean? No."

"Then, Mr. McKenzie, you should be more careful with your accusations."

"Sounds like good advice."

"It was meant to be."

And here I always thought lawyers were supposed to be subtle. I went back on the offensive.

"Where were you Tuesday night, the night Jamie was murdered?"

Casselman waited one, two, three, four, five beats and said, "You should be a trial lawyer. Excuse me." He moved to the entrance of the kitchen. He called, "Lila? Lila, would you come down here for a moment?"

Casselman took another pull of his beer while we waited. Lila was wearing an oversize black T-shirt that barely brushed her thighs and nothing more that I could see. I tried not to stare.

"This is Mr. McKenzie," Casselman told her. "He's investigating Jamie's murder."

"The paper said David did it."

"Apparently the paper is wrong."

"Well, who then?"

"That's what he's here to find out." Casselman asked me to repeat my question. I knew I was wasting my time but I asked anyway.

"I was here, with Lila."

"Is that true, Mrs. Casselman?"

"Yes," she said without hesitation.

"All night?"

"All night."

"How about Friday night between eleven and midnight?"

"Friday night? Isn't that"—Casselman looked to his wife—"The night we went . . ."

"To the movies and for a drink afterwards," Lila finished. "We went to see the new Tom Hanks film. It was a date. We hardly ever have time for dates anymore."

Casselman nodded in agreement. He and Lila danced well together. I knew I wasn't going to get anything more out of either of them until they were separated.

"Thank you for your time, Mr. Casselman. Mrs. Casselman. I can let myself out."

Casselman wasn't as anxious to see me depart as I would have guessed.

"Mr. McKenzie, do you own your own business?"

"I'm self-employed," I admitted.

"Then you certainly qualify for the Northern Lights Entrepreneur's Club Ball. It's tomorrow night at the Minnesota Club. Have you received an invitation?"

"It must have been lost in the mail."

"Please plan on attending," he told me. "I'll arrange to have an invitation sent to you by messenger."

"That's gracious of you."

"It's going to be a great party. A great send-off for Napoleon and the others."

"I'm sure it will be."

"I'll be looking forward to seeing you there."

Through all of this, Lila stood mute, looking first at her husband, then at me, watching our conversation like it was a tennis match. Just for the hell of it, I decided to serve her a high, hard one. I glanced at my watch even though I had no interest in the time and said, "I have to go. I promised to meet someone at Rickie's."

I looked directly into Lila Casselman's eyes when I said that last part. Her smile froze and her face went pale.

"I'm unfamiliar with Rickie's. Is that a club?" Casselman asked.

"Yes. In St. Paul."

"I confess that I rarely get to St. Paul."

"You should make more of an effort," I told him. Lila stared at me without blinking. "Thank you for your time and trouble."

"No trouble at all," he replied.

Lila didn't say anything and probably wouldn't until the blood returned from her feet.

Devanter was nowhere to be seen as I cautiously made my way to the Jeep Cherokee, but I could hear the lawn tractor. It sounded a long way off, behind the house. I turned the SUV around and headed down the drive, under the arches, onto the private lane and drove to where it intersected the main road. I found an unobtrusive spot in the shadow of a large oak tree and parked.

Casselman had made a mistake. He should not have trusted his wife to provide an alibi—she had been with Bruder on Tuesday and Cook on Friday. Apparently, he didn't know.

I switched on my radio, found jazz station KBEM, and waited. During the news break at the top of the hour I learned that one of the three people wounded during the attack on David Bruder had died earlier that morning at the Hennepin County Medical Center. I switched off the radio. That made eight dead since this all began. Good God in heaven.

I waited near the intersection for nearly two hours before Casselman sped past me driving the same Audi Lila had piloted the previous evening. He was alone. I was tempted to follow him as I had followed Napoleon Cook. Instead, I returned to Birchwood.

I parked close to the house and watched for Devanter. I didn't see him and he didn't answer when I rang the bell. Nor did Lila. I circled the house, discovering a twenty-five-foot-high wall of red, pink, and yellow roses climbing a trellis fixed to the south face. Beyond the house I found a carefully manicured lawn about the size of a football field that sloped leisurely to Lake Minnetonka. The lake was blue and quiet—boats in the distance gave it a picture postcard appeal. Having a wonderful time, wish you were here. Closer to the back of the house I found Lila standing next to a lounger by a swimming pool the size of a volleyball court. Why she needed a swimming pool when there was a perfectly good lake only a hundred paces away was beyond me.

She saw me approach but pretended not to, becoming the seductress I saw at Rickie's, slowly discarding the oversize black shirt to reveal a white, scoop-neck tanksuit with shimmery gold straps lacing the back. A swimsuit not designed for water. She pivoted slowly, tugging at this and smoothing that, locking her fingers behind her neck and stretching, giving me a good look at her strong, sleek body, playing me like one of the strippers at Déjà Vu. She sat on the lounger and, with her back to me, slipped the straps of the swimsuit off her shoulders before lying back and stretching out. I stood watching her, not liking the way she made me feel.

"See anything you like?" she asked, her eyes closed.

"One or two things," I admitted.

She moved her hands up her body, taking her time, guiding them to her breasts. She began gently massaging herself with fingertips and palms, her lips parting with a sigh.

"Do you think I'm beautiful?"

"Yes."

"Then why don't you say so? Most men do."

"I hate to follow the crowd."

She smiled slightly, licking her thin lips with the tip of her tongue as she slid her hands off her breasts, across her flat stomach to her thighs. At the same time a German shepherd puppy trotted across the lawn. He sniffed at my leg, wagged his tail, then found a cool spot in the recliner's shadow. The dog broke Lila's spell. I stepped backward, took a deep breath, and asked, "Does this act work with everyone?"

"So far," she said, smirking.

I shook my head, telling myself more than her, "That's not why I'm here."

"Why are you here?"

"I still want to know where your husband was Tuesday night, the night Jamie was killed."

"He told you. He was with me."

"You were with David Bruder."

The smirk froze on her face.

"Bruder Tuesday. Napoleon Cook Friday. And Geno Belloti last night."

The smirk thawed quickly into a soft smile, but her eyes remained hard and shiny. She reminded me of a cat, the kind you find behind the reinforced glass at the Como Zoo, a predator.

Lila swung her long legs off the lounge chair. "Napoleon was sure we were being followed. You?"

I nodded.

She reached down and very deliberately scratched the shepherd's ears. "What I was doing at the Paradise Motel is my affair," she said without irony.

"True. But where your husband was is mine."

The shepherd's wagging tail brushed her ankle. "Sic 'em," she shouted suddenly, pointing at me. "Kill. Tear him up."

I reached for my Beretta but didn't pull it from the holster. No need. The dog jumped at Lila's hand, wagged his tail furiously and let loose with a string of low, playful barks. Just a confused puppy.

Lila scratched his ears again. "Some watchdog. Well, I guess I'm going to have to talk to you after all."

"Where was your husband?"

"I don't know."

"It doesn't bother you, not knowing?"

"Should it?"

"Maybe he was with Jamie."

Lila giggled. "You think Warren killed Jamie and Katherine?" She giggled harder.

"Just a thought."

"Well, think again."

"Was your husband having an affair with Jamie Bruder?"

"Sweet, adorable little Jamie? Sugar and spice, everything nice Jamie? Get serious."

"Why not? You were sleeping with David Bruder."

"I was sleeping with *all* of them. I even slept with Katherine."

"Why?"

"To prove a point about all those wonderful, true-blue, one-for-all, all-for-one lifetime friends of the Northern Lights Entrepreneur's Club."

"The point being?"

"They're hypocrites and they can't be trusted."

"What about all the other men you've slept with?"

"Some people collect stamps."

"You're a wonderful human being, you know that?"

"Mr.—McKenzie, is it? I don't think I care to answer any more of your questions."

"Would it change your mind if I threatened to tell your husband about your activities with his friends?"

"He probably already knows. He's not a fool."

"What if I told him about you and Devanter?"

"I don't think Devanter would like that. Would you, Devanter?"

I didn't know he was behind me until he slammed his fist into my spine. He hit me harder than I had ever been hit before—the pain made me cry out. My entire body went numb and I folded like an accordion. Devanter lifted me by my shoulders and threw me in the general direction of Lake Minnetonka. I hit the ground with my face and upper chest. He picked me up and threw me again. This time I landed on my neck and shoulders. I tried to roll into some kind of fighting stance, but he caught me and tossed me around some more.

Lila sat on the lounge chair and watched, scratching the shepherd's ears, the shepherd licking his paw.

Devanter must have been getting tired because he grabbed my

shoulders and held me. "I told you, didn't I?" He butted my head. Blood spilled over my face. He butted me again. He smiled. I could see my blood on his teeth. Suddenly, there was a heavy weight in my hand. We both looked down. It was my Beretta. Don't ask me how I managed to wrest it from the holster, I couldn't even feel the grip. I thrust the barrel into Devanter's groin. He wasn't impressed. Instead, he grinned. And those eyes. He didn't give a damn. Maybe Lila did.

"Call him off!" I yelled.

"Devanter," she said softly.

Devanter let go of my shoulders and stepped back. I crumpled to my knees, reaching out my left hand to keep from tumbling over. I managed to keep the gun pointed at him.

"Devanter," Lila said again, and he turned and walked toward the house. She rose from the recliner and patted his head as he went past. Just a playful puppy.

Lila came to where I knelt on her lawn, standing before me, the sun directly behind her. Backlit like that she seemed beatified, a halo of light around her head like you see in Renaissance paintings of the Virgin Mary. The sight hurt my eyes. I lowered my chin against my chest. Lila gently stroked my hair.

"You must leave, now," she said.

I nodded and tried to wipe the blood from my eyes.

"Men," she muttered and stepped away. The front of her white suit was stained with my blood. She walked back to her house, the shepherd trailing behind. I kept the Beretta trained on her until she was inside.

With strength I didn't know I possessed, I pushed myself vertical and staggered to my vehicle. I set the Beretta on the passenger seat and slowly pulled the handkerchief from my hip pocket—everything I did was at quarter speed. I mopped the blood from my face and surveyed the damage in the mirror behind my sun visor. There was a four-inch slice along my hairline. I touched it. That was a mistake. The shooting pain made me both dizzy and nauseous.

I shouldn't have tried to drive, but I had to get out of there. I turned the wrong way on the gravel and followed it to the black-and-white-striped traffic barrier. Dead end. I turned off the engine and fell out the door. I rolled a few yards, struggled to my feet and pushed myself over the barrier and through the trees to the lake shore. The shore was rocky—I tripped on it several times, tearing the knees out of my jeans. I pushed myself until I reached the water.

You must leave now, I heard a voice say from far away, and I started to weep again.

"Concussion," I told myself. "Stay awake."

I dropped to my knees and crawled into the lake. I splashed water onto my face. It was cold and I began to shiver. Finally, I lay on my back in the water and watched the sun behind the trees. I stopped weeping and started a long, rambling conversation with myself, discussing whether or not the Timberwolves had the depth to go the distance this season, if the Vikings had finally learned how to defend against the run, what it would take to bring peace to the Middle East, if I had a future with Nina Truhler. I talked to myself for a long time.

Eventually, the nausea and dizziness subsided—my mind cleared. I tried to stand. My knees creaked and my back demanded relief, which I attempted to provide with pressure from both hands. I walked only slightly upright to my SUV. The door was hanging open. It took what was left of my strength to climb in and pull the door shut. The bleeding had stopped long ago—I worried about stitches. Only instead of doing the smart thing and driving to a hospital, I went home. I would rather die in bed.

The light from the refrigerator stung my eyes. I had thought a glass of milk might help relieve the throbbing in my head and settle my queasy stomach. Yeah, right. It was so cold my brain froze—I damn near passed out on my tile floor. Eventually, I made my way upstairs, the house lights off, moving by touch and habit alone. I removed my jacket, shoes, and gun, but stripping off the rest of my wet clothes didn't seem worth the effort.

Later that night I found myself wide awake, shuddering at the thunder and lightning and high wind that shook the trees outside the window. I was surprised but not fearful when a young woman with golden hair crept silently into my bedroom, her white gown shimmering with a light that seemed to come from within. She sat on the edge of my mattress and patted my hands that were holding the blankets tight to my throat. I couldn't make out her face. She told me not to be afraid, that the storm wouldn't harm me, that she wouldn't allow it. She told me my trials would soon be over. She said she was proud of me. I asked her name. In reply she bent to kiss me. As our lips touched I awoke with a start to find that my room was empty and the night was still.

To this day, I don't know if it was Jamie Bruder's apparition that had appeared to me, or my mother's.

14

The mid-morning sun was streaming through the bedroom windows as I stood naked in front of the full-length mirror, inspecting the damage inflicted by Devanter, furious that I had allowed him to toss me around like a lawn dart.

"It's not the size of the dog in a fight that matters, it's the size of the fight in the dog," I said out loud, which was still another of the lessons my father had attempted to teach me. Standing there, examining the bruises that spotted my body like an ugly connect-the-dots puzzle, I decided Dad was full of it. I also vowed that no one would ever beat on me like that again.

Everything hurt—my spine, my hip, both shoulders, neck, my head especially. The cut under my hairline wasn't nearly as bad as I had originally thought, only an inch long and not very deep. I doubted it would leave a scar. I also was surprised that no black-and-blue splotches marred my face. Since the other bruises would be easily concealed under clothes, I was starting to think that, all things considered, I looked pretty good. Until my eyes wandered to the other places on my body where errors in judgment had left their mark—a scar on my thigh, another at the point of my shoulder, the nickel-size spot above my right ear where hair will never grow again. Maybe Kirsten was right. Maybe I should try to get a job with the Minnesota Opera Company.

I spent a long time in the bathroom cleaning myself up. I tried not to think. Thinking gave me a headache. So did tossing corn to the ducks. The mere act of wheeling my recyclables to the curb caused my entire body to tremble with pain, my back especially. I went for a walk. I was afraid if I sat down I wouldn't have the strength to get up again.

I strolled through St. Anthony Park like I didn't have a care in the world, like people weren't trying to kill me. I made my way east, past Murray Junior High School, to the St. Paul campus of the University of Minnesota and south to a small park filled with children and young mothers who eschewed the just-put-your-kids-in-daycare work ethic currently popular in the land. I watched the mothers watching their children and thought of Jamie. *No, don't do that,* I admonished myself. *Don't think.*

To divert my attention, I turned north, found a tennis court, and stopped to watch a pair of college kids. But that only made me feel old as well as out of shape. I meandered to the corner. As the traffic light switched to yellow, I heard the hard acceleration of a vehicle. I glanced up and saw a black van shooting through the intersection just as the yellow went red. It wasn't even a Chevy, yet I was on the ground just the same, hiding my head behind the light pole.

"This is going to stop," I vowed.

I hurried home and changed into my work clothes—Nikes, blue jeans, white shirt with button-down collar, sport coat, and Beretta. I popped a couple of aspirins and installed myself in the office. I spread my notes across my desk—the ones I had addressed to Bobby Dunston and the others in the event of my sudden departure from this earth—and studied them as I sipped my coffee. Who killed Jamie Carlson Bruder? And Katherine Katzmark? And Napoleon Cook? And David Bruder? Why were the Family Boyz trying to kill me? So many questions. So few answers.

I put some Rolling Stones on the CD player and decided they were too distracting, I couldn't concentrate. I replaced them with Bill Evans, whose mellow piano more closely fit my mood. I fired up my PC and searched the file on my hard drive. Nothing. I studied my notes some more. I played with the facts I had gathered, rolled them into a ball, bounced them on the floor and off the walls before smoothing them out again. After a couple of hours I realized that I kept coming back to the same thing. My business card. The one I had given Jamie. The one the Minneapolis cops found on Cook. How did he get it? Did Jamie give it to him? Why would she do that? Maybe she didn't. I had left the card on the patio table. Jamie said that her husband was bringing a business associate home for drinks—around the pool! Maybe Cook found it there. Maybe he palmed it. Palmed it because it proved that Jamie was talking to someone she shouldn't be . . .

A knock at the door. I was careful when I answered it. A courier with a special delivery. The courier was legit. I hid the gun behind my back as I signed for the package, an outsize envelope. I opened the envelope and found a hand-addressed, gilt-edged invitation to the Northern Lights Entrepreneur's Club Ball. The names of the eight founding members were listed on the inside in alphabetical order. And at last, I understood.

"McKenzie, a pleasure to hear from you," Charlotte Belloti said when she answered the telephone.

"I hope I'm not disturbing you."

"No, but that certainly can be arranged." Her giggle had a sort of sad ring to it this time around, or maybe it was the way I heard it. I wondered for a moment if Charlotte knew that her husband was cheating on her.

"As it turns out, I'm going to the Entrepreneur's Ball after all. I was wondering if I would see you there."

"Yes, I'll be there," she told me.

"How about your husband? Is he still in Russia?"

"As a matter of fact, I just spoke to him not ten minutes ago. He's in Montreal with these ex-commie Russian capitalists—at least that's what he calls them. He said he won't be home until late, late, late tonight, sometime after the ball, anyway. So, you lucky dog, I'll be all yours."

"There's a thought," I said, and Charlotte giggled some more.

Thirty minutes later I found Merci Cole. She was dressed in the same white and black outfit, sitting on the same stool at the same bar and conversing with the same bartender as the evening I had first met her. Only the ice in her rum and Coke was different.

She swore between clenched teeth as I approached.

"What do you want?"

"You."

"David's dead." Her tone accused me.

"I know."

"You bastard."

"Cut it out."

"He went to you for help."

"How do you know?"

"Just keep away from me."

"Stop it."

"I said get away from me."

"You heard the lady," the bartender said.

"This is a private conversation, okay, pal?"

"Beat it, chump."

"Don't mess with me today," I told him. "I'm in a real bad mood."

"I got this for your mood." He reached under the bar and came up with a miniature baseball bat, the kind the vendors hawk at the Metrodome during Twins games. I didn't wait to see whose autograph was on it. I yanked the Beretta from its holster—I'd be damned if I'd let someone hit me again—and slapped it down hard on the bartop. The noise startled him. The bartender dropped the bat and backed away, waving his hands in front of him like he was saying no to a second helping of pie.

Merci stared at me, trembling with anger.

"I think I know who killed Jamie and David and all the others and I think I know why," I told her. "I need you to help me put them on the spot."

"Who?"

"I'll explain that later. Right now—look, you're a businesswoman. You work for money. I'll pay you one hundred dollars an hour. What time is it?" I looked for a clock. "Three-thirty? Start now and go until— call it midnight. Nine hundred bucks. Make it an even thousand. Plus, I'll pay all expenses."

"What expenses?"

"Gown, shoes, getting your hair done—we'll have to hurry. We're going to a fancy dress ball."

"Why?"

"Because that's where the bad guys are. Are you in?"

"I don't know," Merci said.

"I'm going to get those sonsuvbitches. Are you in?"

"I need to make a phone call first."

"Call whoever you like."

Merci went quickly to the pay phone attached to the wall between the two rest rooms. She returned five minutes later.

"I have my own gown," she told me. "With matching shoes and bag. It used to belong to Jamie. She gave it to me after TC was born."

Merci shouted at me through the door of what used to be my father's bedroom.

"Why are we doing this?"

"You'll see," I told her as I fumbled with my black bow tie. What was I going to say? I'm using you for bait?

"You know, I never wore this dress before," she called out. I could relate. I had worn my double-breasted tuxedo only a half dozen times in the past five years—most of those times with Kirsten. I had never learned how to tie a bow tie and instead used one of those pre-tied jobs with a strap that winds around your collar and hooks under your throat.

I shoved the Beretta .380 into the holster under my left arm then slipped the tuxedo jacket over it.

"What time do we need to be there?"

Ahh, damn. This was no good. I couldn't use her, hooker or no, not like this. I went to the door. Rapped on it gently with a knuckle.

"Yes?"

I rested my head on the closed door while I explained what I thought I knew and why we were going to the party. I concluded by telling Merci, "It could be dangerous. Probably will be. Eight people have been killed already. If you want out, I'll pay the grand I owe you and we'll call it a night."

Merci didn't answer. I called her name.

"Come in."

I opened the door cautiously. Merci was on the far side of the room, staring at a woman in the full-length mirror. The woman staring back was modeling a long gown of iridescent raspberry lace that hugged her curves from shoulders to ankles. Long sleeves, scoop neckline, a thigh-high side slit that caused my heart to skip several beats. Merci tugged gently at the fabric.

"It's a little snug," she said.

"Works for me," I admitted.

"I'm pretty, aren't I? I'm a pretty girl."

"More than pretty."

"I'm as pretty as Jamie was."

I saw it then. And wondered why I hadn't seen it before.

She spun around to face me. "My life should have been so different than the one I'm living. Jamie understood that. Better than anyone. She wanted me to have the life I had been cheated out of but it wasn't hers to give." Her voice cracked and a sob escaped her throat. Merci turned away from me, but only for a few moments. When she turned back her voice was steady and her eyes were clear.

I thought of Stacy and said, "Let's rethink this."

"No, let's not." In case I wanted to argue, she added, "When do we leave?"

"I thought we'd have dinner first and arrive fashionably late."

Animal rights activists were chanting slogans outside the entrance to the Minnesota Club in downtown St. Paul where the region's best and brightest entrepreneurs had gone to celebrate themselves. It was an interesting performance. Minnesota protesters are way too nice to attack fur wearers with spray paint and plastic bags filled with blood. Here they're usually content with polite heckling. "Get a flea collar."

The entrepreneurs taunted back. "Get a life."

"Do you know how many animals died to make your coat?"

"Do you know how many animals died to make your lunch?"

All in all, everyone was having a wonderful time.

Beyond the protesters was a long line of limousines, some white, some silver, most black—a few of them actually parked legally. Devanter was leaning against the fender of one, cupping an unfiltered cigarette in his left hand, shaking his head at the southeast-Asian drivers who congregated around a limo identical to his half a block up. He was muttering loudly to himself.

"You believe it? The gooks in this state. You'd think a good Minnesota winter'd send 'em back to the paddies."

When he saw us he dropped the smoke and took a step backward. Only it wasn't me who startled him. He was staring at Merci.

Merci turned her head to look at him as we passed by. Devanter tried to say something but nothing came out. We left him standing there, his mouth hanging open.

The Minnesota Club was built in 1915 and remains one of the oldest structures in downtown St. Paul. It used to be an exclusive hideaway where rich old men would go to decide the future of the city and state over a snifter of brandy and a good cigar. Rumor had it that in the twenties the members maintained a tunnel that led to the back door of Nina Clifford's elegant and terribly expensive bordello barely a block away. Personally, I believe the rumor to be true. Especially since a portrait identified as that of the lady in question—a black-haired beauty in a silver-gray dress—hangs prominently on the wall of the club's main bar. And then there's the plaque attached to a red-brown brick salvaged from the ruins of Clifford's brothel that reads, "This brick from Nina Clifford's house is presented to the Gentlemen of the Minnesota Club for their great interest in historic buildings."

Things have changed since the second decade of the last century, of course—for better or worse, you tell me—and now the Minnesota Club is available as a banquet hall for meetings, school proms, wedding receptions, and bar mitzvahs. The Northern Lights Entrepreneur's Club had engaged four full floors of the eighty-seven-year-old building and still the yuppies were wall to wall. People flowed single file through the crowd, moving from floor to floor and ballroom to ballroom like a meandering river, searching for faces they knew and then stopping when they found some, forcing the river to alter course around them. The only comparatively empty space was in the center of the large ballrooms, away from the bars and power corners, an eye of calm surrounded by storm. That's where Merci and I found ourselves, deposited by the current shortly after presenting my invitation to the tuxedo-clad security guards at the door.

I like big parties, the bigger the better. No one asks personal questions at big parties. If you work it right, you can maintain a high degree of popularity without ever needing to reveal a single detail about yourself simply by trading one group for another whenever you exhaust your twenty minutes of humorous small talk.

I spun slowly around, taking in the room. Every man wore a tuxedo, every woman was dressed in a gown. Compared to what some of the women wore, Merci's raspberry lace dress looked like a dust rag. Merci remained unimpressed.

"A lot of thousand-dollar-a-night whores here."

"Seriously?"

"Want me to introduce you to a few?"

"No, thank you." I didn't quite believe her until a comely young woman holding up a strapless gold-lamé gown with her chest approached.

"Moving up in the world, huh, Cole?" Her dark brown hair was cut in cascading curls. She shook it as she brushed past us, hanging onto the arm of a man who was a full head shorter than she was. Merci smiled and nodded in return.

"Love your hair." When the brunette flowed out of earshot she added, "I have a wig at home that looks just like it."

I continued to watch until the woman disappeared into the crowd. *You can buy anything these days.*

"What do we do now?" Merci asked.

"Locate our host."

"Are you sure he's here?"

"His ride is."

We collected a couple of glasses half filled with champagne from a silver tray that was being circulated by a woman who looked way too young to drink, and plunged back into the river. A band played country-western music on the lower floor, but no one danced—the guests all seemed more interested in the strategically placed bars. The huge main floor featured a rock-and-roll band that leaned heavily on golden oldies and everyone seemed to be dancing. The light and airy second-floor ballroom—which used to be the ladies' dining room back when women were forbidden to eat in public with their men—boasted a Count Basie–style jazz orchestra. There seemed to be more people on the second floor than anywhere else. Charlotte Belloti was among them, grooving to the sound on the edge of the hardwood dance floor, spilling champagne in time to "It Don't Mean a Thing (If It Ain't Got That Swing)."

I found an unoccupied space against the wall and asked Merci to wait for me. "Try not to be conspicuous," I told her. My fear was that Casselman would see her before we saw him. Several people had already looked long and hard at Merci as we passed through the crowd. I didn't know if they recognized her as Jamie—looking like Jamie in Jamie's dress—or as one of the few truly beautiful people at the party. In a previous life, with that gown, with her golden hair piled high, she might have passed for a 1940s movie star, she could have been Jean Harlow. At worst, she would have been a nice addition to Nina Clifford's stable of elegant "sporting girls."

"Hi," I said to Charlotte as she danced. When she didn't hear, I loudly called out her name and tapped her shoulder.

Charlotte swung around, stared dumbly, blinked a few times, recognized me, and cried gleefully, "McKennnnnnzzzzziiiiieeeee." She hugged my neck and kissed my cheek like I was a long-lost friend at a high school reunion. "It's so gooood to see youuuuuu."

I returned the hug and stepped back. Charlotte was wearing a short black velvet dress with an off-the-shoulder neckline bordered by ostrich feathers. The skirt ended at midthigh and had an off-center slit that revealed six more inches. Frankly, she didn't have the legs for it, but just the same I said, "Looking good, Charlotte."

"Oh, this ratty old thing . . ."

"I see you're having fun."

"No, I'm not. I'm not having fun at all. No one will dance with me. Dance with me, McKenzie."

"Maybe later. Is your husband here?"

"Ohhh pooh," she said. "Whaddaya gotta bring him up for? He ain't never comin' home."

"Never?"

"Oh, he's still up in Canada. He said he's flying in with the commies later tonight. He said not to wait up, so you know what that means?"

"What does that mean?"

"Goose for the gander," she said.

I was momentarily confused. "Excuse me?"

"What's good for the goose is good for the gander." She enunciated her words carefully even as she grabbed the lapels of my tuxedo jacket and pulled me down to her face. "Dance with me, McKenzie," she whispered into my ear.

"I'm looking for Casselman."

She bit my ear.

"Let's go outside and make love in a limo. Wouldn't that be fun? I'll let you call me Charlie."

Doesn't anyone in this crowd sleep with their own spouse in their own bed?

I bussed her cheek. "Come to me when you're cold sober and we'll discuss it."

"Ahhh, cripes, an honorable man. I don't need an honorable man. I need a dishonorable man. That's what Geno is. Dis-honorable. He's cheating on me, you know."

"No, I didn't," I lied.

"Go away, McKenzie. Go, go talk to Warren, he's . . ." Charlotte waved toward the back of the room, dismissing me and returning to her solo dance.

After renegotiating the human traffic, I found Merci smiling brightly, her arms folded across her chest, her back against the wall. A man was leaning toward her, holding himself up with one hand, the hand planted firmly above Merci's shoulder. He was talking earnestly and gesturing with the mixed drink he held in his other hand.

"Honey, this nice man has just invited me to a private hot tub party at his townhouse," Merci said when I reached her side.

"Really? Can I watch?"

"What? No! I mean—never mind," the man stammered before turning tail and escaping into the crowd.

"What was it you wanted to show me?" Merci called after him.

"Who was he?" I asked.

"Just another man with money in his hand."

Warren Casselman was not on the other side of the room as Charlotte Belloti had indicated. He was on a different floor altogether, the third floor, which was mostly taken up by offices and sleeping rooms and not generally open to the public. Still, there was a large knot of people gathered on the landing, presumably trying to escape the high volume of noise generated by the various bands for a few moments of quiet social intercourse. Casselman was at the far end, engaged in a feverish conversation with the other three surviving founders of the Northern Lights Entrepreneur's Club.

"That's him," I whispered to Merci. "The man with his back to us."

She nodded.

"You're on," I said.

"Wait, I need a prop." Merci glanced quickly side to side, saw still another young woman toting still another tray of half-filled champagne glasses up the staircase. She took one. I moved away, stationing myself at the top of the stairs, hiding among the other tuxedos gathered there.

Merci positioned herself five feet behind Casselman and stared at the back of his head. She stood like that for several moments. Eventually, the man I recognized as Brian Mellgren said something to Casselman and motioned toward Merci with his chin. Casselman spun slowly.

"Good evening, Mr. Casselman," Merci said.

Casselman's eyes swept over Merci's body like a searchlight sweeping the coast. He smiled broadly and so did the other Entrepreneurs—all except Mellgren, who squinted suspiciously.

Merci sipped the champagne.

"Have we met?" Casselman asked in a quiet voice.

"I don't know, have we?"

Casselman licked his lips. "You remind me of a friend."

"Jamie Carlson? No? That's right, you would have known her as Jamie Bruder."

"Yes, Jamie."

"My best friend," Merci said. "This is her dress. We used to swap clothes. Best friends do that. Something else best friends do, they talk. We always told each other everything."

"She told you . . ."

"Everything." Merci nodded to the other Entrepreneurs, reciting the names I had given her. "Mr. Kamp, Mr. Whelpley, Mr. Mellgren. Where oh where is Geno Belloti this evening? Still in St. Petersburg? No, he must be in Canada by now."

"What are you talking about?" Mellgren demanded to know. He moved toward Merci. Casselman grabbed his arm, restraining him. Merci didn't budge an inch. She was playing her part extremely well. I was proud of her.

"Temper, temper, Mr. Mellgren. There's no need for that. I'd be delighted to tell you what I know. Only it'll cost you. 'Course, you're not my only source of income. I understand the ATF and FBI offer rewards for information about people like you."

All four men stood perfectly still. I think they were in shock.

"Gentlemen, do I hear an offer?"

Mellgren made another move for her. Again Casselman held him back.

"It's a party," he said.

"And a very swank do, it is." Merci was grinning, having just a wonderful time.

"Only not conducive for conducting business," Casselman said. "Perhaps we can discuss this matter later? Where can we find you?"

"I'll find you." Merci tilted her head graciously—"Gentlemen"— and slipped back into the river of people. Mellgren wanted to follow her, but once again Casselman held his arm.

"Now what?" Merci asked when I rejoined her on the second floor.

"Now we wait."

"I still don't understand."

"It's very simple," I told her. "They killed Jamie because they were afraid she told me something. They tried to kill me for the same reason. And now . . ."

"They'll come for me."

"That's right. But this time I'll be waiting."

"Then what?"

"We'll see." So much violence in the past ten days and here I was, inviting more.

Merci shook her head just as she had done earlier that evening when I explained my intentions. "Doesn't sound like much of a plan."

"It has the virtue of simplicity," I assured her—and myself.

"Just so you know. I won't die the way Jamie died."

"Amen to that."

I took Merci Cole's hand and led her toward the stairway. Neither of us felt like remaining for the rest of the festivities. The way my back ached I could barely stand as it was. Only at the top of the staircase I was stopped by a female voice calling my name. I recognized it immediately.

Nina Truhler was smiling at me. She wore a long, sleek, searing red tank-dress with tiny beads all over that glittered in the light when she moved, and for a few moments I forgot my pain, forgot where I was and what I was doing.

The words came out in a rush. "You are absolutely stunning."

Nina bowed her head. "Thank you, sir. And may I say that your appearance has improved greatly since last we met."

"It's a new diet."

I released Merci's hand and moved toward Nina, halting a few paces short when a tall man standing behind Nina set a hand on her shoulder. Nina didn't seem to mind the familiarity. She tilted her head up and he spoke into her ear.

"I'll be there in a minute," Nina told him.

The man was at least ten years Nina's junior—which also meant he was ten years younger than me. When he moved away I said, "Your date?"

Nina smiled brightly. "Jealous?"

"I have no right to be, but, yeah. I'm jealous. Isn't that amazing?"

"I like it."

Nina leaned close to my ear. "He's just a friend, I promise. I came here tonight with two vans full of friends. Besides, he has the emotional maturity of asphalt."

"Some women like that."

"Puhleez."

"You do look wonderful." I had been smiling constantly since I first saw her and my mouth was beginning to hurt.

"Thank you again." She took my arm. "I'm surprised to see you here. For some reason I didn't think it was your kind of scene."

"I'm working."

"When do you get off?"

I snickered at that. Suddenly my back didn't seem so sore.

"Are you alone?"

"No." I turned to introduce Merci. "I'm here with . . ." Only Merci Cole had vanished.

I called her name.

"Dammit."

"What is it?"

"Dammit, dammit, dammit."

"What's wrong, McKenzie?"

"The woman who was with me. She was wearing a raspberry-colored dress." I stood on my tiptoes, trying to see above the heads of all the other guests. An impossible task. "Do you see her?"

"I saw a woman with blond hair . . ."

"Where?"

Nina seemed to catch some of the fear in my voice. She pointed at the staircase. I went quickly toward it. The tide of people slammed me right and left, up and down, like flotsam caught in surf. I finally reached the railing and looked down. The top of Merci's blond head was bobbing away from me. She was between two men. Whelpley and Kamp. They were holding her arms tightly, pulling her along. Her face was pale against the color of her dress.

They are moving quicker than I thought they would.

I dove into the river, trying to fight the current, working my way down the stairs. Merci was at the door now. I pushed harder, flailing guests with my hands and elbows and lame excuse-me's. They were dragging Merci out the door when I heard my name.

I pivoted and looked back up the staircase. Mellgren was standing at the top. His right hand was inside his jacket.

"Stop where you are, McKenzie," he called to me.

I ignored him. What was he going to do? Shoot me in front of a thousand witnesses?

"Stop, I said!" He started down the steps quickly but something happened. Suddenly, Mellgren's empty hand swept out from under his coat and over his head, his body spun in a half circle, and he seemed to dive, head first, down the staircase, crashing against this body and that, knocking over at least four guests, finally slamming into a woman in an ivory dress, landing and rolling on top of her. Screams followed.

Mellgren's unexpected tumble caused me to look past him. At the top of the steps stood Nina, her palms turned upward in innocence, her eyes wide, and a most delightful "who, me?" expression on her face.

She had tripped him.

I blew Nina a kiss and moved on.

The swirling tide grew increasingly stronger as people stopped to see what the commotion on the stairs was all about. It took me a long time to get to the door—too long—and when I did, Merci Cole was nowhere in sight. I pushed past the protesters and searched the street, noting that Devanter and Casselman's limo were gone. I had a very bad feeling about that. I reclimbed the concrete steps of the Minnesota

Club, stopping at the top. There. On the other side of the public library building. Three men dressed in tuxedos were pushing Merci Cole into the back of a limousine—not Casselman's, someone else's.

I felt like the guy who got his fingers caught in the mousetrap while setting the cheese.

15

Ass. Bastard. Creep. I called myself every name in the book in alphabetical order as I rushed to my car. Dimwit. Excrement. Fool. Fortunately, every time the luxury car rounded a corner it was slowed by a traffic light. That gave me enough time to muscle the Jeep Cherokee between and around the traffic, speed through the signals and sneak behind the limo as it entered I-35E below the St. Paul Cathedral, going south. Geek. Halfwit. Imbecile.

I-35E in that part of town is only two lanes wide and lightly traveled. It was easy to tail the black limousine while hanging way back. We drove past old suburbs and new suburbs and soon-to-be suburbs, putting over thirty miles between us and the city, speeding south into farm country. The temperature had dropped to fifty-three degrees and I was worried that dressed only in lace Merci would be cold. Like that was her most urgent problem. Meanwhile, I was sweating.

Finally, the limo caught an exit and hung a left, traveling east on a county road just below Lakeville. I chased the limo's red tail-lights, hanging back as far as I dared. The car went three miles east before turning off onto a dirt road that led into the forest. I followed. I lost the limo's lights in the road's twists and turns but that was all right—there didn't seem to be any turnoffs. I continued to hang back, following the road—and the limo's dust—for several miles. I ignored a spur that jutted off in a right angle from the road, then realized when the dust cleared and I was forced to stop for a fallen tree about a half mile beyond it that the limo must have taken the spur. I drove backwards until I discovered a place to turn the Cherokee around near the spur. It was there that I abandoned it—I thought it was safer to investigate the spur on foot.

At first you notice the quiet. Then your ears adjust and you realize that it's not quiet at all. You begin to hear sounds that rarely register in the city—birds and insects and wind blowing through the leaves. I waited next to the Cherokee until my eyes adjusted to the moonlight. When finally I moved, I moved slowly, carefully, holding the collar of my black jacket closed over the white shirt. I tried to remember the lessons my father taught me as a child, the "hunter's rules" about surviving in the forest. I could recall only one. *Stay the hell out of the woods after dark.* A man could disappear in the woods at night, Dad had warned.

I was startled by the *hoot-hoot* of an owl, hesitated, spun around, and jogged back to the SUV. I unlocked the passenger door, reached under the seat and retrieved the hand grenade I had hidden there after my adventure with the Family Boyz. I should have locked it in my safe, but I never got around to it. Now I slipped it into my pocket. It made me feel safer.

I followed the spur for a tenth of a mile. It reminded me of the little-used logging roads that crisscross the woods near my property up north, but I was unaware of any logging operations this close to the Cities. I marched on. Were those my footsteps? I paused to listen, but then pushed on. This was taking way too much time. Merci was in danger and I had put her there. Yet at the same time I didn't want to be careless. Careless would get us both killed.

I finally came to a tight bend in the road. Beyond the bend was the glimmer of a distant light. I left the spur and walked into the woods, trying to sneak up on it. I went about ten feet and tripped over a pile of garbage some environmentally-conscious individual had dumped there. It was a big pile, filled with cans, bottles, disposable diapers. I brushed the debris from my tuxedo. Some people just refuse to recycle.

I circled the garbage and discovered still another road, this one even less traveled than the spur. It led me closer to the light, but I froze when the moon flickered off something metallic fifty yards ahead of me. I waited, listened. I heard no sound so I crept forward. There it was again. Another flash of light on metal. A gun? I had no way of knowing. To be safe, I drifted to my left. So did the reflection.

I slipped the Beretta out of its holster and moved in a crouch toward it. I relaxed only slightly when I realized I was stalking a car, the moon playing off its trim and windshield. The car was much too small to be the limousine. It wasn't until I ran my fingers over the vehicle's front grille that I recognized it. Stalin's Jag, backed in and facing the spur, ready for a quick getaway. The doors were unlocked.

My first impulse was to foul the ignition so the Jag couldn't be started. Then I had a better idea. I crept back to the pile of garbage, almost missing it in the dark, and rummaged through it until I found an empty Campbell's soup can, bean with bacon, mm-mm good. I kept sifting until I found a suitable length of thick string that someone might have used to tie a package. I returned to the Jag and opened the door. The car's interior light gave me enough to work by.

I jammed the can into the opening between the front seat and the floor, working as quickly as I could. Next, I tied one end of the string to the neck of the grenade. I slid the grenade into the soup can. It fit snugly. Sitting inside the car, just above the grenade, I secured the other end of the string to the car door. Next came the tricky part. Lying across the seat, I eased the grenade just far enough out of the can to grasp the pin. I removed it gently. Held by the wall of the soup can, the lever did not detach, the fuse did not ignite.

I hurried out of the passenger door of the Jag, closing it quickly and quietly behind me, and jogged into the woods. I stopped and waited until my breath returned to normal. When I assured myself that an explosion was not imminent, I again moved toward the beacon I had first seen from the road. A few minutes later I reached the edge of a large clearing.

I could see the light clearly now. It hung from a high post about twenty yards in front of a metal shed that could have been a small airplane hangar. Several vehicles were parked around the structure, including two flatbed trucks and two black Chevy vans. The large door to the shed was open. Bright lights shined inside. I could clearly see a limousine. I crawled along the tree line to position myself for a better look, my aching back protesting every inch of the way. There were several figures loitering in front of the vehicle, but I didn't recognize any of them until a tall thin black man roughly pulled a woman from the back seat of the limo. She was dressed in raspberry lace, her golden hair piled high on her head. Merci protested, but Stalin didn't care. He said something to her and then shoved her back inside the car.

At least she's all right, I told myself. Aloud I whispered, "This is not good."

"No, it's not," a shadow whispered back.

The chill that ran up my spine could have frozen ice cream. Someone put a heavy knee in the small of my back—just what I needed— and brushed my cheek with the cold muzzle of snub-nosed .38.

"Not a sound," the shadow whispered. He took the Beretta from my hand and passed it to another shadow behind him. Both of them pulled me to my feet, each taking one arm.

"Come with us and keep your mouth shut," the first shadow told me. I did what he said. I didn't know who they were, but I knew they couldn't be Stalin's people. If they were Stalin's people, I would have been dead by now and no one would have cared how much noise it took to kill me.

The two men hustled me to the spur, down the spur to the dirt road and across the road into the woods on the far side. Neither spoke.

We hiked for twenty minutes through the underbrush. I was the only one making noise—the other two seemed to know the location of every twig, root, or branch that I tripped over or ran into. My damaged body protested their rough treatment but I tried mightily to keep from crying out—I had a reputation to protect, after all. Unfortunately, my body betrayed me and several low grunts escaped my clenched teeth.

"You're such a whiner, McKenzie," one of the men told me.

Finally, we broke into a small clearing filled with men, maybe two dozen of them, who flinched visibly when we emerged from the underbrush. They all carried automatic weapons, M-16s mostly, plus a smattering of shotguns, and they all wore nylon jackets with big, bright letters on the front and back over their dull body armor. Some of the letters read ATF. Some read FBI.

My companions led me to where two men stood, reading a map spread across the hood of a vehicle with a red-filtered light. "Look at what we found." Both men turned in unison.

"Who the hell are you supposed to be, James Bond?" asked the smaller of the two, the one I had dubbed Harry Dean Stanton.

"I told you," said the man I knew as Alec Baldwin. "That's ten bucks you owe me."

"Yeah, yeah, yeah," said Harry as he reluctantly flipped through several folded bills he fished from his pocket until he found the correct denomination.

"We weren't properly introduced," Alec said. "I'm Bullert. He's Wilson."

I preferred the names I had given them.

"So, tell me, McKenzie," said Alec as he took the ten from Harry and shoved it into his pocket. "What brings you to this neck of the woods?"

"It was such a nice evening, I thought I'd take a stroll."

"You know something, McKenzie?" said Harry. "This is the only thing you've done that I didn't anticipate."

I looked from one to the other and then at the small knots of agents waiting in the clearing.

"I have a feeling you guys have been playing me like a violin ever since this thing began. Want to tell me what's going on?"

"It gets complicated," said Alec as his agent handed my gun to him.

"It doesn't look like I'm going anywhere."

"My partner says you're pretty smart," said Harry. "I think you rely too much on bluff and muscle. Why don't you tell us what you think you know."

"Warren Casselman and his pals are gunrunners," I said. "They buy discarded Warsaw Pact ordnance from former Russian communists and smuggle it into Minnesota using their various businesses—Belloti, CK Computers, Mellgren's, Katherine Katzmark's Worldware. I saw their crates and cartons in Stalin's crib. Stalin and the Family Boyz handle distribution and muscle. You can jump in at any time."

"You're doing fine," Alec said. "I told you he was good."

"Dumb luck," said Harry.

"David Bruder probably used his used car lots to help launder the money—he wouldn't be the first car salesman to do it. Jamie Carlson Bruder had worked for his attorneys—maybe she found out about it and threatened to blow the whistle. Or maybe she didn't. The point is, Napoleon Cook learned that Jamie was talking with a former cop and panicked. Cook was a nervous guy. He probably told Stalin that they were all going to prison unless something was done. Stalin killed Jamie or had her killed after torturing her to find out what's what. Then he came after me. I'm guessing Bruder grabbed his son and went on the run to avoid the same fate. When he came out of hiding, the Boyz killed him."

"Oh yeah, he's Einstein," Harry told Alec.

"He got most of it right."

"I want my ten bucks back."

"What did I miss?" I asked.

"You're correct about the Entrepreneurs and the Family Boyz," said Alec. "They've been selling arms for about five years, now. In fact, their operation has become so lucrative for the Boyz that they gave up their daytime job."

"Dealing grass from Mexico," I interjected.

"But September Eleventh changed all that. Suddenly, these fine, upstanding citizens are wondering if they've been subsidizing Osama, if the weapons they buy and sell are going to terrorist groups like al-Qaida. Apparently, the thought had never occurred to them before. In any case, they held a vote—very democratic, our Entrepreneurs. Six to two they voted to get out of the arms smuggling business, with only Belloti and Mellgren in the minority. But they forgot their partners. Stalin and the Family Boyz voted to stay. They also voted that the Entrepreneurs stay, too. The Entrepreneurs didn't like it, but what could they do? Stalin, as I'm sure you've noticed, can be very persuasive."

"Only Katherine Katzmark wouldn't go for it," Harry said. "She walked into my office without an appointment one morning, sat down, and told me everything. She wasn't looking to make a deal, didn't ask for immunity. She was willing to take whatever punishment she received. She had seen the Twin Towers fall on TV and she figured she deserved whatever happened to her. I always admired her for that. Anyway, we called the ATF. . . ."

"We were already on it," Alec assured me. "We knew through our sources in Bonn that Geno Belloti was using his import-export packaging company to move surplus weapons . . ."

"But they didn't know about the rest of the Entrepreneurs or the Family Boyz," Harry said. "We supplied that intel."

"We'll be sure to invite you to the office Christmas party," Alec told him.

"The Boyz and the Entrepreneurs were easy," Harry said. "We could have busted them anytime."

"But you also wanted the Russians," I guessed.

"To get them, we used Katherine," Alec said. "The relationship between the Entrepreneurs and the Family Boyz was strained, to say the least. We convinced Katherine to suggest a solution that would satisfy both parties. Arrange a face-to-face between the Russians and the Family Boyz. They could then negotiate purchase and distribution between them. If they decided to continue using Belloti and Mellgren as mules, fine, but the other Entrepreneurs could then be eased out. That way Stalin no longer had to worry about keeping them in line and he could keep more of the profits. Plus, Stalin gets to be an 'international'"— Alec quoted the air—"'arms dealer.' Believe me when I tell you he liked that idea very much."

"Oh, I believe it."

"The Russians, unfortunately, didn't like the idea," Harry said. "Working directly with a black street gang? They couldn't think of anything more absurd. Except possibly losing their lucrative North American market, and that's what Casselman convinced them would happen if they didn't take the meeting. So, they agreed. Stalin is practically having an orgasm over it."

"If he's so happy, why did he kill Katherine?"

"He didn't."

"We thought he did," said Alec. "We thought Katherine's cover had been blown and Stalin had her tortured for what she could tell him. But listening to our wiretaps—Stalin was as shocked about Katherine's murder as the Entrepreneurs. What's more, both parties were determined not to allow it to compromise their business arrangements. If they had killed Katherine because she was an informant, would they talk like that?"

"Then Jamie was killed," I added.

"And the conversations between the Entrepreneurs and the Boyz increased in volume. Does that make sense?"

"If Stalin didn't kill Katherine and Jamie, who did?"

"We thought it was Bruder," Harry said. "According to our taps, so did both Stalin and the Entrepreneurs. The way that clown Thompson talked to the media, Bruder was all but convicted."

"But Bruder didn't do it."

"We know that now."

"Who did?"

"We don't know," answered Alec. "And as callous as it might sound, we don't care. That's your pal Detective Sergeant Robert J. Dunston's job."

"He's pretty good," said Harry. "What he lacks in imagination he makes up for in tenacity. He'll figure it out."

"I don't understand," I admitted. "If Stalin and the Entrepreneurs weren't concerned that Jamie was informing on them, why did they try to kill me?"

"You were right about Cook. He did some checking after finding your business card. According to our intercepts, he told the Family Boyz that you were 'some kind of cop.' That was enough for Stalin. You have to appreciate that after Katherine's murder, they all became paranoid."

"Why was Cook killed?"

"You tell us," said Harry.

"Same reason, I guess. Cook was a weak sister. He fingered me for Stalin but Stalin couldn't put me down. When I showed up unexpectedly to hassle him, Cook panicked and Stalin became afraid he'd turn."

"Okay," Harry told Alec. "You can keep the ten bucks."

"But why tell me that Bruder was right-handed, that he didn't kill his wife? Why did you want me to keep pushing?"

"We knew the meeting with the Russians had been scheduled," Harry admitted. "But we didn't know when or where. Katherine was killed before she could tell us. Your involvement—your insistence on connecting the Boyz to the murders—kept the parties talking. Each time you survived an assassination attempt the phones would ring off the hook. We hoped that sooner or later one of those conversations would provide us with the intel we needed. And it did."

"You used me."

"Your government is grateful for your assistance in this matter."

"Ahh, stick it."

"You did a good job," Alec told me.

"Sure. So what happens now?"

Harry studied the illuminated dial of his watch. "Thirty-five minutes?" he asked a shadow near him.

The shadow replied, "They entered U.S. airspace forty-six minutes ago. ETA thirty-seven minutes."

"What happens now is that in thirty-seven minutes we are going to scoop up the Entrepreneurs and the Family Boyz and the Russians and approximately two dozen cases of automatic weapons and ammunition left over from the Cold War and put them in our pocket."

I shut my eyes and shook my head against it all. "Gentlemen, you should have told me, you really should have told me."

"It was strictly need-to-know," Alec said. "You didn't."

"Maybe so. But if you had told me all this yesterday, I wouldn't have tried to trap Casselman tonight and he and his pals wouldn't have taken a woman prisoner. She's with them now."

"My God, that's why you're here," Alec realized.

"I changed my mind," Harry said. "I want my ten bucks back after all."

"Dammit, McKenzie."

"I told you he bluffs too much," Harry reminded his partner.

Alec didn't disagree. "Fuller?" he called.

"Sir?"

"Deploy your men."

Quickly, silently, the agents dispersed and disappeared into the night, Alec with them.

I pivoted toward Harry. "I want my gun."

"Get serious. All we need is for a civilian to shoot up the place."

"I'm not staying here."

Harry handed me a windbreaker with FBI in large, white letters both front and back. I wore it over my tuxedo, zipped to my throat.

"We'll try to look out for your girl," Harry said. "But we can't change our plans now. When the plane lands, we go."

16

Harry squatted next to me at the edge of the clearing. I couldn't see his face but I could hear his breathing. It was deep and regular. Mine was shallow and coming fast and I wondered if this was what it had been like in 'Nam, sitting in the jungle, waiting for heavy rain.

The forest was quiet and still. The moon disappeared behind a slow-moving cloud bank and I could see nothing except what was happening below the lamp. I soon convinced myself that Alec's people had gotten lost, had surrounded the wrong shed and Harry and I were going to jump out of the woods and shout "Don't move, you're under arrest" and Stalin would laugh at us. I had participated in several raids in my time, only none like this, none where I couldn't see my backup.

We waited for what seemed like an eternity after moving into position, yet it was only about ten minutes. Where was the damn plane? Finally, I could hear the soft drone of engines. The noise grew louder but I couldn't see the aircraft that created it. A moment later two ribbons of landing lights rolled out from the metal shed like dominos, the ribbons about thirty yards apart and two hundred and fifty yards long. Maybe longer. It was hard to tell from where I squatted next to a fir tree. The plane dropped down from the sky, flying without lights, and followed the ribbons at tree top level 'til it reached the end of the runway, where it banked sharply and once again disappeared into the night. I could still hear it and then I saw it again, coming in low and steady from the opposite direction, its landing gear engaged. The plane was a single-prop job with a huge cargo bay—it looked like a truck with wings. It was silver and maroon—its ID numbers had been masked. Beyond that I can tell you nothing about it. I don't know planes. The fact they can even get off the ground never ceases to amaze me.

The plane touched down at the far end of the runway without so much as a bounce and rolled toward the shed even as it decreased in speed. When it reached the near end of the runway it stopped and pivoted to face the direction from which it came. The ribbons were extinguished, plunging the runway back into darkness. The lamp that hung from the pole now seemed like a candle compared to the light that had been shining. Harry reached over and took my arm. He squeezed it tight. "Easy, easy," he whispered, only I don't think he was talking to me.

The plane engine was feathered. The propeller stopped twirling. A dozen men emerged from the hangar and moved quickly toward the plane. Casselman stood under the lamp. The plane's portside door opened and a stepladder was extended. Geno Belloti stepped out and waved.

"Now!" Harry barked into a hand-held radio. A half dozen shots rang out in unison and the airplane's tires exploded. Before the echoes died away, two dozen agents emerged from the woods, brandishing their weapons like they were just itching to squeeze off a few hundred rounds. They soon got the chance. The two black men I had met in Stalin's apartment, Mr. Mustache and Mr. Non-Mustache, pulled their heavy machine gun from the back of one of the Chevy vans. They trained it on the attacking agents but before they could squeeze off a single round, they were cut down by a prolonged fusillade from M-16s.

I followed the agents, sprinting hard in a straight line past the dead bodies of the gangsters toward the entrance of the shed. There were a half dozen men in the shed. Most of the men were dressed in tuxedos and holding long-stem champagne glasses. They seemed frozen in shock.

"Where is she?" I screamed at them.

Mellgren was the first to come to his senses—sort of. He threw his glass to the concrete floor and rushed me.

"You sonuvabitch," he screamed, trying to throw a punch at my face.

I used his momentum against him, blocking his punch with my left forearm, bringing my right arm up under his left armpit, sweeping his legs out from under him and throwing him over my hip on top of the limousine's hood. I locked my fingers over his windpipe and squeezed.

"Where is she?"

When he didn't answer I squeezed tighter. Mellgren gasped for air.

"Where is she?"

"Here."

I angled my head toward the voice that had called out. Merci Cole was sitting in the back of the limousine and looking out of the window. I left Mellgren gasping on the hood and went to her.

"Are you all right?"

"I am now," she said and smiled. "You want a drink?"

I opened the door and sat next to her. She handed me a square crystal decanter filled with scotch that she had found in the back of the limousine. I gladly took a long pull.

"The FBI and those other guys, were they part of the plan?" she asked.

"Yes, they were." 'Course, I didn't explain that it was their plan and not mine.

"How come you didn't mention 'em before?"

"Must have slipped my mind."

I took another sip of scotch. As I drank, Harry and Alec and their band of happy warriors led Warren Casselman, Stalin, the airplane pilot, three disgruntled Russians, and Geno Belloti into the hangar. Not a shot had been fired since the two gangsters went down.

"Congratulations," I said, raising the decanter in salute.

"Your girl okay?" Harry asked.

"Safe and sound."

If looks could kill, Casselman's expression would have put me six feet under.

"Is this yours?" I asked, displaying the scotch. I made a production out of taking another sip. "Smooth."

An excited agent spoke to Harry. "The trucks are on their way. ETA fifteen minutes."

I turned back to Merci. "Are you sure you're all right?"

She shook her head. I gathered her up in my arms. She rested her head against my chest. I held her tight.

"I kept thinking of Jamie. I kept thinking . . ."

"You're safe now. It's all over."

"Is it?"

"You're safe," I repeated.

I held Merci for a while longer. I thought she might cry, but she never did. Instead, she asked for more scotch. While she nipped at it, some of the agents busied themselves reading Miranda-Escobedo to the suspects and chaining them together for the drive into Minneapolis. Another group isolated the three Russians.

"Welcome to America, comrades," Alec told them. "I know you'll enjoy your stay. We have the best prisons in the world."

"Look what we found," an agent said, walking toward Harry. He was carrying a briefcase. He set the briefcase on the hood of the limousine and opened it. It was filled with American currency.

"At least half a million dollars," he said. "Maybe more."

"We'll count it later."

Harry was smiling brightly. In fact, everyone wearing a windbreaker was smiling, including me. Only the prisoners looked like they were in mourning. It would have made a great picture, except you never have a camera when you need one. Casselman's mood had already swung from anger to despair. He was standing next to Stalin near the limousine, a single agent training his weapon on them. Stalin glared at the agent and muttered, "Fucking F, fucking B, fucking I . . ."

Merci took another sip of scotch and handed the decanter back to me. I raised it toward Casselman.

"Why?" I asked him. "You're a wealthy, respected man. All of you are wealthy, respected men. So, tell me why. Why did you do it?"

"The supply of product had decreased sharply following the collapse of the Soviet bloc, yet the demand had remained consistently high, not only here but throughout other markets in North America that we were able to identify. We determined that a comparatively low-risk invest-ment would reap significant rewards, especially if a streamlined distri-bution system could deliver the product to our customer base in an efficient, secure manner."

I chuckled at Casselman's response. Even now, with his world col-lapsing around him, Casselman was unable to appreciate the moral or legal implications of what he had done. To him it was simply a business decision.

"Be sure to tell that to the jury," I told him. "I'm sure it'll appreciate your logic." I shook my head. "You're never gonna see the sun again, you moron."

"Kiss my ass," Stalin snarled contemptuously.

"Whatever you say, *Raymond*."

Oh, he didn't like that at all.

After securing the others, two FBI agents moved toward Casselman and Stalin, chains in their hands. The rattling of the chains sounded like small bells and when one of them fell to the floor, everyone glanced down at it. Except Stalin. He grabbed the barrel of the M-16 held by the guard, spun the agent around, and kneed him hard in the groin. The agent released the gun and Stalin started running, weapon in hand. He ran about fifteen yards, whirled, and fired the M-16, the shots pounding high into the ceiling of the hangar. He sprinted for the woods as we picked ourselves off the floor. Several agents fired wildly at him, missed, and began pursuit.

"No, no, stop. Call your people back," I told Harry. "Keep them out of the woods."

Harry was confused by my request.

"Trust me. Please."

Harry recalled his men.

"This had better be good."

I held up my hand and gazed into the woods in the direction Stalin had escaped.

"Wait for it," I said.

The agents, the prisoners, Merci—we all silently watched the dark trees, although only I knew what we were watching for. Suddenly a dim light flicked on. "There," I said, pointing. It was the Jag's interior light. It came to life when Stalin opened the car door, when he jerked the string that pulled the pinless grenade out of the tomato can, releasing the trigger and igniting the fuse. I started counting, "One football, two football, three football . . ."

I could see the woman in my mind's eye, the Rosie Riveter who raced to the factory to do her bit during World War II, the last good war—who bent to the task of cutting fuses, a thankless task as tedious as any assembly line job, as tedious as putting bolt A into nut B ten thousand times a day. She was young and she was pretty and her mind would wander and she would think about what she was going to have for dinner on Meatless Tuesday and if her friend who had a friend who had a friend would come through with the nylons in time for the Friday night dance at the USO and what she should do about the 4-F down the street who made her feel like a woman, who made her almost forget her fiancé who was fighting in North Africa. And during those brief reveries she would sometimes cut the fuses short.

"Four football, five football . . ."

I felt no guilt, no remorse when the grenade exploded, lifting the Jag three feet into the air, twisting and dropping it lengthwise across the road. My hands did not shake and my stomach did not churn as I watched the fire slowly burn itself out. This was four, I told myself. Four dead men. Yet the revulsion and nausea and dizziness that had accompanied the others was not present this time. I tried to make it come, repeated silently to myself, "You're sick to your stomach." Only I didn't feel sick. I felt indifferent.

Harry stared at me, not quite sure what to do or say.

Alec stepped between us and sighed.

"Suspect killed while resisting arrest. I hate it when that happens."

17

The drive back to Falcon Heights was unencumbered by traffic. At three a.m., we had the freeways to ourselves. Even the drunks had gone home.

Merci sat next to me. She wore my jacket over her shoulders and my heater was going full blast, yet she shivered just the same. Several times I asked her if she was all right and each time she said yes. Despite the early hour I felt refreshed, invigorated the way I usually felt after a tough workout. I asked Merci if she wanted to stop for a bite—there was an all-nighter on the strip that served a fair omelet. She wasn't up for it. She had spent too much time with the decanter of scotch.

"I thought they were going to kill me."

"They moved faster than I anticipated. I'm sorry."

"Sorry." She repeated the word like it was something she had never heard before. "Sorry isn't going to cut it. You owe me money."

I nodded my understanding.

"You said a hundred bucks an hour."

"So I did."

"I figure you owe me twelve hundred. Plus another fifty to have my dress dry-cleaned."

"Make it fifteen hundred," I told her, feeling generous.

"Twelve-fifty is fine. And I want cash. I don't accept checks. I ain't no bank."

"No problem."

Merci sat back, pressed the palms of her hands against her eyes. She continued to tremble.

"Are you okay?"

"I wish you would stop asking that," she told me.

"I feel responsible."

"You are responsible."

"I know. I'm responsible for a lot of things. For example, there's still the matter of why Richard and Molly Carlson came to me in the first place."

"To find Jamie," Merci reminded me.

"No. To find a compatible bone marrow donor for Stacy. Remember Stacy? Little girl who's dying of leukemia?"

"Little Stacy." Merci tugged the jacket tighter around her.

"Don't you think it's about time you hustled your ass up to Grand Rapids and took the test to see if you're compatible?"

"Why me?"

"For the same reason they wanted Jamie to take the test. Family members are best. And you're family."

Merci gazed out the windshield at something well beyond the reach of my headlights. After a few moments, she asked, "How did you know?"

"This and that. Richard Carlson wanting me to find you—the fact he was so happy when I did. I figure he was holding you in reserve, just in case. And then there was the way he knew exactly when your mother died. . . ."

"Bastard didn't even go to the funeral."

"Probably he didn't want his wife to know. Then there was Bruder insisting his son was safe with *friends*. What friends? The way the cops were hunting him, you know they were watching everyone he's ever known. So, who would he have left his son with? How 'bout his unclaimed sister-in-law, the boy's Aunt Merci? I figured that when you had to make a phone call before you could accept my offer last night, like you first needed to ask permission. Of who? The baby-sitter, was my guess.

"But to be honest, I didn't put it all together until I saw you in the gown Jamie gave you."

"I said I was as pretty as Jamie."

"And you are. Every bit as pretty."

We drove a full mile in silence. Finally, I said, "It's pumpkin time, princess."

"You're right. Jamie and I were sisters. We figured it out during our senior year of high school. We weren't sure what to do about it—deep, dark family secret, small town, all that bullshit. Jamie wanted to tell the world. Richard said he'd disown her if she did. She disowned him first. She came down here to live with me. For seven years I had a family."

"And the night Jamie was killed?"

"David brought TC to me. He asked me to hide them both and I did. David was terribly confused. A lot of the things he said didn't make sense. He kept muttering that *they* were out to get him. That *they* had killed Jamie and *they* were going to kill him and TC. At first I thought *they* were you. Eventually, I learned about the Family Boyz and the Entrepreneurs and about Warren Casselman."

"Casselman?"

"David admitted that he slept with Casselman's wife and he believed Casselman might have killed Jamie outta revenge."

"The thought hadn't occurred to me," I admitted, wondering why.

"I tell you, if it weren't for TC I would have turned him over to the cops right then. He was cheating on my sister."

"The night you came to my house, it wasn't to kill me, it was to find out what I knew."

Merci nodded.

"Later, you realized Bruder couldn't hide forever, so you sent him to me, hoping I'd help."

"Instead, you got him killed," Merci muttered. I ignored the remark.

"Where's his son?"

"Good people are taking care of him," she confirmed. "Not like me, they're straight."

After a half mile of more silence, Merci asked, "So now what?"

"I think it's time Richard Carlson accepted his responsibilities, I think it's time he acknowledged his daughter. Don't you?"

"Like that's going to happen. I'm a prostitute. A convicted felon."

"Yeah, but you're also family. And you'll be bringing him and Molly their grandson."

"I hate the idea of letting Richard turn TC into some kind of tobacco-chewing, back-slapping, ass-kicking, north county good ol' boy."

"Perhaps his Aunt Merci will be around to help him out."

Merci shook her head slowly.

"God, how I hate Grand Rapids."

I parked the Cherokee at the curb and escorted Merci to my front door.

"When am I going to see my money?" she asked.

"As soon as the bank opens."

I unlocked the door and stepped inside the dark house ahead of her. It was an impolite act on my part and I was soon punished for it. Before I could switch on a light, someone hit me on the head from behind with the proverbial blunt instrument. Twice. The first blow drove me to my knees. The second knocked me unconscious.

There was something in my hand, something small and oddly shaped. It was driving me crazy. I lay there on the living room floor, my eyes shut, and played with the object, squeezing it, rolling it between my fingers. When at last I was able to open my eyes, I found I couldn't see. Blackness everywhere. Was I blind? No. It was night. I was at home. Someone had hit me from behind. Must've been Merci. I tried to rise. It was hard work. I managed to kneel. My eyes grew accustomed to the lack of light and I could make out shapes of furniture. But why would Merci hit me? Money? Surely, she didn't think I had it on me, that I had it lying around the house. I managed to stand. My mind cleared a bit more. I heard noises coming from upstairs. The thudding sound of someone walking across the hardwood floors above me. What would Merci be doing up there? I continued to roll the object between my fingers. Oddest damn thing. I held it close to my eyes, tried to catch it in the dim street light shining through my windows. It looked like a bullet. The .22 I had ejected from Merci's gun. How many days ago was that? I turned it in my fingers again, squeezed it tight. A muffled scream from upstairs. My God in heaven! I dropped the bullet and reached for my Beretta as it clattered on the floor. Only my gun wasn't there—Alec never returned it and I forgot to ask.

I stumbled unsteadily up the stairs, making entirely too much noise. Light spilled out from under the door to my guest room—the room that once belonged to my father. I leaned on the door. It flew open. It wasn't even closed all the way, much less locked. I nearly stumbled to the floor, but regained my balance. Devanter laughed at me. He had been waiting, a knife in his hand. One of my knives from the wooden block in my kitchen. In his other hand was a lit cigarette. He flicked it to the floor. Merci Cole was behind him on the bed. She was nude. Small, round burn marks dotted her flesh. Her hands and feet were bound to the headboard and baseboard with strips of raspberry lace, the rest of her gown was shredded and lying on the floor. She screamed. Panties in her mouth muffled the cry.

Devanter rushed at me. Or rather, he rushed at someone I recognized as me. See, I wasn't there any longer. Instead I was up high, floating near the ceiling somewhere, looking down. Watching. Watching what this person did, this person who looked like me, who staggered on quaking legs like a drunk about to pass out. He didn't seem afraid, this person. He just stood there when Devanter rushed at him, the knife held high above his head. And when Devanter tried to strike down at him, this person who looked like me crossed his right forearm over his left forearm and thrust them above his head, meeting the blow straight on, blocking it with the V of his crossed arms, absorbing the shock of the blow with those already impossibly weak legs.

This person who looked like me but who couldn't possibly be me then grabbed Devanter's wrist. He grabbed the wrist with both hands like it was a baseball bat. He swung the wrist down in a clockwise motion. Swung it down and then up again even as he stepped in under the arm that was attached to the wrist. He turned his body and pivoted on the balls of his feet—amazing that he could still stand—and kept swinging that arm upward until it reached twelve o'clock and then back down again, winding Devanter's arm like a corkscrew until Devanter's body simply had to follow that arm, up and around in a clockwise motion.

Then boom. Just like that, Devanter was on his back on the floor. His wrist broken. He had dropped the knife when the bone cracked. It skittered across the floor and the person who looked like me went to fetch it. "Hurry," I kept telling him. "Hurry." But he seemed to take forever to get that knife. While he was getting it, Devanter struggled to his feet. It didn't bother him a bit that his wrist was broken—he didn't seem to mind at all. He rushed again at the person who looked like me just as he retrieved the knife and spun to meet the attack, holding the knife low with both hands, the point of the knife tipped upward.

Devanter's momentum carried him forward. The person who looked like me brought the knife up. Devanter tried to parry the knife aside with his hand. But he forgot. His wrist was broken. His hand didn't respond. He missed the knife.

A look came over his face. Devanter knew he had made a mistake. Only there was nothing he could do to correct it, nothing he could do to check his forward momentum. The person who looked like me thrust the knife into Devanter's chest just below his rib cage, angling the blade upward toward the heart muscle. Devanter's weight and speed did the rest. His body fell onto the blade. The blade went in cleanly all the way to the hilt because of Devanter's weight and momentum and because of the upward thrust and because the person who looked like me but who couldn't possibly be me enjoyed working in his kitchen and had always kept his knives razor sharp.

For a moment Devanter hung on the knife, literally hovering in the air, the person who looked like me holding him maybe two, three inches off the floor. His mouth was open and from where I was up by the ceiling I could see that it was filling with blood and that the blood was trickling from the corners of Devanter's mouth and down his chin. Devanter's eyes were open, too, and the person who looked like me could see them roll backward into Devanter's head until only the whites were showing. And then the knife broke. The blade snapped off at the hilt. And Devanter fell to the floor, the blade buried in his chest. And the person who looked like me was left holding the wooden hilt.

The person who looked like me dropped the hilt and moved unsteadily to the bed where Merci Cole lay spread-eagled between the bedposts. He worked the knots in the lace but they were so tight. Then he did a remarkable thing this man who looked like me. He pulled the knife blade out of Devanter's chest with his fingers and used it to saw through the lace. Even so it seemed like forever before he freed her. She removed the panties from her mouth and screamed at him, but he didn't understand what she said, her words were incomprehensible to him. He helped her from the bed. Her screaming became deafening sobs. He led her past Devanter's body. Her bare foot stepped in blood, warm and sticky, and the sobs became screams again.

Merci Cole and the person who looked like me stumbled from the room. He held her with one arm. The other he dragged along the stucco wall of the hallway, supported them both as they moved toward the master bedroom. Once inside the person who looked like me locked the door. Merci Cole collapsed on the bed and curled herself into a fetal position. Shaking uncontrollably. Weeping as if she would never stop. The person who looked like me pulled a blue-green comforter over the woman, a final act of chivalry before he reached for the phone. He punched 911 on the number pad. The phone rang once. Twice . . .

I don't recall what happened next.

18

I was dreaming. I dreamed I was in a hospital room. I was seriously injured. There seemed to be a tube protruding from my left forearm that led to a plastic bag hanging from a metal stand. Another tube. No, it was a wire attached to what looked like a clothespin, the clothespin squeezing the middle finger of my left hand. The wire ran to a small machine with a numerical display that reminded me of the depth finder on my bass boat. The light above me was dim and cast everything in shadow. It was hard to see. A woman with butterscotch hair was sitting in a chair near my bed and reading a magazine.

"Turn on the lights," I told her.

Her head came up abruptly and she closed the magazine without marking her place.

"Hi," she said. "How are you feeling?"

"Feeling?" I didn't understand the question.

She placed her palm against my forehead the way my mom used to.

"I love you." I think I told her that.

"I love you." I think she told me that.

Everything went dark.

I thought I heard someone calling.

"Don't you die, McKenzie. Don't you dare die on me."

She was dressed in white and hovering above me like an angel. Only she didn't act like an angel.

"McKenzie, McKenzie," she called while she slapped my face lightly. I used an open hand block to grab her wrist and pull her down across my chest. Muscle memory.

"Where am I? What happened to me?"

"Do you mind?" She tried pulling away.

"Sorry." I released my grip.

"You're in Regions Hospital," she answered, massaging her wrist. "You were hit on the head real hard."

She looked like someone I should know, only I couldn't place her. "How are you feeling, cowboy?"

That's when I recognized her.

"Lilly?"

I glanced at the photo ID that hung from a tiny chain around her neck. Lillian Linder, MD.

"Lilly."

"I thought I told you I didn't want to see you in here again."

"I've missed your kind and gentle bedside manner."

She grinned. "It's starting to get old, you know, having to save your life every couple of years."

I was that close? Again? I refused to think about it. "What's my status?" I asked.

"Surprisingly good, but then you always were a quick healer."

"Merci Cole?"

"The woman you came in with. She's fine. Physically, anyway. Emotionally she's still a bit unhinged—she's been through quite a trauma."

Her and me both, I nearly said.

"She's been visiting a couple of times each day. Quite a few people have dropped by, in fact. I'm amazed that an arrogant jerk like you has so many friends."

"Have I told you how much I've missed you, Lilly?"

"There's good news and bad news, cowboy."

"Tell me the bad news."

"You suffered an epidural hematoma."

"Sounds serious."

"It is serious. There's a blood vessel—the middle meningeal artery—under the skull that lies alongside the brain. When you were hit, the artery was torn and you started to bleed. The bleeding put pressure on the brain. That's why you lost consciousness."

"But I came out of it. At least I think I did." My memory was still a little foggy on the subject.

"That's not unusual. The initial trauma—the blow itself—knocked you unconscious the first time. You came back. You did what you had to do."

I liked the way she put that.

"Meanwhile, the lacerated blood vessel was bleeding. When enough blood built up, the pressure forced you into unconsciousness for a second time. We did a CAT scan immediately after you were brought to us. The CAT revealed the hematoma. So we drilled two burr holes smaller than a dime into your skull to drain the fluid and alleviate the pressure."

"You drilled into my skull?" The thought of it shocked me. My hands went to my head. There were two patches where my hair had been shaved that were covered by bandages.

"It took forever, too. You have a very thick skull, McKenzie."

"What about the artery?" I asked.

"The meningeal should repair itself. We'll do another CAT scan later today to make sure there's no additional bleeding."

"I'm all right, then?"

"You're off the ventilator, oxygenating well, your BP and heart are much stronger than you have a right to expect, you're going to be fine."

"What's the good news?"

"That's the good news. We'll keep you here for a while, observe your functions, your kidneys, make sure everything is working the way it's supposed to. I'll send up an OT and PT . . ."

"Occupational therapist and physical therapist."

"You remember from last time, good. They'll do an assessment. If you pass, you should be out of here in two, three days."

I expected it to be worse and told her so.

"It could've been, cowboy. If you hadn't been brought to us immediately, if surgery hadn't been in time, you could have suffered brain damage. Or worse. As it is, we don't expect any deficits."

I heard everything she said, but the words "brain damage or worse" seemed much louder than the others.

"We don't expect any brain damage," Lilly told me, as if the thought had leaked out of the holes drilled in my head.

She patted my cheek. The thing about Lillian Linder, MD—despite her brusque manner, you knew you were in good hands.

"I need to go and see some sick people now," she told me gently.

"Thanks, Lilly."

"McKenzie, we have to stop meeting like this."

"The doctor says you're going to be all right," Merci Cole assured me.

"What does she know?"

Merci was holding my hand against her smooth cheek. Tears collected in her eyes, but none fell.

"Thank you for saving my life."

"You're welcome."

She tried to smile but couldn't. There was a sadness in her that I had not seen before.

"I'm going home," she said.

"To Grand Rapids?"

She nodded.

"Good for you."

"We already took the tests. The doctors say I'm a perfect match. B-negative blood, all that. Stacy should be fine after we do the transplant."

"That's great. Just great."

"My father and I—we had a long talk. Several, actually. With Molly. Molly's like the arbitrator. She wants me to stay with them and Richard says okay. Me and Jamie's son. I think they were so delighted at getting their grandson that taking me in, too, seemed like a small price to pay. I probably won't stay long, though. Just until I decide what to do next. I was thinking of going back to school, see what the Vo-Tech or Community College has to offer."

"Good luck." I didn't know what else to say.

"Richard wants me to tell you he expects to see a bill for all your time and expenses, hospital expenses, too, if you're not insured. He hasn't changed much. All he cares about is money."

"He cares about much more than that," I told her.

"We'll see."

Merci smiled ever so slightly. In the end she was just like the rest of us. She needed to be loved. Eventually, it's what life comes down to, a few people loving us and us loving them. Sometimes it takes a tragedy to impress that upon us.

"Don't be too hard on him," I told her. "I admire a man who pays his own way."

Merci held on to my hand for a while longer.

"Will you come visit me?"

"Sure. I have property near Grand Rapids."

"Better hurry. If things don't work out, I might take off again."

"If you do, don't let me find you."

Bobby Dunston entered my hospital room carrying a bouquet of flowers. "These are from Shelby," he announced so I wouldn't think he'd give another man flowers. "I tried to smuggle you a six-pack, but the nurses stopped me."

"Sure."

"Shelby sends her love. You might not know it, but she's been here almost without a rest since they brought you in. But now that they say you're all right, she's packing."

"Packing?"

"We're sneaking up to your place for a few days."

"Just you and Shelby?"

"Just me and Shelby. Mom is taking the kids."

"Good for you."

"Shut up, McKenzie."

He sat on a chair and crossed his legs.

"I had him, you know. Devanter. I had him. I knew he killed Katherine and Jamie eight hours before you killed him. I had a warrant for his arrest, only I couldn't find him. I couldn't find him because apparently he was hiding at your house. Why I didn't think to look there first I'll never know."

"Don't be bitter," I told him.

"Who? Me?"

"I didn't know it was Devanter," I confessed. "I didn't have a clue. Not until I saw him hovering over Merci with the knife. Hell, the people I accused were innocent. Innocent of that, anyway."

"Maybe so, but the way the papers are playing it you'd think you were the greatest thing since Dick Tracy."

"A very underrated investigator, I might add."

"You realize, of course, that you look ridiculous with those bandages on your head."

"I'm starting a new fashion—next week I'll be on the cover of *GQ*."

"It was the twine," Bobby said. "The twine used to tie down both Katherine and Jamie. Microscopic examination indicated that the lay, circumference, and strand number were identical. So was the reason they each had it—to secure the rose bushes to the trellis on the south side of their houses. They had the same gardener. Devanter. That's why he knew precisely where the twine was kept. I would have figured it out sooner only I let you distract me with all that Family Boyz nonsense."

"It really was a coincidence, Jamie's murder and the Boyz," I admitted. "You guessed right the first time."

"I made a lot of mistakes."

"Why did Devanter do it? Do you know?"

"No, I don't."

"He was at the VA—I saw his wounds. Maybe the answer is there. An honest-to-God deranged Viet Nam vet like you see in all the movies."

"Except Devanter was never in Viet Nam, or the Persian Gulf, or anywhere else for that matter. He never served. He suffered his wounds working on an off-shore oil rig fifteen years ago."

"But he was a patient at the VA."

"He was a groundskeeper at the VA. We interviewed his former coworkers, the hospital staff. Apparently, he didn't have any friends. Everyone who remembered him, and there were only a few, said he was scary, but quiet—a loner, but a good worker."

"Aren't they all?"

"We traced his movements. Born in Des Moines. After high school he drifted south, more or less in a straight line, working for a farm co-op in Iowa, a nursery in Missouri, another nursery in Oklahoma, a golf course in Texas, then an oil rig in the Gulf of Mexico. He was engaged to be married to a woman in Fort Worth, but he called it off just before the wedding and moved here. I spoke to the woman. She said Devanter broke off the engagement when he found out she couldn't have children, something about a botched abortion when she was sixteen."

"Was there anything about her that resembled Jamie and Katherine?"

"Not that we could determine. Little over a year ago, Devanter went to work for Warren and Lila Casselman. The Casselmans introduced him to their entrepreneur friends—by the way, did you hear that the feds busted them and the Family Boyz and a couple of Russians . . ."

"I was there. Front-row seat."

"Then you know why everything happened the way it did."

"Pretty much, but we can talk about that later. What about Devanter?"

"The ladies of the Northern Lights Entrepreneur's Club apparently admired his handiwork. He agreed to help them with their gardens. They paid him for his trouble. That's all we know and are likely to know."

"No motive then?"

"Jealousy. Frustration. Obsession. Pick your own."

"I thought you were the psycho expert."

"Obsession, then. You were a little obsessed yourself. Why else would you put yourself through all this?"

"I was just doing my job."

"Job? What job?"

I recalled the mission statement that Kirsten had attributed to me. *Live well. Be helpful.*

"Uh-huh. Speaking of which, I have a message from Chief Casey of the City of St. Anthony Village Police Department. 'All sins are forgiven.' Whatever that means."

"Whatever."

"Are you thinking of getting back into harness, Mac?"

"I honestly don't know what I'm thinking."

Bobby didn't push. Instead he told me I had had another caller while I was unconscious.

"Nina Truhler."

That made me smile.

"Nice," Bobby suggested.

"Very."

"I like her."

"She is likable."

"How do you do it?"

"It's a gift."

"Speaking of gifts, Shelby is waiting for me."

"Thanks, Bobby."

Before he left, Bobby found the remote control and aimed it at the TV set suspended on the wall at the foot of the bed. He surfed past several channels until he found WGN—the Cubs were playing Houston. Sammy Sosa was up with two on base.

"Are you going to be all right, alone like this?"

"What do you mean alone? I'm in a hospital."

"I have a few minutes. Let's watch the game."

"Get out of here. Shelby's waiting."

"McKenzie?"

"Dunston?"

"Screw it. I'll see you in a couple of days."

"Love to the family."

"Back at ya."

After he left I turned up the volume.

"Whaddaya say, Sammy," I said to the TV screen. "Just me and you, man. Just me and you."